Advance Praise for *Love at First Spite*

"*Love at First Spite* had me hooked from the first page! The playful banter, steamy love scenes, and delightful cast of secondary characters made this debut an unputdownable read."

—**Alexandria Bellefleur, author of *Written in the Stars***

"Filled with sizzling chemistry and delicious revenge, *Love at First Spite* had me smiling from start to finish! Get ready, rom-com fans, this is one debut you don't want to miss!"

—**Kate Bromley, author of *Talk Bookish to Me***

"*Love at First Spite* delivers on every level with humor, heat, and heart. Collins has crafted characters I was so delighted to spend time with, and whose love story was full of emotion and sparkling sexual tension."

—**Denise Williams, author of *How to Fail at Flirting***

"A delightful twist on a classic tale of revenge—packing plenty of tenderness and heat."

—**Brooke Burroughs, author of *The Marriage Code***

ANNA E. COLLINS

LOVE AT FIRST SPITE

A NOVEL

GRAYDON
HOUSE

GRAYDON
HOUSE®

Recycling programs
for this product may
not exist in your area.

ISBN-13: 978-1-525-89979-9

Love at First Spite

This edition published by arrangement with Harlequin Books S.A.

Graydon House
22 Adelaide St. West, 41st Floor
Toronto, Ontario M5H 4E3, Canada
www.GraydonHouseBooks.com
www.BookClubbish.com

Printed in U.S.A.

To my husband—Ménière's fighter and the best person I know.

LOVE
AT
FIRST
SPITE

1

MY WHITE DRESS trails me as we make our way across the small clearing to where the others are waiting. The heavy fabric rustles against the ground, a few leaves catching in the hem, but I ignore them, concentrating instead on what's ahead. All eyes are on me.

"Are you sure?" my cousin Mia asks at my elbow. My partner in crime.

I glance her way. I'm nervous, but I don't want to be, and the simmering excitement in her expression reassures me. This is the right choice.

"Hundred percent," I say.

She smiles and squeezes my hand. "You'll rock this, I know it." She lets go and steps away to assume her position with a wink. "See you on the other side."

Then it begins.

I take off at a sprint. The paintball arena is at least a football field in size and strewn with steel drums, crates, and sandbags.

A few larger structures in the middle resemble a small-scale Old West town complete with porches and a saloon sign. The guys Mia and I've been teamed up with run that way, while she and I head for the trees along the sides. The large pines tower stoically above the fray, and I choose one of the largest trunks for my first cover.

"Did everyone else go the other way?" I call out to Mia but get no response. Wasn't she behind me?

I peer around the trunk only to catch the whisp of her braid beneath her helmet as she dives for shelter by a tree trunk twenty yards in front of me.

"Don't be a baby, Porter," I chastise myself, before following her. It's a thirty-minute game of most-hits-win, so she's got the right idea: it's go time.

As fast as my skirts allow, I jog in the direction of the rapid *pops* and *ka-splats* of active battle, paintball gun at the ready. The staff told me I'd be at a disadvantage playing in my wedding dress, and they had a good point. But then again, I didn't come here expecting to leave in virginal white.

I barely get my finger on the trigger before two shots in succession hit me squarely in the chest, and a green stain blooms before me. It hurts less than I anticipated, but I still freeze too long and another round easily finds my shoulder. Blue paint drips off the white lace of my sleeve.

Oh yeah? That's how it's going to be?

Something akin to glee bubbles up my chest and I let out a loud cackle. *All righty, then.* Shouldering my gun, I aim at the culprit—some kid a full foot shorter than me—and one, two, three splotches of paint hit his belly.

"Yeah!" I shout, as he hightails off. Adrenaline pumps through my arms.

"Dani, over here!" Mia runs sideways behind me from the cover of a fake building to a stack of boxes. "I'll shield you."

Yeah, right. She already looks like she's wrestled with a rainbow.

I consider darting the opposite way, to a smattering of hay bales, but Mia sounds increasingly desperate. I hike up my skirts and do my best to make myself small before jumping to safety next to her.

Back up against the boxes, I peek around the corner. "Two of them," I say, still breathing hard. "On my mark." I count down with my fingers and, on three, we spring out, guns leveled at opponents who don't see us coming. I'm a vengeful angel, gliding through the sky—at least that's what I picture until my toe catches the hem of my dress and I stumble forward into a mouthful of dirty straw.

"Take that!" Mia shouts from a distance, accompanied by a fresh round of shots volleying through the air.

"What the fuck?" a deep voice yells out.

Another voice: "We're on the same fucking team."

I lift my face off the ground. Mia is backing up toward me, pursued by our imagined foe who's indeed wearing the same beat-up Timberlands I spotted on our teammates earlier. It's fair to say they're about as excited to be paired with us as my taste buds are about the straw. I spit out the horse fodder and push myself up.

"We should have never teamed up with them," the first guy complains. "That one *wants* to get hit, and this one..." He gestures at Mia.

She exhales as if he's punched her.

"What?" I say, moving to stand between him and my cousin. "This one, what?"

"Dude, come on," the second guy says. "Let's just play."

"Well, she's not exactly agile, is she?" guy number one sneers.

"Ha, that's funny." I bob my head a few times and train my gun on him. "What do you think, Mia?"

She appears at my side. "I think someone's about to get pummeled."

His eyebrows jerk behind his protective goggles, but that's all he manages before we shoot. And shoot again.

Who needs a team? The sight of them running away is totally worth losing for.

Before we know it, the game is over, and Mia and I hobble back to the arena gate. The kids ambushed us in the last few minutes, and I'm still on a high from the attack, from fighting that flight response and accepting my colorful defeat. In the end, I threw my hands up in the air and twirled as the paint splattered, each hit another glorious nail in the "Dani and Sam" coffin.

"Probably not the best idea to shoot our own team. Did you see them watching?" Mia asks, referring to our teammates laughing as the kids got in round after round on us.

"Watching? Pretty sure they partook. But whatever. Winning was never the point."

Mia rips open the velcro holding her armor together and lets out a breath. "Agile, my ass. Hardly my fault places like these never carry gear that fits those of us with more *natural* padding. I'd like to see him join my yoga class. He wouldn't last a minute."

"That would be a sight," I agree.

Once inside, I assess the state of my dress, admire the streaks of color weeping down the fabric. "I think it's a definite improvement."

Mia nods, but now that the deed is done, she's not quick enough to hide the pity in her eyes.

"Let's get some drinks," I hurry to add before she can put words to her feelings, and drag her along by the elbow.

The bar in the middle of the rec center is busy even though the afternoon hasn't fully turned into Saturday evening yet. Fortunately for us, I'm still in my wrecked wedding dress, and people make way at the sight of my ghoulish visage. I pretend I don't notice the stares and whispers, and soon we have seats at the bar, as well as two margaritas with tequila shots on the side.

I pull the scrunchie down my ponytail and shake out my wavy tresses, blue-and-yellow streaks now adorning the long, chestnut strands. "To not getting married," I say, raising my shot glass.

Mia hesitates. "Dani…"

"Nope." I shove her shot into her hand. "A toast."

"Fine." She smiles. "To wrecking dresses. It was pretty fun."

"Hell yeah, it was." I tip the tequila back and relish the burning in my throat before holding up my margarita glass, too. "To no more guys. Ever!"

Mia squints. "Ever?"

"Yeah, who needs them?"

"Well, I mean…me…a little. For certain things."

"Come on." I set my glass down. "You're still not doing this right. We hate men right now."

"Okay." She lifts her glass and pauses. "To schlongs, the only good guy parts."

I almost spit out my drink, but I have to say—it's as fine a toast as any.

After our loaded nachos arrive, I snap a picture of us. "Think I should send it to Sam?"

"Sure." Buzzed Mia is a lot more game than the sober version. "Rub it in if you can. Always thought he was a douche."

She slurps up the remnants of her margarita with a straw, then leans forward to flag down the bartender.

A wave of tenderness washes over me. When I moved to the Seattle area from Idaho a year ago, Mia was the only person aside from Sam I knew here. I'll admit I had little intention of becoming friendly with her again after a decade—my memory was of a younger cousin (by two years, but still) who was as straightlaced as they come and whose one claim to fame in our hometown was having given up candy for Lent one spring and then sticking with it for the next ten years. Not my idea of a good time. I'd agreed to get in touch mostly because it felt like something you do as family, but I hadn't expected her to have grown up into a truly cool person I now consider my best friend.

"What?" She's staring at me. Scrutinizing.

"Nothing."

"Are you crying?" She reaches out but stops short of my cheek.

"What? No." I turn away. Damn tequila. It always gets me.

"Fine. We need more drinks. Did you send it?"

"Send what?"

"The photo, dummy."

"I was joking." Not that Sam doesn't deserve a picture of me in this dress, especially since he hasn't bothered to have his buddy delete the Instagram photo that broke us. The one with *her* in it.

"Another round of the same?" The bartender smiles at Mia and steals a glance at me. Or, not at me, at my ruined getup. He looks younger than us, cute, with fashionably unruly hair in a mop that flops across his forehead.

I know he's dying to ask.

"I was supposed to get married today," I say with a shrug. "Shit happened."

His smile stiffens, and Mia places the order.

The din around us ebbs and flows as people come and go, and slowly, the air fizzles out of me. I've been fueled by stubbornness and adrenaline since this morning, but now the bodice of this dress is too tight, the paint-stained sleeves too heavy. Plus, if I don't get to pee soon, bad things will happen.

"I'm gonna go to the…" I hike my thumb toward the restrooms.

"Are you okay?" Mia grabs my arm as I get up.

No, I'm not okay. I'm not supposed to be here, drunk in a bar, cinched into this splattered gown. Right now, this gown should be a dream of white rocking it on the dance floor of my wedding reception. We took classes, for God's sake. Sam was going to spin and dip me in front of our families.

I pout. "Men are stupid."

"So you keep saying." She pats my arm. "You go do your business. I'm going to get you a surprise drink that will cure all. No more tequila."

"Okay." I have no idea what I'd do without her, and not only because I've been crashing on the couch in her one-bedroom apartment for the past three and a half weeks since ending my engagement. "Be right back."

It requires effort, but I manage to navigate my multilayered garment both in and out of a bathroom stall without any major issues. Considering my blood alcohol level, this is truly an accomplishment, and perhaps it's making me a bit cocky as I amble back to the table. If you can pee without assistance in a poufy wedding dress, you're pretty much invincible. I can do anything. I can party all night. I can dodge bar patrons at full speed like a beleaguered quarterback, jump obstacles like a graceful gazelle, and—

"Aaah!"

I trip on the skirt again, but this time, instead of getting a mouthful of straw, a pair of steady hands grab my shoulders, yanking me upright so fast I go flying into their owner's solid chest.

"Sorry, sorry," I mumble, trying to regain balance and untangle my legs from too much tulle. "This stupid dress…"

"Yes, it's an interesting choice," comes a low, familiar voice.

My head jerks up, and the confidence of mere moments ago is replaced by the gravest sense of misfortune.

2

WYATT MONTEGO, ONE of the architects at the house-building firm where I work as an interior designer, peers down at me in that disdainful manner of his. As if I smell bad or am too stupid to stay out of his way. He's the big boss man's golden goose after all—dreaded by all except maybe said boss man.

"Danielle," he says, curtly.

This is bad, really, really bad.

I step back, away from his hands on my shoulders. "I'm so sorry."

His gaze flicks to my dress. I must look like technicolor roadkill to him. Will he hold this against me? Get me kicked off client-facing projects for being unprofessional? I'm still working to establish myself at the firm and I've heard stories about him and how little he already thinks of us in "pillow fluffing" on the sixth floor. Could just be rumors, but when I had my orientation walk-through nine months ago, he was also the only one on the fourth floor who didn't greet us as we dropped by. I've done my best to avoid him since then—that is, until I was moved to the north-side team two weeks ago. Now he's in my weekly meetings whether I like it or not.

In the midst of my fretting, I spot it—a small cobalt stain on the sleeve of his (surely) expensive shirt. I can't stop staring at it.

He notices and, in what feels like slow motion, reaches up to touch the paint. "Themed wedding?" he asks, examining his now-inked fingers.

A bitter laugh escapes me as I shift to allow another patron to pass. "No. No wedding."

His mouth opens, but nothing comes out. I don't know what's worse—his silence or the idea of a possible condolence. He's so tall standing only a foot away from me, the light above us casting shadows beneath his jaw that disappear into his collar. Not that this is news. It's kind of his thing, towering above people. But I've never seen his lips up close like this, and there's something about them that makes me want to bite mine.

No. Nope. I squeeze my eyes shut. Fucking booze goggles. What's he even doing here? Doesn't he have some uppity steak house to visit or a wine tasting to attend?

"Waste of a good dress," he says, finally, looking off above my head.

Like every other guy here, he's probably distracted by one of the many flat screens mounted around the room. Either that or he doesn't deem me worthy of even five seconds of his attention. It's getting on my nerves how much he can't wait to get away, how he doesn't do anything to hide it, down to the snide remark. I was going to offer to wash his shirt, but now—not so much.

"It was worth it," I snap back. "Sorry about the shirt." I sidestep him and, as I do, a glint of amusement crosses his face.

What a prick. I barrel down the aisle toward Mia. She'd better have that drink ready because I now have one more item to add to the list of things I need to forget.

I plop down into my seat and snatch up the full martini glass in one swift motion. It's an appletini—the vilest of vile concoctions—but at this point, I'm not picky. I guzzle half before setting it back down.

Mia nods slowly. "Told you I'd get you something good." She's unraveled her thick braid and is combing through the bronze-colored strands with her fingers.

I don't have the heart to break the truth to her. Instead, I smile and breathe out through my nose.

"So?" she says, leaning in. "That seemed cozy. Who's the Tom Hardy lookalike?"

I stiffen. "Who?"

"The tall drink of top-shelf vodka you had your hands all over a minute ago?"

"Just someone from work. One of the architects. Actually, he's that guy I told you about who couldn't be bothered to say hello when I started. And I did not have my hands all over him. I tripped, he caught me. End of story."

A twinkle of mischief, then, "The story was a lot longer than that. The look he gave you when you walked away deserves a whole epilogue."

"Mia…" I say in my most cautioning tone, before I down the rest of the martini. It takes all of my willpower not to grimace at the drink's cloying sweetness.

She raises her arms in defense. "He's pretty hot, that's all. No need to bite my head off."

"Sorry. But he's a total asshole who thinks everyone is way beneath him, and even if he wasn't that way, I'm done with guys. I don't—"

"Want them, don't need them, and the world would be better without them," Mia fills in. "I remember."

"He's just another pompous jerk who likes calling the shots."

"And yet we're still on the topic," Mia mutters around a nacho chip.

"Oh stop it." I punch her lightly in the shoulder.

She giggles. "Fine. Hey, Matt." She waves to the bartender. "My cousin's glass is empty."

"Matt?" I turn to her, eyebrow arched.

"I think he's flirting with me," she says, holding up a slip with his phone number. "You were in the bathroom a long time."

I order a cosmo. Pacing is a virtue, but here I am, almost thirty, newly single, without a place to live, in a city where I have one friend, and I've now made a fool of myself in front of not just someone I work with, but Wyatt Montego of all people.

"I need a plan," I say. "Are you sure I can't convince you to move into a bigger apartment with me?" As if I don't already know the answer. Mia's been in the Seattle area since college and her parents helped her buy her place. She's settled.

Mia swallows a big gulp of her drink. "Oh, I have a lead for you, actually. Matt's aunt has a room to let. Like an in-law suite—bedroom, bathroom, kitchenette. Up in Bridle Trails, near the Microsoft campus. I may have spilled some of your backstory..."

Was I really gone *that* long?

"What's the catch?" I ask. All other places I've looked at should either be condemned or the rent is exorbitant.

Matt joins us on the other side of the bar with my cosmo, and Mia awards him a smile. "No catch," he says. "My aunt is super nice. You like dogs, right?"

Dogs? "I guess..."

"Of course she loves dogs," Mia offers enthusiastically, kicking my shin. "Why?"

"Only because she has two, and those beasts are her children."

Sounds like it could be worse. "Sure, I'll take her number." How about that? Mia's flirting may just pay off for the both of us.

He scribbles a few digits on a sticky note and hands it to me. "Her name is Iris. Tell her Matt says hi."

3

I'M EARLY TO the staff meeting Monday morning. Wyatt is typically seated well before the room fills up, and the sober light of day has convinced me I need to right our interaction from Saturday night. Workplace harmony is important regardless of what you think of the other person. I will not risk my career suffering.

While I wait, I review requirements for a subdivision in North Creek. I've recently been named interior design lead for the model home, the first project where I'm officially in charge. The designer who prepared the initial drawings was moved to a large, brand-new development two towns away because he has more experience. He wasn't happy about being replaced, and while I don't doubt my ability to pull it off—let's just say I know several pairs of eyes are watching.

I have time to scan my notes twice and fill up my water bottle before Wyatt enters with one of the lead engineers, enmeshed in a conversation about a development I have nothing to do with. Neither of them acknowledge my presence as they find seats diagonally across from me at the rectangular conference table.

I hide behind the protective veil of my hair and pretend to be busy scribbling notes. "Danielle is a chicken," I write, next to a very poor sketch of a googly-eyed birdlike creature. My design skills do not extend to fine art.

"Shoot, I forgot the Holstead folder," I hear the engineer say a minute later as he riffles through his paperwork. "I'll be right back."

I take a sip of water. Here's my chance.

"Less colorful today," Wyatt says, beating me to it, his focus on the papers in front of him.

I straighten abruptly as if I've been called out in class. "I'm sorry, what?"

"The dress." He nods toward me.

Crap. He's still annoyed.

"Yeah, about that." *Chin up.* "I need to apologize. There's no excuse, the way I was… And I got paint on you—"

"At least it wasn't orange or red." His lips press together.

I choke down the rest of my ramblings and for a moment we stare at each other in silence. Am I supposed to ask why this is a good thing? Is it a riddle? A trick? Voices are growing closer in the hallway outside.

"You were saying?" he asks.

What was I saying? "I'm… I mean, I'd be happy to get your shirt cleaned for you. Since the paint stain was my fault and all. It was a rough day, and I'd had a few drinks. I didn't mean to—"

He cuts me off again, this time with his infamous squint. The one that usually foreshadows a Statement of Weight of some sort. "You…want to do my laundry?" he asks, sitting back in his chair.

No, this is a different squint. If I didn't know better, I'd say he's confused.

Just then, we're interrupted by the rest of the staff trickling in, and I make a show of searching for a pencil in my bag.

Disapproval emanates from Wyatt's side of the table as the meeting begins. My blouse clings to my back. All I wanted was to pay for dry cleaning and let him know I usually don't spend my weekends in paint-stained wedding dresses throwing myself at random men. Mission *not* accomplished.

Today he's even more self-important than usual, questioning Regina on a build *she's* lead on, and challenging the timeline for another in which he's only tangentially involved. As we adjourn, I no longer give a flying fuck what he thinks. The confident slant of his jaw, the false humility at the praise for his latest project, the way he never bothers with niceties once business has been handled, but instead hurries off as if he's allergic to chitchat—I'm not wasting my energy on that. If he uses Saturday against me, I'll go to HR. Why should I tiptoe around any man? Answer: I shouldn't.

My irritation lingers throughout the morning, a bone-deep itch I can't scratch. At lunch, I text Mia to complain, hoping for her usual support.

What's he wearing? she asks.

Not exactly the commiseration I need.

4

AFTER WORK, I head over to bartender Matt's aunt's house. She sounded nice enough when I spoke to her yesterday, but the uneven rhythm I tap on my steering wheel still speeds up as I near the house. What if "likes dogs" is code for "lures desperate, midlevel professionals into dungeon?" Maybe I should have let Mia come with me.

Iris's house is a white stuccoed bungalow with a deep porch. It's not cute exactly, could use a coat of paint and some landscaping, but the door is an inviting carmine red, and the doormat makes me chuckle. "Ring the doorbell and we'll sing you the song of our people," it says. Signed, "The Dogs."

I opt to knock, but if the ruckus coming through the door is anything to go by, it didn't make a difference.

"Cairo, Cesar," an authoritative voice calls out right before the door opens. Miraculously, the barking stops. A bespectacled woman with a dark Joan of Arc bob and short bangs offers a fine-boned hand. "Sorry about that. You must be Danielle."

"Dani," I say. "And you're Iris?" I'd assumed she'd be younger, because my aunts and uncles are all still shy of sixty, but Iris has for sure passed seventy, with soft jowls and a diminutive frame. And yet—the expression behind the trendy black glasses is sharp, her outfit more young Audrey Hepburn than *Golden Girls*. Is that a cigarette holder between her fingers?

"Indeed I am." She grins and a decade falls off her. "Come on in. And I'm a shoes-off kind of house."

As I toe off my Keds, she bestows praise upon two of the biggest Great Danes I've ever seen—one dark, one sand-colored. They sit stock-still, tongues out, observing me until Iris says, "Greetings?" and they saunter over and bump their noses near my pockets.

I scratch their ears. "Sorry, fellas, I don't have any treats."

"Here." Iris hands me a couple of biscuits from a jar on the entry table. "Cesar is the tan one. He'd eat all day if I let him."

"Hi, Cesar." He pushes against the treat in my hand, forcing me to take a step closer to the wall. "Yeah, he's hungry all right."

"And the polite one waiting is Cairo. Cesar, sit," Iris commands. "There you go." She ushers Cairo forward.

The black beast looks up at me with intelligent brown eyes, sits, and lifts his paw as if to shake.

"Aw, you're a sweetheart," I coo, giving him the cookie. "How old?" I ask Iris.

"They'll be five this year. Brothers, and a bonded pair." She watches them affectionately.

I see what Matt meant when he said they're like her children.

"But come on in." She turns around, snapping her fingers, and instantly Cairo and Cesar follow. "Do you want some tea? Coffee?"

"Sure. Whatever you're having is great." I take a seat at the table that's against one wall of the small kitchen. The place has been updated at some point, but the bones are likely original. No open concept. 1920s maybe. The decor feels Scandinavian—light woods, minimalist lines, white airy curtains, lots of plants—but the wall art is primarily architectural drawings of landmarks like the Eiffel Tower and the Notre Dame, save for a few photographs of Iris and another woman.

The dogs head to a huge pillow in the living room and lay down with audible sighs.

"They're really well trained," I say. "My parents' dogs were never like that."

"You get what you give." Iris sets down two mugs with hot water along with boxes of tea. "True with animals *and* people."

We sip our beverages, she has a few questions, answers mine. I'm surprised to learn she used to be an engineer for Microsoft—she doesn't have that vibe—and she wants to know everything about my ventures in textile printing—a hobby from my college years I don't have much time for anymore. It's like talking to an old friend, and I'm about to ask when I can move in, room unseen, when my cell phone rings. I expect it to be Mia, but the name lighting up the screen makes me do a double take. Sam's mom.

"I'm sorry, I should take this." I gesture to the phone. "I'll be right back."

Iris gets up. "No. You stay. I'll go print a contract for you."

I know it's rude, and I'd decline the call if not for the fact that she'll keep at it if I do. The first week after I left him, it was every day, nonstop. You'd think Sam was a five-year-old needing help navigating the kindergarten playground, not a thirty-two-year-old venture capitalist with a mortgage and a brand-new mistress.

"Christy," I answer. "What can I do for you?"

"He's beside himself," she says, not bothering with formalities. "I've never seen him like this. He stayed over on Saturday and barely ate anything."

Sam never eats at his parents' house because his mom is a terrible cook.

I plead with the crown molding where wall meets ceiling for strength. "Like I've said before, that's no longer my problem. Sam and I are not together anymore."

"But people make mistakes. If you'd only listen to him explain…"

I know this tune well enough by now, I lip-sync what comes next: "We all have moments of weakness."

I shake my head. "I don't know how much clearer I can be, Christy. Sam cheated on me a month before our wedding. With the Realtor who sold us our house."

"And he's all alone in that big house now, constantly reminded of what could have been. Hasn't he suffered enough?"

I push up from my chair at the same moment Iris returns, but the way she startles at the sight of me stops my impending outburst in its tracks.

"I'm going to go now," I say instead, teeth clenched. "Please don't call again." I hang up and shove the phone into my back pocket before I dare look at Iris.

"Sorry, I should explain." I sink back into my chair.

She shrugs and taps her ear. "It's a small house. Your fiancé cheated on you. Pretty self-explanatory. Matt said you're living with your cousin temporarily."

"Have been for about a month now."

Cesar comes to investigate the commotion in the kitchen, but Iris nudges him back out.

"Sam and I were together over three years," I say as if she asked. "I moved out here to be with him a year ago. My things are actually still in the house we bought."

"The one with the Realtor?"

She'd heard that part, too, then. "The same."

"And now his mom is calling you?"

I let out a deep huff. "Yeah, it's a lot."

"Indeed. Incidentally, why I prefer dogs." She slips her hands into the pockets of her houndstooth cigarette pants. "But maybe things are looking up. Ready to see the room? It's guaranteed in-law-free."

I smile. "Sounds perfect."

I follow her down the hall, Cairo and Cesar at my heels, thankful she doesn't seem deterred by my drama. I'm usually in better control of my emotional displays. These past few weeks have gotten the better of me.

"You'll have a key to the garage entry if you prefer to let yourself in that way." She points. "And then, this is the room." She opens the door at the farthest end of the hallway.

It's about the same size as Mia's apartment, completely furnished, and there's an alcove with a sink, hot plate, and microwave oven near the window. A half-size fridge sits underneath the counter.

"If you need more space for food, there's a full-size fridge and freezer in the garage. And of course, you can use my kitchen to cook as long as I'm not in the middle of doing the same." Iris opens another door in the room. "The bathroom. I had it all updated a few years ago after my wife, Ellen, passed. She used this space as her office."

That must be the woman in the photos. I peer into what's an average, unexciting bathroom—or a blank canvas, as I like to think if it. A new shower curtain and some plants will work wonders.

I do a full 360 of the room, which is as good as anything I could hope for. I might even be able to fit my high-back armchair next to the bed. Of all the furniture I had to leave behind at Sam's place, that piece broke my heart the most. It was my college graduation present to myself—soft caramel leather, sleek modern design. The rent is on the high side of what I can afford, but utilities are included.

"Very nice," I say. "Also, I'm sorry for your loss."

Iris gives me a tight smile. "Oh, well, that's nice of you. Rent is due the fifth of the month."

❧

"She called you again?" Mia is on the opposite end of the couch, messy bun and glasses. It's ten at night and I've regaled her with a play-by-play of my meeting with Iris, including the interruption from Christy.

"Sounding like a broken record."

"What part of her son being an unfaithful douchebag does she not understand?"

"No, no. Darling dearest can do no wrong." I drink my mango-flavored sparkling water as memories of my would-be in-laws play in my mind. I'm still so resentful of Sam that I'm willfully ignoring what I also know to be true—that Christy was over-the-moon excited about our wedding. If I had a dollar for every time she's told me I'm the daughter she never had…

"Okay, I have two questions." Mia pulls the blanket tighter across her lap. "What are you going to do about it? And how am I going to stand the loneliness when you move out?" She pouts.

I toss a pillow her way. "You'll probably have a dance party as soon as I'm gone to celebrate your reclaimed space. And either way, I'm not that far—you'll still see me all the time."

"Can I be your wingman when you go for your rebound?"

"As for Christy…" I say, disregarding her question. "I think I have to talk to Sam. I hate having to ask him for anything, but I don't have a choice here."

"You're going to have to get your stuff from the house anyway now that you have a place, won't you? I can come with you if you want. Moral support *and* muscles." She flexes.

She's right. Finally, after living out of a suitcase for a month, I'll be able to officially get all my belongings out of there. Chop off that limb. "No, that's okay. This is something I have to deal with myself. I'll call him tomorrow when he's at work. That way he can't throw a fit."

"See, you've got this. If he puts you on speaker, promise me you'll sprinkle some of the sordid details into the call. I can't stop wanting him to suffer a bit."

"That's why I love you so much," I say, a big yawn swallowing the last syllable.

Her phone chimes and she glances at it while she says, "Aw, me, too." Whatever the message is, it sucks her in and soon her thumbs are a blur as she types. She waits, giggles, types again.

"Who's that?" I ask.

"Huh?"

"Must be pretty important."

No response.

I reach for the pillow I threw at her earlier and toss it again. Now I've got her attention. "Anything I should know about?"

Mia's face flushes pink. Her fingers are still perched above the screen, but at least she lowers the device. "I've been texting with Matt."

"Oooh."

"Stop it." She wrinkles her freckled nose. "He wants to do happy hour this week. Should I?"

"Why not. 'Cradle robber' is a good addition to anyone's résumé, I always say."

She throws the pillow back at me. "He's twenty-four, I'm twenty-seven—it's hardly a huge gap."

I put my hands up. "I'm kidding. Go for it. I liked him." Mia hasn't exactly been lucky in love the past few years. "But take the sexting into the bedroom, please. Some of us need to get some sleep."

She sticks her tongue out at me but gets off the couch and saunters into the other room with a quick "good night" over her shoulder.

It takes me a while to fall asleep, knowing what awaits me tomorrow.

5

MIDMORNING, I SNEAK out to a sunny spot next to the office parking garage. Sam answers right away, his voice firm, but with the same cheerful lilt that drew me to him when we first met. After growing up in a house where my mom basically eradicated herself to accommodate my dad's moods and whims, an easygoing disposition was pretty high on my list of traits I wanted in a partner. Turns out even cheerful, charming guys can be uncompromising asses.

"Dani, how the heck are you?" he says, as if we're long-lost friends and he can't believe his good fortune at hearing from me. Well, maybe the latter isn't too far off the mark. I have been avoiding him completely since I moved out.

"Never better." *Say what you need to say and be done with it.* "I'm only calling to ask you to get your mom to stop contacting me."

"Oh, she called you?"

Why did I never realize what a terrible liar he is? "Will you tell her to back off, please? I have no beef with your parents, but it's getting weird."

"Mmm-hmm."

I picture him nodding along, that look of fixed intent on his face that makes it feel like you have his full attention and then some.

"And I got a new place, so I need to stop by and get my things."

He's quiet for a beat. "Dani..."

"I'll do it while you're out. It'll be quick."

"Can't we talk about this first?"

"There's noth—"

"I miss you." He lays it on thick, voice quaking. "I've said I'm sorry a million times. How can you throw away all the time we put in like this? I don't get it."

I take a deep breath and jab my toes into the concrete wall.

"All I ask is one more chance. Please. She meant nothing to me."

He still doesn't understand the Realtor was only part of the problem. I had two conditions for agreeing to the much-too-big colonial he wanted. One, that we also buy the un-developed sliver of land next door for a small textile printing studio I'd daydreamed about, and the other, that we invest in the house *together*. He knew I'd saved up for my share, even if he'd put down the bulk of the money, trust fund baby that he is, but in the end, he covered the full payment, and there was no studio space. So while the cheating was the tipping point, the whole process of purchasing the house—how my wishes were ignored—also illuminated what kind of life partner he'd be. I'll die before I become dependent on a man like that.

"It won't be until this weekend since I'll need to rent a truck," I say. "Possibly Friday after work. I'll text and let you know. I'll leave my key, too."

The sound of a door closing comes over the line. "So, that's it?" There's an edge to his voice now, one he rarely uses. "I thought you were smarter than that, *Danielle*. What—you're going to go live in some rathole somewhere when you could be in our house?"

"*Your* house."

"Eat alone? Sleep alone? You hate sleeping alone."

He hates sleeping alone.

"What about that trip to Rome we planned?"

"It would never work," I say, cutting off a rant I know is imminent. "I don't trust you anymore. It's as simple as that."

"But that's not fair. Everyone makes mistakes. You're always too serious about stuff."

"Oh, I am, am I?" The fucking nerve. "You know what? I'm gonna... I'll text you later this week. Bye, Sam." I hang up and lean against the building. "Fucking fucker," I mutter under my breath. "Smarmy, self-righteous, brainless assho—"

"Everything okay?"

My eyes fly open and I push off the wall as if I've been caught red-handed smoking behind the bleachers in high school. Wyatt is standing eight feet away, his blueprint portfolio across one shoulder, a to-go coffee in hand. The sun is behind him, morphing him into some kind of otherworldly man-god.

I use my arm as a visor, but it's still impossible to make out his expression. If I was to guess, it's a mix of scorn and pity. The question is: How much did he hear?

"Yep. All good."

He regards me awhile longer. "Hmm," he says, finally. "If you say so." And he turns on his heel and heads toward the office.

As if today couldn't get any worse.

6

I USUALLY DON'T take advantage of the company policy that allows cutting out early on Fridays, but today it's warranted: I'm moving. By three I'm at the home improvement store, where I've rented a small truck that should fit my few belongings and then some, and by 3:40 I pull into my old neighborhood. Sam's neighborhood.

When I texted yesterday about stopping by, his only response was Leave the key, so maybe he's finally realized I'm serious about us being over. Small miracles.

I hit the brakes hard as I turn into his driveway and spot a car parked in front of one of the garage bays. I have no reason to think he's home, and it's not his Tesla, but then again, I wouldn't put it past him to buy himself a new toy as a Band-Aid for everything that's happened. A bumper sticker next to the Audi insignia that announces "I'd rather be on the beach" clarifies things. Not his. Sam hates everything to do with big bodies of water.

Before I can even make it out of my car, the front door to the house opens, and there's the sun-and-sand-worshipping culprit.

"Hey, Danielle," Catrina the Realtor calls as she sets something down on the porch. She's daintier than I remember, annoyingly precious in a loose-fitting off-the-shoulder T-shirt and matching yoga pants.

"Hi?" I close the car door behind me and take a couple of hesitant steps her way. Is Sam selling the house already?

"Sammy said you'd be coming by, so I thought I'd give you a hand," she says when I reach her. She's barefoot, her toenails painted a rose-colored hue. The situation takes a moment to compute. *She's barefoot. In my house.*

The coin drops.

No, not my house. She's barefoot in *Sam's* house because she's made herself at home here. Because he's let her. My brain short-circuits. Was she there in the background all along, listening in on the messages he left me about how "she didn't mean a thing" and how I was "making the biggest mistake of my life"? Were they laughing at me? Together?

The world goes hazy and then I register what she's brought out of the house. Suitcases. I don't have to ask to know what's in them. She's gone through my stuff.

"Sam didn't say you'd be here." It's a daft comment, but the only one that comes out.

"Oh no?" Her eyebrows rise in fake confusion.

I climb the two steps to the porch, but she doesn't budge, blocking the doorway like a tiny linebacker. As if I couldn't easily pick her up and toss her over my shoulder. I consider it for a split second, but then again, I wouldn't be surprised if she takes Krav Maga or some other combat sport to compensate.

"Got your things here." She nudges one of the suitcases with her foot. "You're welcome." She meets my eyes directly, and the message couldn't have been clearer if she'd donned a pair of boxing gloves and raised her guard.

Little does she know I'll gladly take a right hook to the jaw if it means I'll leave here with my pots and pans, memory foam pillow, and armchair.

"That's sweet of you," I say, my voice dripping with sarcasm. "Obviously, I have a few more things to pack up, but this should save at least a few minutes. I'm going to grab some boxes out of the truck. If you have places to be, no need to wait around. I can lock up and leave the key under the planter when I'm done."

Her smile vanishes. Did she really think she'd get rid of me just like that?

On the way back to the truck I text Sam, rage building.

You've got some nerve! What the hell is means-nothing-to-me Catrina doing at the house? Touching my stuff!!

I don't know if I want a response, but it comes anyway:

We're hanging out a bit. Don't think it should matter to you who is or isn't at my house.

I force myself to tuck my phone into my purse instead of smashing it against the concrete and yank a stack of boxes out of the truck bed. If he was always this petty, then what does it say about me that I almost married the guy?

This time, Catrina steps aside when I approach, and I head straight to the kitchen. There's a pile of dishes in the sink, and an empty pizza box on the stove. Bachelors around the world would be proud. I go through drawers and cabinets as quickly as I can and take only what I brought when we moved in. Same goes for the office.

In the bedroom, all the throw pillows are in a forgotten pile on the floor, a jumble of cream and mahogany that I picked out especially for Sam since he didn't want the room to be *too girly*. My closet and dresser are completely empty, so I'll have to assume that's where Catrina focused her efforts. My nose wrinkles at the sight of Sam's clothes heaped on top of my armchair. He's basically used it as a laundry basket. I clear it with my foot and drag it to the hallway. It takes maneuvering to get it down the stairs, but there's no way I'm leaving it to be desecrated by these two.

"Watch the wall," Catrina hollers when the chair swivels precariously, as if it's her house.

Sheer fury boosts me and my burden safely down and out to the truck.

Back inside, I continue my frantic packing until I enter the bathroom in search of the curling wand I'd forgotten. Next to what was once my sink sits an unfamiliar toothbrush, and a blush-pink robe rests haphazardly over the edge of the tub. I bite down hard on my tongue as reality finally pierces my carefully constructed chain mail. I need to get out of here.

Eyes stinging, I fill up the last box and balance it in my arms down the stairs.

"Is Sammy okay with you taking all that?" Catrina asks from one of the stools in the kitchen.

I don't bother answering—I don't want to give her the satisfaction. After I bring the box out, I return one last time and toss the key onto the hallway floor without awarding her so much as a glare.

The first tear breaks free as I put the truck in Reverse, and by the time I'm fully in the street, the deluge blurs the world to the point where I can't drive. All I can do is pull over and hope she's not watching through the window.

For the first time since the Instagram photo popped into

my feed, I don't hold back, and once the floodgates are open, there's only letting the whole mess wash over me. I'm a heap of snot and tears, until I'm completely wrung out and gasping for breath, my chest hurting. The humiliation of it, the pain—I wish it on them, too. On Sam. The house is in my peripheral right, and Catrina's car is now gone. If only I'd still had that key, I'd... I'd...do something. Show them.

New tears spout, and in the midst of this round I'm dialing my mom before I even know I have my phone out. It's instinct wanting to curl up in a safe space, to hear a familiar voice telling me everything will be all right, like in fourth grade when friendship drama and making the soccer team were my biggest problems.

"Hello?" she answers after three rings.

"Mom," I sniffle.

"Who is it?" my dad asks in the background.

"Danielle," Mom says to him. "How are you doing, honey? Do you have a cold? You sound like you have a cold."

"Tell her to get Theraflu. It's the only thing that works."

"You should get some Theraflu," my mom says.

I wipe my nose with the back of my hand. "No, I'm not sick. I just..." I rest my forehead against my fist. "I had to stop and get my things at Sam's, and I was feeling a bit—"

"How is Sam?" Dad asks, louder now. I must be on speaker. "Still killing it at work?"

I close my eyes, irritation effectively replacing gloom. "I wouldn't know. We broke up, remember?"

"Now, don't take a tone with your mother," he says, as if the tone-taking wasn't directed at him. Deflecting, as always.

"And how is Mia doing?" Mom asks. "I saw your aunt just the other day, but we talked more about the younger ones. Can you believe Aaron is graduating high school now?"

I sigh. "Yeah, wow. Time flies." If I'd stopped and considered whether to make this call, I'd have been able to predict the exact feeling now engulfing me.

Mom keeps on about Mia's siblings, but I tune her out. Out the windshield, the pale March sun illuminates the downward slope of the street, the green tips of evergreens, and farther still the glittering waters of Lake Washington. The view was one of the reasons Sam wanted to buy the house and the main one I didn't flat out refuse. I trace the contours of the bedroom windows, down the side to where I might have created a small, raised garden, and onward to the low hedge that marks the end of the property. The overgrown sliver of land between the hedge and the street is still for sale, and I curse Sam again. It would have been ideal for a studio.

If only I'd realized sooner that Sam's choices always reflected whatever directly increased his own happiness. Making *me* happy wasn't enough for him. After everything I did for him—attend work parties with his jerk colleagues (in heels, mind you), cancel plans last minute when something "came up" at his firm, fucking relocating—and now I'm left with nothing and *he's* moving on.

The letters on the For Sale sign start to blur again, but, blinking the moisture away, a spark of something flashes in my subconscious, a synapse firing out of the dark, first a lone pulse, then a steadier rhythm. He shouldn't get away with this. I can't let him. I need more, something that will drive the consequences of his mistakes home, something to give me closure. A big fat F-U in his face every time he looks out the window, signed by yours truly.

"Um, Mom. I think I have to go now," I say into the phone before hanging up.

Catrina's smug face flickers past my inner eye. Sam's patronizing voice saying I should consider his ignoring my wishes "a wedding present." The fight we had after I found the paperwork in only his name and questioned how any part of the house could be a present when I didn't own it.

I trace another line from the empty lot to the house and back again. Sam's refusal to use my money to purchase the house means I still have my savings.

It would be the perfect thing. Poetic justice.

The For Sale sign shines more intensely red now. It sways in the wind, taunting me.

This is either the best idea I've ever had, or the worst by far.

7

I HANG UP the phone, thankful to have found an empty conference room on the eighth floor so no one can see my red face. One hundred thirty thousand for a mini lot that's not even level? The property alone would eat up most of my savings. I'd have nothing left for the actual build.

It's Monday, at lunch. My head is in my hands and I'm wallowing in the depths of despair like my girl Anne with an *E*, when the door swings open and the powers that be once more dump Wyatt into my path. He pulls up short at the sight of me, turning us both into deer in headlights. Almost ten months I've worked at this company, most of which I've managed to keep Wyatt-free, and now he's everywhere.

"Are you stalking me or something?" I ask, my capacity for deference (or even politeness) depleted.

His mouth pinches at the corner, and he checks behind him as if there's someone else here also intent on interrupting every unfortunate moment of my life. Once he seems to confirm my accusation was aimed at him, he says, "I suppose I could ask you the same. This is my space."

I cross my arms. "Your name's not on the door." I don't know what's gotten into me, but whatever it is, it feels great.

He takes a step into the room as if challenging me. *Oh yeah?* his feet murmur against the blue carpet. *I beg to differ*, says the creaking strap of his workbag.

I follow his movements as if he's a large cat about to pounce, but he just places his things on the table, sits, and takes out his laptop. Nodding toward my phone in front of me, he asks, "Bad news?"

When I don't answer, he shrugs and opens the computer. Types, thinks, types again.

I frown. "What are you doing?"

"Working."

The gall. "What if that's what I'm doing, too? I was here first."

He keeps typing. "The room is big enough for two."

I stare at him. At the focused set of his brow, his tan neck against that white collar, those square shoulders. All business. Is he serious?

His fingers fly across the keys for another minute before he pauses. "Unless you're going to keep ogling me like that the whole time." He looks up. "It's pretty distracting."

I whip my attention to the tabletop. "I wasn't ogling."

He chuckles. "Okay."

"I wasn't. Why are you here anyway?"

"I come up to this floor for the silence. I get more done that way."

"Fancy corner office downstairs doesn't do it for you?"

"Corner *fishbowl* downstairs invites a lot of interruptions."

"Yes, must be so hard." He has the best space on his floor.

Glass walls, bright and airy. Leave it to him to find something to criticize.

"It is when there are piranhas circling who all want something from you."

I want to say more, something clever that will stump him—but the aquatic detour has thrown me off. Instead, I grab my phone and stand. I can't take another interaction where I come out at a disadvantage. Not now.

I feel his eyes on me as I walk around the table to the exit, the rush of blood in my ears matching the sounds of my footsteps against the synthetic fibers.

When I'm at the door, he clears his throat. "Whatever is going on, I hope you figure it out."

I pause, fingers on the knob. "What's that supposed to mean?"

Finally, he removes his hands from the keyboard. One of them goes to his neck. "You seemed upset about something earlier, that's all."

If he's mocking me, he's hiding it well, but I wouldn't put it past him.

"Not that it's any of my business," he adds.

Damn right, it isn't. Before he can make any other observations, I'm out of the room and halfway down the hall.

The rest of the afternoon, I bury myself in work. And the next day, and the day after that, until finally, Thursday night, I decide to tell Mia about the empty lot. The idea just won't leave me alone.

"You're nuttier than a squirrel in a Nutella factory," she says as we sit down at the table for a gourmet meal of grilled cheese and potato chips to refuel from the exertion of unpacking, which for her mainly has involved lounging on my bed, leafing through my extensive pile of home decorating magazines.

Before I can respond, Iris returns from walking the dogs. How they don't run away with her, I haven't the slightest. I offer to move into my room, but she waves it off.

"I'm fine with the company if you are," she says. She busies herself heating up leftover jambalaya that smells delicious.

"Back to this scheme of yours," Mia says, between bites of her sandwich. "I get the whole 'investing in property' thing, but why there? I'd think you'd want to be as far away as possible from them."

Them. As if they're already an item.

I push my plate away, no longer in the mood. "Because he'd hate it. Because he deserves it. Because I can."

Iris takes a seat. "What are we talking about?"

"Oh noth—"

"She wants to buy the lot next to her ex's place and build a house on it," Mia volunteers.

So much for keeping my landlady out of my personal business.

"It's complicated," I say. "And I doubt anything's going to come of it."

"This is the bulldozer who cheated on you?" Iris puts a forkful of rice and sauce in her mouth and chews slowly.

Mia continues oversharing, oblivious to my attempts at stabbing her with my eyes. "She's as good as moved in with him. The other woman. Ugh, he's just a lying liar, lying all the time." She crunches down on a potato chip.

I give Mia another glare before addressing Iris. "I know I should turn the other cheek or whatever, but I can't stand it. That he's getting away with it."

"You want him to share the pain," Iris says, matter-of-factly.

"A little," I concede. "Is that bad?"

She shrugs. "Depends. Is it only revenge or do you get something else out of it?"

I hadn't considered it from that angle. All I know is I need to do something he won't like.

"Would you live there? Or what's the plan?" Iris has me locked in her sights, and I shrink back at the scrutiny.

"I mean, I don't know. I guess I haven't thought it through all the way." But no, I could never live there. Which means it's a stupid idea to begin with and I should spend my savings on something smarter. Something less rash.

"It could be an Airbnb," Mia says after a long silence. "You could market it specifically to girls' weekend getaways, make revenge a whole theme." She works at a publicly traded tech company that was little more than a start-up when she joined. She's somewhat of a marketing genius.

Images of light hardwood and big windows instantly present themselves to me as facts.

"That's clever," Iris agrees. "Posters of *Kill Bill*, and that dragon tattoo movie on the wall." She turns to me again. "I hear real estate is very lucrative."

"You could call it…" Mia taps a finger against her lower lip. "The Revenge Hotel. No, too big and formal."

"Killer View Bed-and-Breakfast?" Iris suggests. But both she and Mia shake their heads.

A bright and charming interior to contrast an exterior designed to stand out like a boil on silken skin next to Sam's manicured lot. "The Spite House," I say under my breath. Apt for a vision borne from the basest of human impulses.

"The Spite House," Mia repeats. "I kind of like it. A bit on the nose, but also cute."

"You forget this is not actually a thing. Don't get too excited." I groan. "Why is revenge so hard? It's a piece of cake in the movies."

"What about doing something else?" Mia asks. "Online rumors? Releasing ants in his house? A glitter bomb?"

We're quiet as we ponder ways to make Sam share the fall-out of our split.

Finally, Iris sets her empty glass down with a clang. She nibbles on her cigarette holder as if thinking hard. I've seen her smoke only twice; the holder functions more like a fidget from what I've gathered. It also looks fancy as hell. "The Airbnb is the best option," she declares.

I lick my finger and swipe a few chip crumbs from my plate. "Yeah, well…"

"What if I told you girls I have some savings?" She rests her elbows on the table, then adds with a crooked smile, "A fair amount, actually."

The air around us stills. An interlude to allow the meaning of her words to sink in.

That's the worst idea yet. I begin to object only to be interrupted by Mia.

"I do, too," she says. Her eyes sparkle in the light of the setting sun coming through the window.

"Guys." I lean forward. "While I appreciate your support, I've already told you I'm not taking any loans for this—not from a bank and certainly not from you. Being in debt afterward would leave me worse off."

"No, you misunderstand." Iris places the cigarette holder beside her plate. "Not as a loan. We'd be partners. And when the Airbnb starts making money, we'd share in the profits according to what percentage we each put in." She looks from me to Mia, who nods.

Where are all those solid counterarguments when I need them?

"So, we'd pool our money, buy the lot, hire builders, and then rent it out as a business venture? What if we can't agree on something?" I face Iris. "No offense, but we've only just met.

If we're going to do this, it's still with the intention of pissing Sam off, and I wouldn't want to compromise on the details."

"Well, I for one don't care what you build as long as it has the basics for a weekend getaway," Mia says. "This is a freaking high concept situation. I can market the shit out of anything you put together. Plus, I know how much you hate group projects, you adorable control freak." She blows me a sassy kiss.

I shrug. You want something done right, it's always better to do it yourself.

"I'm not interested in being involved with the build either," Iris says. "Think of me as a silent investor. My only ask is that everything is legal—permits and what have you."

Two pairs of eyes are on me as I absorb their words. The clock on the microwave blinks to 7:00 p.m. Do I want this? To take on a construction project next to Sam's house? To mess with his peace, with his view, his smooth sailing into the future? Do I want to build a house just to spite him? A spite house?

Hell yes!

8

BECAUSE WE'RE PAYING with cash, the process is far less complex than what Sam and I went through buying the house. A surveyor comes out to inspect the plot within a few days, and Iris knows a good real estate attorney who helps us with the purchase contract. We even manage to negotiate the price since the lot's been vacant for a long time. When property easements and zoning rules are taken into account, the area available for actual building won't be much bigger than a couple of school buses lined up. But tiny houses are in, and the height is all that matters.

The attorney confirms the zoning restrictions and assures us our (loosely) planned build will be A-OK, we sign on the dotted line, and that's it. Champagne all around. The property is ours.

A week later, things are decidedly less celebratory. It's not enough to own land—we also need permits, blueprints, and a contractor, and so far, I don't have much to show for my efforts in procuring any of those. The one contractor who's interested doesn't have an architect on staff, and the architecture firms I've spoken with are either not interested in a one-off job for a small house or they're already booked solid.

Mia and I are watching a movie in her apartment after Friday Happy Hour, but I can't concentrate. Halfway through I pause it and turn to her.

"What if this is it?" I ask. "What if we can't get someone to build it?"

She sets down her wineglass and rests her elbow against the back of the couch, leaning her head in her hand. "It's not ideal," she says. "But it's only been a week. A week is nothing."

"But the longer we have to wait, the more it feels like he's getting away with everything."

"Isn't revenge best served cold?"

"That's assuming we'll find someone later. We're going into our busiest time—if other builders don't need new business now, they sure as hell won't need it in three months."

"Well..." Mia falls silent even though it's obvious she has more words at the ready.

"What?"

She looks away. "You can always ask at work."

I've already explained to her in detail why that wouldn't be a good idea—this is not exactly the kind of project they'd want their name associated with—but I'm about to do it again when her phone beeps.

"One sec," she says. "It's Matt. We're going on a day date tomorrow. A hike." She smiles to herself as she types.

At least one of us isn't a complete romance pariah.

When she's done, she takes a sip of wine. "Look, here's what I think. We can either be patient and wait for someone to call back..."

I'm not sure I like where this is going. "Or?"

"Or you talk to one of your work friends." Before I have a chance to protest, she continues, "I get it—it's a small, unorthodox project, you're stretched thin as is, etcetera."

She has listened to me after all.

"But maybe someone wants to make some extra money on the side. Maybe we don't have to go through official channels and hire JM Archer Homes."

As much as I don't want to involve my company, she does have a point. Maybe it wouldn't hurt to ask a colleague. But who? It would have to be someone who could use the extra cash and who wouldn't rat me out to HR—I'm sure this at least skirts the edges of our noncompete clause. Someone I'm friendly with.

"Maybe Alaina would do it," I say, more to myself than to Mia.

"The girl you have lunch with?"

I shrug. "She's a solid architect. New, but she knows her stuff." The more I think about this, the more sense it makes. It shouldn't be that difficult of a project, and no one at work has to find out. All I'd need her to do is draw up blueprints and hope the contractor I talked to will do the build. "Yeah, it could work." I nod to myself, finally easing into the plush pillow behind my back.

"Start the movie again?" Mia raises the remote, trigger finger ready.

I pop an M&M into my mouth. "Go for it."

❁

Alaina Santiago started at JM Archer Homes around the same time I did, and thus by tenure is my closest work friend. She knows about Sam and me going south, and I know she's single, lives for her job, and volunteers for anything that involves boosting company morale. She even got me a birthday card with a sloth on it last year since she'd noted I love sloths from my screen saver. Got everyone to sign it. But that's about as far as our friendship stretches.

Come Monday, I seek her out in the cafeteria at lunch. She has her nose in a book, but I sit down at her table anyway. If she's annoyed at me for invading her space, she doesn't show it. We make small talk as I unpack my lunch, exchange work updates, plans for the week. I'm well through my salad before I find a good enough segue to the million-dollar question.

She asks if I've seen the proposal for the new waterfront duplexes we're currently bidding on, and isn't the upswing in sustainable construction something to promote even further? "That's what I wrote my thesis on," she says. "It's right at the top of my list for the kind of stuff I want to do."

I could make my spite house sustainable, I think. Why not? It would be another selling point and, to be honest, another way to set it apart from Sam. When we moved in together, it took me a several-weeks-long lobby campaign to convince him paper plates are not the be-all and end-all of kitchenware.

"I actually have a project I want to run by you," I say when she finishes. I share the basics of the situation—have lot, need architect—but leave out the sordid details.

"Why not go through Archer acquisitions?" she asks.

I squirm in my seat. "Well, our pipeline is already pretty full, and I'm hoping to build sooner rather than later."

"But it sounds like a small job. We usually fit those in in between."

When I run out of reasons, and she still isn't swayed, I have no choice but to disclose the true purpose of the house. If I want her on board, I'm going to have to be honest.

"Okay fine." I drag my fingertips across my forehead. "Here's the thing…"

Alaina stands. "I actually need to head up. Tell me on the way?"

I pack my stuff, and we walk toward the stairwell. "You know about my ex and my wedding. Well…"

I confess as we climb, and once we reach the landing to her floor, I put it out into the universe. "I'm sure you understand, I can't go through JM Archer. What I'd like to do is hire *you* to draw up the plans."

She stops short, the hand she's already extended for the door falling to her side. I don't like her hesitation, but in my mind I still will her to say yes.

She shakes her head. "I don't think so. I… It doesn't sound like the kind of project I'd want to put my name on."

"We can pay," I try. "Weren't you talking about wanting to go to New Zealand next year?"

"Dani, come on."

"But—"

"No. Sorry." She raises her voice, and it echoes throughout the stairwell. When I retreat, her expression softens, but she opens the door to the office floor all the same, marking with no uncertainty our conversation is over. "I can't do it," she says as she steps over the threshold.

I take hold of the door to avoid it slamming in my face and follow her into the carpeted hall. The offices beyond are abuzz with activity.

"You're going to have to find someone else. Someone who doesn't mind bending the rules for you. Sorry again." Her eyes flick past me, and her mouth clamps shut.

I spin to the right and there he is—Wyatt. Because of course.

"That sounds interesting." His mouth turns up in a quick smile, but snaps back to neutral instantly as if moving his lips was a struggle. "Alaina, I emailed you the Holtz file. Let me know if you have questions. You guys talking about a new project?"

Alaina straightens, a nearly imperceptible change from lunch companion to colleague. "Thanks, I'll get back to you shortly. Dani was telling me about a design she needs help with. But it won't work…uh…with my schedule."

"Oh yeah?" He looks to me. "What's the project?"

Alaina gives me a wave and hurries off. Great, now I'm stuck here alone with him.

"Um, it's this…" I pause. "This house…project."

He's listening intently, his eyes not leaving mine. They're the rich hue of ripe blueberries.

I avert my gaze and zero in on a freckle on his right ear instead. It's shaped like a star. "Some friends and I bought a lot, and we're building a small house on it," I manage to say. "Or, we want to, that is."

"And you need an architect?" I brace for the suggestion I know will come—why not hire JM Archer? But instead he rocks back on his heels. "I'll do it," he says.

The offer rolls off his tongue in such a flippant way, at first I'm not sure I heard him right.

"You?"

"Sure."

I squint at him. "Why?"

"Oh." His eyebrows shoot up as if he hadn't thought about that. "I… Well… As luck would have it, I actually need an interior designer. Yeah. So, you know, we could help each other out."

I have a hard time imagining him *needing* design help. He's the best dressed guy in the company, and he has a great instinct for detail. Every project he touches is gold. Unfortunately, he's also aware of this.

As if he senses my skepticism, he elaborates, "It's my nan.

She's getting all new window treatments, which, you know, is not a small job, and I can't think of many things that excite me less. Fabric and ruffles and all that... Not exactly the best use of my time." His nose wrinkles, then he nods once and says, as if he's surprised himself, "Yeah, so that's why."

As expected—my job is beneath him.

"I don't know. This house project is pretty important to me. I'm not sure I could take on yet another thing after work." I'm not as convinced as he is of the merits of this arrangement. It might save us some money, but—I'd have to work with *him*.

"My nan isn't in a hurry. She can wait until we're done with yours. One at a time."

I try to picture what that would be like, having him survey the lot, translate my vision into a plan. Who am I kidding— he'd try his best to make it all *his* vision. He's not exactly known for his collaboration skills.

I shift my stance. "I..."

"Why don't you think about it?" Wyatt starts backing away. "Talk to your friends."

He glances at his watch then walks off without any other parting words.

He's so damn sure of himself.

It's too bad at this very moment, he's also my only option.

9

I RUN THE offer by Iris and Mia that evening. It has become a routine for me to cook dinner while Iris eats hers, and more often than not, Mia joins. While I like Cairo and Cesar fine, Mia has absolutely fallen in love with them, and the feeling is mutual. Iris says she doesn't mind the company. This joint venture of ours has turned out to be the best icebreaker for our new friendship. It's also why, even though I'm leading the project, Wyatt's possible involvement is a decision we have to make together.

"He's good at his job?" Iris asks, sipping her red wine at the kitchen table.

She's wearing black and white today, a pair of huge sunglasses perched atop her bob even though it's dark out. I'm balancing the universe in old pajamas, my long tangles piled up into a messy bun barely kept in place by two pencils.

"Understatement."

"But he's a jerk?"

Whatever is going on, I hope you figure it out. The sound of his concerned voice in the empty conference room echoes in my mind, but I push it away with a determined "Yep."

"I don't know, Dani," Mia says from her spot on the floor wedged between the two Great Danes, as if she heard Wyatt, too. "He did offer to help. In my book, that's not something a jerk would do."

"Because his grandmother needs window treatments, and he thinks interior design is a waste of time. Not out of the goodness of his heart. But I've called everyone and no one's calling back unless it's with an exorbitant quote. Everyone's so busy they don't need to take on new stuff, especially something small like this. The one guy who got back to me—Loel Hubbard—is our best bet for a builder, and as much as I hate to say it, we might need Wyatt to get him to do it."

"Did you tell him why we're building it?" Mia asks.

I glare at her. "Yeah, right."

"Well…" Iris taps her cigarette holder on the table. "Beggars can't be choosers. If you ask me, I say let's at least show him the lot and get a quote. Then we can go from there."

It's the rational thing to do. But also, working side by side with Wyatt Montego for months on end is about as close to my idea of a good time as a drawn-out root canal. Minus the anesthesia. And no, it makes no difference that the dentist is attractive; the pain remains the same.

❧

I shoot Wyatt an email when I get to the office the next day, suggesting we meet at the lot at some point if he's still interested. It does occur to me as I hit Send that his offer might have been a joke, but now it's too late.

He responds right away: Let me check when I can fit you into my schedule.

I roll my eyes.

A new client presentation due next week consumes the rest of my morning. They want a completely open concept home with large windows for most of the exterior walls, and it's my job to source materials and ensure Regina, the architect on the job, can find solutions for any pipes and wires that would otherwise get in the way. It's been a fun problem to solve.

A little after eleven, I check my email, where another response from Wyatt waits for me: Thursday 5:30 p.m.? Address?

"A man of many words," I mutter as I open my calendar to confirm that the time works. As if I have a social life that demands my attention.

I send him the address, hoping this isn't a huge mistake.

10

FROM WHAT I can glean, Wyatt isn't in the office in the days leading up to our meeting, which is a good thing, or I might get cold feet. I do, however, have lunch with Alaina, who apologizes profusely for leaving me with him in the hallway the other day.

"I never know how to be around him," she says. "I shadowed him for a week when I first started, and he answered all my questions and really helped me feel prepared, but he's so impersonal. Like there's nothing beneath the surface. And that blank expression when you try to make small talk?" She shudders. "I try to avoid him if I can."

Too bad that won't be a possibility for me if I agree to this arrangement with him.

Wyatt is already there when I pull up to the curb Thursday evening. I choose the side of the property downhill from Sam's house so my car won't be as visible. While I one hundred percent want my ex to know I'm behind this build, I don't want him to discover it too soon and interfere. The re-venge will be all the sweeter if I let him put the pieces to-gether little by little.

I check myself in the mirror and half expect a hand-rubbing villain to stare back, but no, it's only me. I lick the tip of my finger to flick off a speck of mascara beneath one of my eyes, then exit my car.

Wyatt has his back to me and startles when I say his name.

"I have twenty minutes," he says after I thank him for showing up. "Perhaps we can start with the property lines?"

I extract the plat survey from my portfolio and hand it to him. He studies it and, occasionally, scans the land for refer-ence, then strides onto the property where grass and weeds reach past our knees. The lights at Sam's aren't on, so I'm rel-atively sure no one's there, but I'm still glad I remembered to bring my Steelers cap to hide beneath.

We're standing in the middle of the overgrown lot when the first drops of rain hit my brim. The wind is picking up, too, and I wrap my arms around myself.

"Let's talk in the car," Wyatt says abruptly, and stalks off as if he's seen enough.

I stare after him for a moment before following. Is he going to rescind his offer?

The cabin of his impeccably detailed Infiniti smells faintly of campfire and wet dog, but I resist the urge to ask if he has one. How would I explain that question if he doesn't? *Well, your car sure smells like damp fur.* I don't think so.

"It's an unconventional choice of land," Wyatt says once we're both inside. "Great view, but the slope…"

"I know."

"You do realize there's only room for a small building, right?"

As if I'm unaware of the foundations of building design.

I force myself to swallow a snarky response, and say instead, "It's not for me. My friends and I are putting up a vacation rental property, which means location beats size." It's at least half the truth.

"Oh." He runs his teeth across his lower lip and nods. "Interesting."

"How much of an issue is this slope? We've done worse with Archer."

"Sure." He makes a couple of notes. "I'm not really worried. Who's your builder?"

"I have a tentative agreement with Loel Hubbard over in West Seattle." Another half lie.

Wyatt lights up. "Oh yeah, Loel—we go way back. We went to high school together. I've worked with him a few times. Good guy."

The cabin is getting warm with both of us inside and I've started to sweat. I try to find somewhere to rest my gaze that isn't him, but it's not easy considering he takes up so much space. I'm going to have to come clean. "He may not have actually committed," I confess. "He wanted an architect on board first."

Wyatt sizes me up. "I see," he says, and I'm sure his next words will be ordering me out of his car. Instead, he picks up his phone and dials, only averting his eyes from me once someone answers on the other end. It's beyond disconcerting how difficult it is to read this man.

"Hey, Loel, Wyatt here, how's it going?" He's quiet for a while then continues, "Yeah, listen, I'm here with Danielle Porter. She says you guys have spoken?"

I watch him on the phone, the pounding of the rain threatening to drown out his voice, and it's the strangest thing—in that instant, the carefully tailored seams of his exterior come apart to show something different. A sign of life. He has one arm casually draped against the window, fingers brushing the door handle, and his face animates in a way that allows me to keep up with the conversation. As he moves with the phone, a muscle in his forearm plays beneath his skin.

"He's in," Wyatt says suddenly, bringing me back to earth. I hadn't noticed the call was over.

"Great," I say. "Does that mean you are, too?"

His chin retracts. "I thought I already said I was."

"We haven't discussed payment, though. I'll need to run your quote by my friends."

His jaw tenses, and he shifts his attention to some imagined dust on the dash. "I think you misunderstood. You help my nan with her window treatments, I help you with this. No other payment required. It's an exchange of services." He stops fussing, his hands settling on the steering wheel, and, after a moment's hesitation, the full weight of his eyes returns to me. "I wouldn't have volunteered in the first place if I wasn't planning on following through."

My thoughts jumble as if he's Kaa and I'm his surprisingly willing, jungle-dwelling victim. Right. Of course. Wyatt Montego doesn't joke around. I know this.

What he doesn't know is that I, too, can be all business when I choose.

I look away and grab a firmer hold on my purse. "As long as we agree it's my project, and you'd work for me. Just because no money would exchange hands doesn't mean it's an equal partnership or anything like that." I barely recognize the bossy inflection in my voice, but I don't apologize for it.

His mouth puckers in what had better not be an attempt to temper a smile. "As you wish," he says, then he reaches into the back seat for his bag and scribbles a number onto a business card. "My personal cell."

I take the card and put it in my pocket, marking the end of the meeting. "Thanks," I say, reaching for the door handle.

"Hey, did you really cancel your wedding?"

You could knock me over with a feather. "What?"

"That night at the bar. You said there was no wedding." When I don't respond, he grimaces and puts up a hand as if to erase the question. "Never mind. It's none of my business. Again."

He's right. Again.

But then his eyes land on mine, head tilted. Earnest.

"It was supposed to be that day," I admit, shrugging.

"Was he at the company Christmas party? Bit of an ass? Really into craft beer?"

That would be Sam. Unfortunately, he was outspoken about what he thought of the open bar selection—something I'd hoped no one would remember. No such luck.

I want to sink through the floor. "Uh-huh. Guess I dodged a bullet there." I try a small laugh, but he doesn't join, and now I know what's coming next—the big question, the one that assigns blame. I steel myself for *What happened?*

"I'm sorry," he says instead. "I shouldn't have asked."

"It's okay."

"His loss, right?" Something else flickers in the depths of his eyes.

I'm not sure what to say other than "Thanks." He's not wrong. And it's the most supportive thing I've heard from someone other than Mia and Iris since everything went down. My dad predictably still thinks I should cut Sam some slack because guys will be guys, and my mom has no training in forming opinions. If I was to ask her, she'd only regurgitate Dad's stance.

I'm about to step into the downpour and make a run for it, when Wyatt calls out, "Hold on," and comes around with an umbrella. He escorts me to my car without a word, and before I have time to thank him, he's already on his way back to his truck.

The rain on my windshield blurs his retreating contours.

I must be imagining things, but the distortion makes him look suspiciously like someone who cares.

11

EVEN I KNOW a good deal when I see one, and what Wyatt is offering is unbeatable. Mia and Iris cannot believe our luck, and to some extent I'm with them, except they're not the ones who'll have to work with him.

I flip his business card over in my hands that evening in bed. Archer Homes is a flat organization, so it's not like he's my superior, but he's been with the company longer, and his proficiency at what he does paired with the way he carries himself is intimidating. But like I told him, he'll be working *for me*, on *my* project. I already laid down the law, and I'll do whatever it takes to stay in control. I'm a capable, independent woman, and if I've learned anything, it's that guys will assume the opposite if you so much as give them an inch. No more.

With that pep talk, I grab my phone and text him.

We'd like to move forward. What's the next step? Then I add, This is Dani Porter, since I never gave him my number.

My finger hovers over the send button. It's free, I remind myself. He'll work well with Loel. We're out of other options.

I touch the screen and it's done.

Somewhere in the house, the clink of dog nails against tile announces Iris is taking Cairo and Cesar out before bed. I'd been obsessing over this text for far too long when I should have been sleeping. I toss my phone on the nightstand and get ready, but I've barely turned out my lights when it buzzes against the wood. I guess Wyatt is up, too.

Let's talk tomorrow. If you're free over lunch, we can use my office.

I grunt at his text. While I'm all in on this venture, I'm also fully aware my motivations are, at best, ethically gray and might reflect poorly on me both personally and professionally, noncompete clause aside. I don't want any part of The Spite House to be mixed up with work, but how do I tell him that without having to explain this isn't exactly a run-of-the-mill tiny rental house? No way am I giving him reason to pull out before we've even started.

I choose my words carefully. A partial truth. Would prefer other location since I'm not enlisting you on official Archer business. Afraid it would look bad?

The hovering dots that announce his typing appear right away. You're up late.

"Astute observation," I mumble.

The dots again and then, I didn't realize there'd be secrets to keep.

What? I gape at his message, regret at having texted in the first place setting in.

Not secrets. I'd just like to keep it separate from work, I say, hoping he won't press further.

Got it.

The phone is silent, and I'm about to put it down when he texts again. How about Sono's?

Sono's is a café two blocks from the office that has great sandwiches and lattes, and doesn't frown upon people bringing laptops. It's a good suggestion.

It's a date, I type, before realizing my mistake. Face flushing, I erase it and replace my close call with See you there.

I really should not be texting after midnight.

I'm in the midst of filling out insurance paperwork for the build when Wyatt DMs me midday Friday.

Heading out shortly. See you in a bit.

I'd totally lost track of time, so I finish up and tuck the envelope in my bottom drawer. To avoid the elevator lunch-rush, I take the stairs, and as I approach the fourth floor, the stairwell door opens and Wyatt enters. He doesn't spot me a flight above, but now I face the dilemma of whether I call out or creepily trail him at a distance. I opt for the latter. At least I didn't wear heels today.

I stay close to the wall, quiet as a mouse, and, at each landing, peer over the railing to make sure he's still far enough ahead. At the first floor, he stops to check his phone. Is he taking a selfie? I crouch down to get a better view and almost lose my balance, my hand clutching the railing just as he scrubs a finger across his front teeth then puts the phone away. I remain a statue as he jogs down the last flight, and wait another ten-count before I follow.

Unfortunately, my triumph only lasts until I make my way

through the lobby and find him holding the door for several other people. Damn it.

"Oh hi," I say, as if I had no idea he was nearby.

"Hey." Up close, subtle navy stripes in his black shirt bring out the dark blue of his irises. The coordination is too striking to be a coincidence.

I steel myself as I slide past him and outside. This is one of those situations everyone dreads, like when you've said goodbye to a bad date only to realize you're both parked in the same direction.

The silence is painful as we walk, and he's not yielding. Finally, I can't take it anymore.

"Any plans for the weekend?"

His head swivels my way. "Huh?"

"Do you have anything fun planned for this weekend?"

"Oh. Getting some work done." He pats his portfolio.

"That's it? No parties? Good movies? Dates?"

"I don't date," he says flatly. "How about you?"

This is not where I intended this conversation to go. "Yeah, I don't date either."

There's a brief pause in his step. "No, I mean, are you doing anything fun?"

I do a mental facepalm. *Of course, he doesn't want to know if I date.* "Not really." No need to tell him I'm planning to cringe-read all my old diaries from middle school that I discovered in a box.

Still another block to go. I catch a glimpse of us in a storefront window as we pass and groan internally at the awkwardness. We're two robots maintaining enough distance that an onlooker might assume we're not together. Tongue-tied robots. Note to self—next time, be fashionably late.

Sono's is unexpectedly busy when we arrive, but we manage to snag a round café table in the loft area half a flight up. It's an unusual space with twenty-foot ceilings and ducts painted bright yellow, which works against the gray-and-white interior. I might have painted the sales counter yellow, too, but whoever designed it had a different vision. It's okay. I still approve.

I head downstairs to order first while Wyatt watches our things. "I wasn't sure what your order is or I would have gotten it," I say when I'm back, more to make small talk than because I actually would have bought him coffee.

"Pardon?"

I repeat myself, though the words sound even more vapid the second time.

"Yes, why would you?" he says. He shrugs out of a gray moto jacket that I suspect costs more than I make in three months and drapes it over the back of his chair.

As charming as ever.

But I'm determined to have a good working relationship whether he wants it or not, so when he returns from the barista station I point to his cup with a smile. "Let me guess—extra shot Americano?" Dark and bitter seems fitting.

He looks up at me. "It's a decaf mocha." He pulls his tablet from his bag and places it next to his cup, then adds, "With caramel drizzle." His expression is daring me to judge him.

I wouldn't do that. No matter how unexpected his answer. Whatever floats his boat.

"You?" he asks.

"Me what?"

"What's your drink?"

"Oh. A rooibos latte." I have a sip to hide from his attention but curse that choice instantly when the foam of my tea scorches a trail down my throat. My eyes water and I take a gulp of water. So much for setting a professional tone. "Sorry." I push my cup to the side and position my notepad front and center in an attempt to reclaim control over this meeting. Swallow the sting away. "Perhaps we can begin by looking at permits. Since those will take a few weeks, I'd like to get them in as soon as possible. And we'll need to get on Loel's schedule, as well."

Wyatt takes a beat to respond. "Right. I'm happy to be the go-between with Loel if you'd like."

Here he comes, swooping in... "I don't know. It is my build."

"Yes, I haven't forgotten. But I've worked with him before—we already communicate well. I'll stick to your directives, don't worry. How about we divide and conquer?"

I don't want to start off our collaboration by arguing, so I accept his compromise. I'll file the permits, and he'll talk to Loel.

"As for the house," Wyatt says. "What style are you thinking?"

I turn on my tablet. "I have some preliminary drawings to show you."

He scoots his chair my way, and faint notes of cologne bridge the remaining foot of space between us. Not at all like Jim in Sales, who could knock out a horde of olfactory-challenged buffalo without lifting a finger. Or even like Sam, who, when we met, was still using the stuff teenage boys buy at the mall with their allowance. I had to teach him a thing or two about adult grooming, but he insisted on the body spray. I shake my head to banish him from my thoughts, focusing instead on Wyatt's pleasing scent.

"What?" Wyatt asks, studying me.

Stop being weird, Porter. "Nothing." I angle my tablet to give him a better view. "I was thinking something like this." It's a rough sketch of a rectangular building with the foundation partly set into the slope. One side of the first story is supported by posts to frame a deck that faces the lake view. If we can make that happen, it will be one of the main selling points when we rent it out.

"Hmm." Wyatt opens his own tablet to a 3D rendering program. He works fast, and when he's done, he tilts it my way. "Like this?" His program lets us move the house around and assess it from all sides. I hate to admit it, but I'm impressed at how quickly he pulled that together.

"Yeah, that's great," I say, "except this area here can't have a window." I point. "If the entryway is here, and we have a circular staircase down to the basement—which will only have storage and maybe a small bath/laundry, plus the exit to the deck—then the stairs to the second floor would have to go somewhere in that corner. The first floor would be kitchen, living room—open concept, of course—plus a full bathroom, and the second would ideally hold two bedrooms."

He rests two fingers against his chin. "Yeah, I don't think a second story is possible," he says.

"Why not?"

"The footprint is too small. The proportions will be off."

"Then we extend it."

He frowns. "Where?"

"Toward the back of the lot." I yank the folder with the plat survey from my bag with a little more force than intended, bumping my cup in the process. The dregs of my tea jet out and form a rusty constellation on Wyatt's sleeve.

Splat, splat, splat.

12

MY EARS GO NUMB, and I freeze, one hand suspended above the cup, the other halfway to my mouth. He's similarly immobile, his arm in the air, body leaning away. A slow-motion game of charades. Man attacked by beverage.

I've ruined another one of his shirts.

With a *whoosh*, I return to my senses, grab the tiny insult of a napkin next to my plate, and swipe at the soiled fabric.

"I'm so sorry," I say on repeat. "I'm so sorry."

"Don't worry about it." Wyatt tries to free his arm, but I, the queen of making everything worse, don't let him. My hand is around his wrist, locked in place. All I can think is that the stain resembles a restless ghost, and I need to banish it now.

"Hey." He puts his hand on mine. "Danielle?"

I still, the novelty of his firm touch flustering me enough to release him.

"Sorry," I say one last time, voice small. "And also, my friends call me Dani."

He looks at me for a long moment as if considering this. Or maybe he's measuring out my punishment?

"I know how to do laundry," he says, finally. He sits back, uncuffs his sleeve, and rolls it up. Inch by inch, more skin becomes visible, the healthy contrast between his complexion and the fabric captivating me.

"But tea is hard to get out," I squeak out.

"It's fine. Really. It was an accident."

"I just feel bad because…"

He tips his head forward, gaze soft beneath dark lashes. "Dani, let it go. I have other shirts."

"For now," I say, dryly. "Give me time."

His eyes widen, and a split second later, the face that's earned him the moniker *Wry*att among certain colleagues transforms with a luminous grin. "You have plans, huh?" he says, sitting back again. "I'll be sure to stock up."

As much as I try to stop myself, his smile is contagious. Our eyes meet, crinkled with glee, and my chest expands. The shirt staining is forgotten. Ancient history. We're two smiling fools.

Just then, someone drops a glass on the floor below, startling us both.

Rein it in, Porter.

"So, anyway…" I spread the papers out in front of us.

He pulls his shoulders back. "Yeah."

I pretend to flip a page in my notebook. "Where were we?"

Wyatt takes a moment to respond. "Proportions."

"Right." I go to pick up my tea but catch myself. "Right." I slide the plat survey in front of him, willing a seamless transition back to professionalism.

Initially our visions clash, with Wyatt pushing for a sleek, organic one-story build—the opposite of what I want—but after I stress the view as a selling point, and note the depth of the lot, which would allow for extending the house length-wise, he starts to come around.

"So, two stories, an emphasis on hospitality, open living space, two bedrooms…" he says, sipping his mocha. "I'll need to see the lot again."

A tiny drop of foam lingers on the top of his lip where the Cupid's bow dips. The white stands out against his five-o'clock shadow, but he wipes his mouth, and the vision disappears, righting my treasonous mind. Time to wrap this up.

"Sure." I pack away my tablet and finish the last of my water. "How much time do you need for an initial concept?"

"I'll let you know where I'm at after the weekend. Head-ing back?"

My chair screeches against the floor as I stand. "Yeah. Lots to do." I pause to make sure I have all my stuff. He's watch-ing me, and it's making me fumble. "And that sounds like a plan. Thanks."

"No problem." He smiles, still relaxed in his seat as if he has all the time in the world.

With a cursory "See ya," I flee down the stairs and onto the sidewalk without a backward glance.

I run into Alaina in the lobby on the way back. She's also re-turning from lunch with the PM on her current project—a woman named Jenya I haven't worked with yet.

She introduces me and Jenya, then peers over my shoulder. "Did I see you leaving with Wyatt earlier?"

Jenya balks. "You had lunch with Montego? I didn't think he took lunches."

The two of them laugh as if that's a funny joke.

"It's a…work thing." I hope my vagueness is enough for Alaina to get my meaning and not give me away. Outside of

Mia and Iris, she's the only one who knows about the build, and I'd like to keep it that way.

"Oof, my condolences." Jenya lowers her voice. "I've heard he makes almost every new person he works with cry."

I frown.

"Oh, I don't think he means to, he just can't help it. He's kind of like—" Jenya stops to think "—like a handsome ogre who is forced to work with the local villagers but ends up scaring them half to death. He's Shrek, basically. Good luck with that one." She steps back and cocks her head toward the elevators in a got-to-go motion.

"Is that true?" I ask Alaina when Jenya is out of sight. "He makes people cry?"

"I don't know about that exactly, Jenya might be exaggerating there, but he's definitely a perfectionist. No time for bullshit, that's for sure. Sometimes he'll just talk over you if you don't get to the point fast enough, and with the way he talks, I suppose someone might feel like they're being reamed out."

I've noted this in our team meetings, too—not yelling, but interjections coming with a speed and authority that can be unnerving. Oddly enough, one-on-one his voice has been perfectly pleasant. Maybe he's just like that in group settings.

"Can you imagine what someone like him must be like in a relationship?" Alaina shakes her head. "Who could ever live up to his standards?"

Is that why he doesn't date? I wonder.

She leans closer. "I heard he and Cal Archer's daughter, Madeline, used to be a thing, but that it went sour and she left the company." Her forehead creases. "Was one of them sick, maybe?"

"Really?"

"Yeah. But that was a couple of years ago, before our time.

If he's dating now, I doubt it's someone from work. People would know, and HR doesn't like it."

"That's true." My mind chugs away at this news. I wonder who broke up with whom.

Alaina has pulled out her phone and is typing. "There. I sent you an invite to my annual Spring Fling party in a few weeks. Let me know if you can make it."

13

SUNDAY MORNING, I find Iris on the couch guarded by her two beasts. She coughs when I approach and waves at me to stay away. "Spring cold. I don't want to get you sick," she says between hacks. "I've been up all night, trying to get comfortable."

Her skin is pallid and her eyes glassy. Underneath a blanket, nestled among Cesar and Cairo, she looks delicate enough that a mild breeze might carry her away.

"Maybe you should call a doctor. Do you have a fever?"

"Fever schmever. Doctors are guessing most of the time anyway."

Well, she's definitely still alert. If she's running a temperature, it can't be that high. "How about some cold medicine, then? I have some. It would help you rest."

She sneezes, and Cairo swings his head toward me as if saying, *See what I have to deal with here?* Once she's blown her nose, she concedes. "Fine, fine. I'll take your meds. And while you're at it, could you be a doll and make me some tea, too? And get me another tissue box."

I gather what she needs and place everything on the coffee table. "Anything else?"

"It depends." She squints up at me as if taking stock.

"On?"

"I won't be able to take the boys to the park today. Are you busy?"

Cairo and Cesar flank her like silent sphinxes. They're well-behaved enough. How hard could it be? "The one at Marymoor? I can do that."

Iris nods. "Take my car since it has their blankets in the back already. It's a short walk from the parking lot to the field. How strong are you?"

I mean, I'm pretty sure I could take her in arm-wrestling any day of the week. "I think I can handle it."

"Yes, you should be fine." She sniffles. "If they run too far, whistle. And bring their treat bag."

It's a beautiful April day and the sun has reached its zenith by the time we get to the park. Cairo and Cesar start whining as soon as we turn into the parking lot. It sounds like they're complaining to each other about how long I'm taking.

"Okay, boys, calm down. One moment." I find a spot at the far end and manage to wrangle them out of the car without anyone making a run for it. Trying my best Iris impression, I tell them to heel as we walk. It's not lost on me that if they decided on a mutiny, I'd have little to put up against it. "That's it, good boys. Cesar, no pulling."

They dash off like greyhounds at a track the moment I free them. Lap upon lap in larger and larger circles until they're roaming a football field away. Since it's forty partially fenced acres, I'm not worried. I sit on a bench near the entrance and whip out my phone. A message from Wyatt appears on my screen.

I have drawings. Short notice, but lunch same place?

How typical, assuming I have nothing better to do with my time. Though I suppose I did tell him I had no plans this weekend.

That was fast. Unfortunately, I can't. At the dog park. (landlady's dogs)

Which one? he asks.

Marymoor.

I'm 20 min away. I can swing by?

My stomach summersaults. What do I say to that? I scan the field for Cairo and Cesar. A third large dog is with them, and they're chasing each other without a care in the world.

Or I have some time Wednesday, he adds when I don't respond right away.

No, I don't want to wait that long. But seeing Wyatt, here, on a weekend?

Now is fine, I type before I chicken out.

Great. Picking up a sandwich. Want anything?

He wants to get me food? I'm good, I say. Whatever I can do to keep this professional.

See you in a bit.

I spend the minutes leading up to his arrival wondering why I had to wear taco print sweats out of the house, checking my teeth, and convincing myself it is absolutely possible to stay formal in this less-than-businesslike environment. But my inner pep talk is cut short when a red car I recognize enters my view. It's him.

Wyatt waves as he spots me from twenty yards away.

"Not very busy here today," he says, setting his portfolio on the ground next to the bench I've claimed. He glances down at my legs. "Nice sweatpants."

As usual, he looks fresh out of a cologne ad in his moto jacket. Today he's paired it with dark jeans and a dark shirt. Still approximating business casual.

"I wasn't expecting company. Be glad I didn't wear my SpongeBob leggings—they're even better," I blurt before I can help myself.

He smiles slowly. "I love SpongeBob!"

"No, you don't."

"You're right, I don't."

I shade my eyes in the direction of the dogs so he won't notice the way his smile hits me square in the chest.

Taking my cue, he nods at the field. "Which ones are yours?"

"The two Great Danes."

"Beautiful. Ha, look at them go."

We watch the dogs play for a minute in silence, before he pulls out his tablet. "So," he says. "Want to see what I've got so far?"

"You don't want to eat?" I nod at his take-out bag.

"You don't mind?"

"It's a nice day. I'm not in a hurry."

"In that case." He unfolds the bag. "I got extra chips in case you changed your mind. And a bottle of water." He holds the latter out to me, and I take it.

"Thank you."

"No problem." He opens the cardboard container with a hoagie-style chicken sandwich, and rummages in the bag until he finds a wrapped plastic silverware bundle. As if it's the most normal thing in the world, he proceeds to use the utensils on the fast food.

A knife and fork. To eat a sandwich.

I try not to gawk, but in addition to this unusual eating style, there's something about the precise movements of his hands, the gentle but firm grip of his fingers on the plastic, that mesmerizes me.

"What?" he asks after swallowing another forkful.

A snorted laugh forces its way out my nose, a mix of amusement and protection against a threatening blush.

"You know most people use their hands, right?"

He rests the knife and fork against the container. "And?"

I gesture to his utensils. "That seems unnecessarily complicated. Fingers deliver food faster."

"Maybe I like to take my time…" He cocks his head, dark blue eyes sealike in the bright sunlight. There's a brilliant burst of silver closest to his pupils.

I lunge for the bag of chips between us, desperate for a distraction. "It's just unusual, that's all," I say as I tear the bag open, sending crumbs flying everywhere. A good amount lands on Wyatt's food and in his lap. "Oh shit. Not again." I reach out to try to brush them off, but this time he shimmies back before I can get my hands on him. "Sorry. Clearly, I'm the one whose eating habits should be mocked, not yours."

"Is that what you were doing? Mocking me?" With studied slowness, he cuts another piece of his sandwich and brings it to his lips. "For eating like this?" He chews leisurely, one cheek bunching on a smirk.

I pick up a chip and toss it at him. That awards me a full grin.

"I don't get you at all," I say when another few minutes have passed, and he's packing up the now-empty box.

"What do you mean?"

"You're...nice."

He pauses the movement of his water bottle to his mouth before taking a sip. Then he screws on the cap and leans back against the worn wood of the bench. "This surprises you."

"Well, yeah." I wait for him to say more, but he doesn't. Instead, he puts on his sunglasses. I wish he hadn't—now I can't see what he's thinking. "Do you do it on purpose?"

He faces me again. "Do what?"

My reflection is distorted in his mirrored lenses. "The work thing. The whole 'Hello, I'm Wyatt Montego. Don't mess with me, I mean business' thing. You're clearly capable of being perfectly cordial." I emphasize the sentiment with the brush of an open palm around us.

He removes his glasses. Rubs them against his shirt. Puts them back on. Removes them again. "First, that was a terrible impression of me. Second, thank you for the compliment."

"And third?"

"Third?"

"The work thing?"

He raises the shoulder closest to me and lets it fall again. "I think a lot of people are different at work and at home."

"So, you admit you do it consciously?"

He sighs and shifts forward, resting his elbows on his knees. "Maybe we should look at the drawings now."

"It's a simple yes or no question."

"Dog with a bone," he mumbles, before tilting his head

toward me. Somehow, I don't think he's referring to Cairo or Cesar. "Then yes, I guess. I don't need to make friends at work. I like taking charge, for others to see me as a…"

"Know-it-all?"

He feigns indignation. "An authority in my field, is what I was going to say. I know what I'm doing there so why pretend otherwise?"

"But everyone already knows you're a great architect. It's the social bit. Why put people off?"

"You think I'm a great architect?"

"Obviously."

"Thanks."

"But your people skills suck."

His mouth snaps shut and he squints off into the distance. One hand tightly clasps the other. "I'm probably supposed to say I don't intend to be that way, but honestly, it makes things easier. No blurred lines. People let you down if you get too clo—"

Midsentence, he pushes off the bench. "What the…?" He points toward the field. "I think something is going on out there."

14

IT TAKES ME a moment to switch gears, but then I follow the line of his finger to see a woman chasing the dogs and waving her arms in the air. She's yelling something, but she's too far away for us to hear.

Teeth on skin comes to mind, tufts of fur flying.

"Shit!" I take off. Cairo and Cesar are huge—what if they're ganging up on a smaller dog? They're gentle, but they wouldn't need to intend injury to hurt a terrier or a bichon.

The legs of my pants flap in the wind as I run, one hand fisting the loose elastic at the waist to avoid giving Wyatt an eyeful. "Cairo! Cesar!" I call, but the dogs keep circling, and now it's clear the woman is yelling for them to "let go" and "drop it." I don't want to imagine what *it* is.

I've not sprinted like this since oversleeping for the high school bus, panic nipping at my heels, but as I draw closer, I spot the same third dog running with Cairo and Cesar, and nothing about their game appears aggressive. In fact, they're having a blast rushing one another.

I come to a stop within earshot of the woman. "What's going on?" I ask.

Her face is stark red, and there's dirt on her jeans. "Are they yours?" Her tone makes me want to say no.

"I'm dog-sitting. Did something happen?"

"Well, I'm trying to throw a stick to Benji, but the big ones keep getting it first. I need them to stop."

I look at the dogs, and back at her. She's playing fetch with her dog at the dog park and she's surprised other dogs want in on the action?

"Seems like they're all having fun together," I say.

"That's not the point." She moves toward the dogs. "Hey! Benji! Here."

Benji ignores her. Can't blame him.

"Everything okay?" Wyatt approaches, carrying my purse in his hand.

"Yeah."

The woman hollers again. Seriously—how does she expect Benji to play fetch when she keeps the stick shoved so firmly up her own behind?

"But I think it might be time to round up the beasts," I say. "Some people have no chill. Cairo! Cesar! Let's go!"

Cesar barks once and takes off. Cairo hesitates, but when his brother barks again, he, too, runs for it.

"The hell?" I start walking their way. "Come on, boys— you want a treat?"

Wyatt chuckles. "I think they're having too much fun. Maybe you should have brought some real tacos along to bribe them."

"Ha. Ha." I give him a sarcastic smile. "They always do what Iris tells them."

"She's their person. Want me to help?"

"No, they're picky about people. If anything, you'll scare them off."

He throws his hands up and backs off as I hurry forward.

Why are they being like this? "Cairo! Cesar!" I yell again. What did Iris say—to whistle for them? I give it a go, but I have a feeling she wasn't referring to the weak chirping of a baby chick, and I've never learned how to whistle with my fingers. "Come here!" I scream as loud as I can. Nothing.

"I guess they're wild dogs now," Wyatt says from behind me. "Maybe your landlady can come visit them from time to time."

I turn and cross my arms. "Again, very funny. A regular comedian today. Will you please whistle for them?"

"I won't 'scare them off'?"

"Just do it, please."

He puts his fingers up and whistles.

Cairo and Cesar halt in their tracks and drop Benji's stick, and a second whistle sets them galloping toward us. Victory.

"Here, give me a leash." Wyatt holds out his hand. "Come here, Cesar." He pats his legs, and, lo and behold, Cesar practically bounds into him as if they've known each other forever. It takes effort not to stop and stare.

"How did you do that?" I ask, as we head to the parking lot. Both dogs are panting hard and I'm trying to keep Cairo from dragging his feet. They must have hit a wall.

"I grew up with dogs," he says, simply. "They know a friend when they see one, but if that's not how they usually are, I'll consider it a compliment. Another one." He grins, and it does that thing to me again. A spark crackles at the small of my back—as if he's touched me there.

We walk the rest of the way to the car in silence. I click the key fob and it beeps a few cars ahead of us.

"That Volvo is yours?" Wyatt asks.

"It's Iris's."

"Was the window broken before?"

I pull up short, tugging Cairo back on the leash. "What the…?"

The rear window is shattered, shards of glass scattered across the wayback. This corner of the lot is empty of people. Row after row of parked cars—the ideal spot for a smash and grab. It'll be the first and last time Iris entrusts me with her car.

"Was there anything of value in there?" Wyatt asks, examining the jagged hole.

"No. At least I don't think so. Oh wait, is there a small black duffel in there?"

"No."

"Then that's what they got. Jokes on them. Assholes."

"What was it?"

"Iris's dog bag—leashes, towels, toys… Easily replaced." I hope.

"Still, you should report it to the nonemergency line. They'll want to know."

Cairo pushes his nose into my hand, bringing another issue to the forefront of my mind. "Shoot. There's glass everywhere. The dogs will get hurt if I put them in there."

"I'll drive them in my car." Wyatt makes the offer without batting an eye.

"Are you sure? I don't have any extra blankets and they're filthy…"

"It's fine." He scratches Cesar's ears. "You'll be good, right? No shenanigans?" Cesar yawns. "Yeah that's what I thought. You're such a good boy." He peers up at me and smiles slowly. "See, we're cool."

If you had asked me weeks ago, I'd have said there'd be no way in hell Wyatt Montego would do any of these things—

bring me a snack, talk goofy with dogs, offer up his pristine back seat to muddy paws. And yet here we are.

"I'll follow you, okay? Piece of cake."

We make it back to the house without incident, though Cairo and Cesar are quick out of Wyatt's back seat upon arrival. I imagine they're used to more legroom. Together we get them in the garage, where Iris has a rinse-off area with a hose and a drain—none of those fancy shower stalls Archer's clients usually want. Wyatt holds one dog while I wrestle the other.

Cairo is compliant enough, letting me lift each leg for a rinse, but Cesar wants nothing to do with the cold water. All it takes is a 180 with his hips and I'm sprawled on the ground in a puddle, laughing at this inevitable misfortune. As Wyatt goes to help me up, I raise the hose without thinking and soak one of his legs. He lets out a surprised yelp that makes me drop the nozzle, before he, too, starts laughing, steps on it, and *accidentally* gets me back.

"Sorry, sorry, I yield," I howl, trying to protect myself from the spray, and that's when the door to the house opens and Iris peeks out.

"I thought I heard voices," she says. A confounded pause as she gives us a twice-over. "I see Cesar is being his usual helpful self."

I shake water droplets from my hands and get up off the floor. "They got really muddy. I didn't want to bring them in without cleaning them."

"Did you get muddy, too?" She smirks. "I probably should have told you he's not keen on water. Are you, boy?"

Cesar pants at the end of Wyatt's leash, straining to get to the door.

"And you are?" Iris asks him.

I introduce them, and she views him at length, but if she has any thoughts about how his wet pants and hair on end contrasts with the stern professional I've described, she keeps them to herself.

"Let me give you a hand with Cesar." Iris opens the door wider. She still has a blanket around her shoulders, and her hair is pulled back with a scarf.

"That's all right, ma'am," Wyatt says. "We've got it." He gives a short whistle and snaps his fingers toward the hose, and like that, Cesar obeys. "Dani, why don't you dry off Cairo. I've got this guy."

Iris's eyebrows are well on their way to jumping off her head. I shrug in response. I don't have an explanation for any of this.

When the dogs are finally toweled off and inside, I tell Iris I'll be right in. I still need to come clean about her car, which is currently parked in the street.

I close the door behind me and face Wyatt, who's hanging the towels on a rack to dry.

"Thanks." I nod at his wet pant leg. "And sorry about that."

He jiggles it out as if that will make a difference and runs a hand over his hair. "It'll dry."

I pull my sopping shirt away from my body, where it's doing its best to imitate a bawdy spring break contest. "Maybe not what you had in mind when you called earlier?"

His gaze drifts along with my hand, but when I stop talking, he looks away and clears his throat. "Yeah, and I still haven't shown you the drawings."

"Show me now?"

How about that? I'd almost forgotten why he came out in the first place.

15

I GET IN the passenger seat of Wyatt's car and he pulls his tablet from his bag.

"So, I know a two-story build is important to you," he says, tapping the screen.

"But?"

He falters. "No but. Here." He shows me the drawing, and not only does the house have two stories, it also has the walk-out basement and posts I requested, a longer footprint, and he's added the extended overhang to reflect that Northwest modern style I love. The only problem is that the house resembles a matchbox set on its long end. While I hate admitting he was right, I don't like how it looks. At all.

I'm about to tell him as much, when he says, "I have another one to share with you if you don't mind. I played around with it, in case you wanted options."

I gesture for him to go ahead, and he flips the screen to a second drawing.

"It's a compromise," he says. "There's a second story, but it doesn't extend the full length of the building. Instead you get—"

"Another deck." I take the tablet from him. It's brilliant and I could kick myself for not thinking of it. "Because I wanted to—"

"Optimize the view," Wyatt says, and is that...? Why, yes, it is. Another real smile.

I can't turn away from the magic of his transformed expression, especially this close up—how it softens his eyes, lends yield to his rigid jaw. I'm not discreet enough, because he reigns it in too quickly, his attention back on the screen.

"The nautical feel is interesting." He outlines where there'd be a door from the bedroom out onto the deck. "But if that's not what you're picturing, we'll rework it."

"No, I think it's great." It's hilarious, actually, because Sam gets seasick easier than anyone I've ever met. And now he'll have a boatlike structure blocking his view. I should put a flagpole on that deck, like a mast. I giggle to myself at the thought.

"Something funny?" Wyatt asks.

I try to wipe the smug smile off my face and pretend to study the illustration closer. "No, just excited."

"I was thinking of continuing the concrete up to here to add more modern vibes." He points to a line halfway up the first story. "Natural cedar siding will turn gray with age, and monochrome is in right now."

He continues describing his vision, and the warm fuzzies from a moment ago fade as he waxes on about "natural light" and "sustainably sourced wood." It's not that his concepts are bad, but design is my area of expertise.

I put a hand up to stop him. "Do you think you could send me these drawings, so I can get to work on the look and feel some more? Windows are key, and I want to make sure that the flow of the rooms won't be too cramped."

"Oh, it'll be fine."

"Still. It's *my* job." I recline and cross my arms over my chest. "And I'm not into the concrete. I'm thinking a lighter wood with black details." It's the first thing that comes to mind. Usually, I go through my idea books for inspiration before creating a plan, but I can't very well shoot him down without offering another option.

"Right." He considers me in silence, then grabs the tablet and taps the screen a few times. "What's your email—or should I send it to your work one?"

"No, don't do that."

I hesitate. I don't remember the last time I gave someone my personal email, but I don't want work involved in this any more than it already is, so here goes.

"It's *wooliscool@yahoo.com*, all one word." I brace for his reaction.

"Wool is cool?" Wyatt raises an eyebrow. "Let me guess, you grew up on a sheep farm."

I should have totally had him send it to my work email. "It's my Etsy shop. I haven't done much with it lately, but I used to make and sell felted wool figures when I was in college and I never saw the point of changing my email to something less..."

"Nerdy?" A quick flutter of light across his lips.

"Says the guy who eats bread with cutlery. Pot, meet kettle."

"You're really stuck on that aren't you?" Another flash of pearly whites.

"Well, I was going to say *niche*." I unwrap my arms from my chest and his eyes flick downward again. "But I suppose a nerd by any other name... I still get orders on occasion, especially around holidays."

"That's cool." He closes the cover of the tablet. Then he deadpans, "Like wool."

I nod at the corny joke. "I see what you did there. Nice one."

"That's all I've got, though. It gets worse from here."

"Good to know. So, I guess I'll work out the details and touch base?" When we bring the plans to Loel, it'll be best to have everything in one document. That way his quote will leave less room for surprises.

"Yep. And I should…probably head out." He fastens his seat belt.

I reach for the door handle. "Yeah, me, too, or Iris will think we're on a date or something." I tense up, thankful I'm facing away from him. Curse my wayward tongue.

There's an empty beat, then Wyatt says, pretend horrified, "Yes, and what a crime *that* would be."

I dare a glance back and find him watching me expectantly. "I just mean, obviously it's not," I say in a rush. "Since neither one of us is the dating kind."

He rubs his chin with one finger. "As we've already firmly established."

"Right." A puff of air leaves my nose. "Right. So, anyway, I'm going to…" I swing my legs out of the car and take care not to stumble or drop anything. Once they're on the ground, I lean back in. "Hey, thanks again for all your help today. I really appreciate it."

"Anytime," he says, starting the engine. He looks at me like he's containing a whole dictionary of words within, then puts his sunglasses on. "I had fun."

High praise indeed from Wyatt Montego.

16

I WORK ON my drawings all week and don't stop until I'm happy with them. I even drive by the lot for inspiration and to confirm that the two-story part of the house will line up with Sam's bedroom window. His view will go the way of the woolly mammoths like the revenge gods intended. Knowing construction will take a while, I've also decided to put up a fence to give him something to stew about sooner.

My sketches come to life: an all-glass front framed by redwood on the lower level for warmth. White stucco above the concrete base, with modern steel windows, some floor-to-ceiling to let in as much light as possible. More redwood accent around the windows and in the deck railing. I might even echo it in the interior.

Structurally, I don't change a whole lot of what Wyatt already proposed—only the layout of the basement powder room, and some of the kitchen dimensions. Since people aren't going to be cooking gourmet meals in a weekend rental, the living space should have more of the square footage. I add a small loft on the top floor for an extra bed. I'm pretty sure the slope of the roof can accommodate it, but maybe it's overkill. I write a question mark next to it to get his opinion.

Thursday near midnight, I finally email the materials to Wyatt. I finish my iced tea and brush my teeth, and when I'm back in my bed, he's already responded.

A loft would fit little more than a twin mattress. Gain vs. cost? Everything else looks good. We have enough to finalize. My day is pretty full tomorrow, but I could meet Saturday before noon. Also, Loel can fit us in asap. Small enough project. I've attached his quote.

I open the file and let out a sigh of relief at the number. It's less than our cap, which is fantastic. Affordable and with no wait. How did I get so lucky? I pause to bask in the knowledge that I'm actually doing this, before checking my schedule. I have a yoga class at one, but nothing else. It feels a little odd to make more plans with Wyatt on a weekend—intimate, almost—but on the other hand, time is of the essence.

Your office at 10? I type. It will be empty and I'm hoping the environment will keep things focused. On a whim, I add, Do you happen to know anyone who could put up a fence on short notice?

A minute later my inbox dings again.

10 works. Yeah, I know a few. What kind of fence?

A tall one. I smirk to myself. A chain-link fence would be the ugliest option, but I have to remember it'll be visible from the rental, too. Plus, you'd be able to see right through it. No,

I think a solid wood fence, eight feet (the maximum height allowed without a permit for my zoning), should do the trick.

I wait for a good fifteen minutes, but this time there's no reply. It's twelve forty-five in the morning, and he's in no way obligated to offer polite closure. But cliff-hangers are the worst. They raise too many questions. Did he not respond because he went to bed, or could it be because he thinks a fence is a bad idea?

The more I think about it, the more convinced I become he'll try to talk me out of it on Saturday. An argument takes shape in my mind, completely tanking my good spirits as I trace the dark corners of the ceiling. His friendly demeanor last weekend was probably a bait and switch to bring my guard down. He'll say a fence will detract from the house, or that it'll be an eyesore.

I kick off the duvet and roll onto my side as I come up with rebuttals of all varieties—the neighbors won't want to see our tenants come and go; it'll look cozy; I'll do whatever I want—until, finally, I drift off. Unfortunately, my dreams are little better. Wyatt morphs into Sam, who wants a picket fence line built down the middle of a church aisle strewn with rose petals. *So we know what's yours and what's mine,* he says. Catrina is the minister waiting for us at the altar.

I wake up too early and have a cup of bitter, black coffee, but not even that can match my mood.

17

I CAN'T SHAKE IT. When I swipe my key card at the office Saturday morning, I'm still pricklier than a hedgehog at a snake convention. I'm not sure why the excessive reaction. Maybe because Wyatt wasn't in the office yesterday and he never responded to that last email I sent about the fence? Whatever the reason, I know I shouldn't let it get to me like this. I am totally prepared to defend my fence should it come to that. More than prepared; I'm eager. I didn't back down when my high school tried to bump start times earlier (you're welcome, Wildcats!), and I won't back down now. Bring it on.

Wyatt's floor is mostly dark, but there's light at the far end where his office is located. I push open the stairwell door and am met by carpeted silence. Without the AC humming, printers whirring, phones ringing, and the backdrop of conversations, the cubicles and hallways are a dystopian landscape moments after a blast. My senior year, when I snuck into the school with friends in the middle of the night, it felt the same way. Places where people make up the heart and soul should not be visited when empty.

I shrug off a chill as I reach Wyatt's doorway. He's at the window with his back to me, talking on the phone, and the sight of him in a slate gray Henley and jeans stops me in my tracks. The soft fabric flatters his arms and shoulders in a way his dress shirts could only ever dream of.

"Yeah, for sure," he says, and then to make matters worse, he stretches one arm behind his neck as if to release a muscle knot. The Henley rides up, revealing a small wedge of skin at his side.

He turns, catching me, and my cheeks flare instantly. I excuse myself with a bumbling gesture so he can finish up, but he beckons me in without missing a beat.

"I'll let you know," he says into his phone. "Yeah, sounds good… Okay. Love you, too."

My ears perk up. Did he lie, after all, about not having someone in his life? A strange pang skips like a flat rock across the surface of my core.

"Hey. Sorry about that." He places the phone on his desk. "Come on in."

"Hi." I put my stuff down on one of the upholstered chairs by the wall. "I didn't mean to interrupt."

"No worries. I talk to my dad every Saturday."

Oh. "That's nice."

Seeing him like this in his office—the way he moves around it not with his usual intention, but with the ease of someone unleashed from the bonds of a schedule, adds even more contrast between work Wyatt and the man I've glimpsed during our one-on-one meetings.

"I have everything up over here if you don't mind coming around." He taps the digital drawing board by the wall near the window, essentially a giant screen set horizontally—the kind that's at the top of any designer's list. When I've been at the company ten years, maybe I'll have one, too.

I cross the room and join him. The sun has not yet climbed higher than the tall buildings of downtown Bellevue, so the shadows inside make the office its own contained space bound by the artificial light above. Though anonymously furnished, it's still very *Wyatt*—the methodical layout of office supplies on his desk, the diplomas in thin gold frames on the wall, the ambitious energy infusing the air...

"I appreciate you getting together today," I say, putting command in my voice. Maybe he's onto something with the work persona thing. It's like playing a role to achieve a certain outcome. If he can convince the whole office he's Mr. Serious, I can do *this*. "Did you have any questions about what I sent you?"

"Not really. I made adjustments here and here." He enlarges the first-story floor plan on the screen. "Good thinking on the kitchen."

I lean over the board to confirm everything matches what I've asked for, trying to ignore the proximity of his body to mine.

"What I wanted to work through was your loft suggestion." He switches to a 3D rendering of the shorter second story. "We'd need some sort of ladder access and a railing at the top of the loft. The accessibility might be a problem."

"Hmm... May I?" I ask, since it's a big no-no to touch other people's work surfaces without permission.

I reach in front of him to swivel the model, and without intending to, my shoulder grazes his arm. Neck to elbow, my skin lights up as my hand hovers above the screen. I wouldn't be surprised if the wall clock above us came to a temporary stop.

"Go ahead," he says, finally, voice tight, but he remains in place.

I don't dare look up at him. We're so close, a mild case of goose bumps would bridge the gap. Just the thought of it makes the downy hairs on my arms rise. His fingers curl under his palm where it rests on the edge of the table.

Get a grip, Porter. Head in the game.

I force my focus back to the drawing. If we do a loft, the space wouldn't be much more than a mattressed ledge.

A tendon near his knuckle flexes slightly.

Then again—a mattressed ledge is another bed.

Slowly this time, I extend my hand to rotate the rendering. The heat from his arm flows through my sleeve for another fleeting second, and I press my knee hard into the table as a distraction. "Yeah, I'm not sure. It's extra work, and pullout couches in the living room might be better. Let me think about it some more."

"No problem." He returns the screen to the view of the exterior front, and for a while we just stand there, side by side, staring at it. "You have a good eye," he says, nodding. "Black steel windows…"

Warm tendrils spread from my belly up my sides. "Thanks."

"Cedar siding could still work, you know."

I've never been so intensely aware of my arm.

"Or even concrete if you'd reconsider that."

Or my hip. It's like I— Wait, what did he say? I lean away, introducing space between us once more, and it's like shaking off a dream. "I already said I'm not into concrete as a look. For the foundation, sure, but that's it." I need to wrap this up and get out of here. I clear my throat and reach for my bag. "So, the fence. You said you know some people?"

It takes him a moment to catch up. He's good at the inscrutable facade, but not perfect, and now that we've talked a few times, I've figured out his tell. When he's thrown off, he blinks twice and lists his head a tad to the left. Like Cairo when you ask if he's hungry.

"Uh, yeah," he says. "But is that really something you want to spend money on now? We could save it for after completion."

I knew there was going to be pushback. I cling to it like a lifeline, the relief of having been right—right about men, right about *him*—a buoy that I can let haul me out of danger. "Now is ideal since we'll be waiting for Loel. Plus, I spotted some of the neighbors using the property as a shortcut when I was there the other day." A white lie won't hurt anyone. I move toward the door. Three feet away from him. Three more. "If you send me the info, I'll handle it myself."

He agrees, albeit without enthusiasm, and I pivot to leave, eager to be gone.

"Dani."

The way he says my name, though—like he's always known it...

"Yeah?"

His hands tap a quick rhythm against his thighs as he takes a step closer but then stops. A tentative first ray of sunlight skates across his left shoulder, but his face remains in shadow. How does he manage to come off chiseled no matter what he wears? The thought is there before I can suppress it, doing strange things to my stomach.

"Ah, never mind." He pulls at the cuff of his Henley.

I hike my thumb over my shoulder. "Okay, well I should get to my class," I say.

"Sure."

This time I do walk away, but I'm aware of him watching as I do. My arms lock in an even stronger grip around that lifesaving buoy. Maybe we can be friends, and maybe this collaboration won't be as painful as I'd anticipated, but I can't let myself be swayed by pretty.

I. Will. Not.

"You're quiet today," Mia whispers next to me when we're both perched in downward dog toward the end of our yoga class.

"We're not supposed to talk," I whisper back.

"Your hamstrings will thank you later," the yogi says from somewhere behind us. "One more deep breath."

"Still. Your whole person is off." Mia releases her stance and lowers herself to the floor.

I follow suit. "It's nothing."

"Namaste," the yogi says.

We roll up our mats and head outside.

"Is everything going okay with the house?" Mia asks.

"As planned. I've filed for the permits, Loel is lined up—all we have to do is wait." It's not supposed to rain today, but the darkening sky suggests otherwise. It's the exact same shade as Wyatt's shirt.

I grind my back teeth together. *No.*

"Dani." Mia stops in the middle of the sidewalk.

"Huh?"

"Where the hell are you today? I was asking if you wanted to go bowling with Matt and me tonight. He's bringing a friend." She says the last word in a singsong voice, dangling it in front of me as if it's a ball of yarn and I'm a kitten. Does she not know me at all?

I scrunch up my nose. "I don't know."

"Come on, please. I've barely seen you this week." She does her best imitation of a pleading puppy. "You need to let loose. For me."

My resolve cracks. She's right, I do need to live a little.

"Fine. But only if we invite a few more people. A group thing I can do, not a double date."

No sooner have the words left me before Mia stops and grabs my wrist. "Dani, two o'clock."

I scan the street, but don't see what she's referring to.

"To your right," she hisses.

I try again, and there they are—Sam and Catrina exiting a brunch place he and I used to frequent. In fact, it hasn't even been three months since we were last there. She pulls her hair over one shoulder and smiles up at him before they stroll off.

"Are you okay?" Mia asks.

I should be. I don't want to be with Sam anymore. And yet... "Did you see how happy he looked?"

Mia drapes her arm around my shoulders, and we keep walking. "Do you want to rant? You know I'm happy to listen."

I shoot a murderous glare at the street corner behind which the smitten couple disappeared. "I'm about to do much more than rant." I tell her about the fence, or as I like to call it: phase 1. "That'll show him happy."

Mia laughs. "Revenge looks good on you, cuz. He won't know what's hit him." She squeezes my arm tighter. "Aw, you'll be all right. A kick to Sam's nuts, some rebound bowling tonight..." She wiggles her eyebrows.

I groan. "Nuh-uh—I don't do rebounding. I told you. Invite a group or I'm staying home. I have no interest in men anymore."

But as I get ready for a night out a little later, two insidious questions sneak into my mind:

Is Wyatt, by chance, a regular at the rec center?

And would it be so bad running into him again?

18

I'M NOT TOO ashamed to admit I throw around JM Archer's good name when speaking with the fence contractors Wyatt sends my way. As a result, I don't have to wait more than a few days before someone goes out to the lot. The posts should be in before the end of the weekend.

That checked off my to-do list, I immerse myself in work. I spend most of the week on-site in North Creek but am back in town right in time for the Spring Fling.

When Mia and I arrive at Alaina's that night, the party is already going strong. The condo she shares with three others is packed, but they have rooftop access, and most of the guests are mingling there while Latin rhythms pump through two speakers propped up on chairs. I recognize several people from the office, but most I haven't actually worked with. JM Archer Homes occupies multiple floors, and while I generally collaborate with other designers, architects, and project managers, as an architect, Alaina knows many of the engineers and developers, too.

We make our way to the edge of the roof, balancing our red Solo cups. It happens to be one of the first warm evenings of the year, so all of Bellevue has come alive, and a steady city buzz rises from the streets below. Celebration is in the air.

"To taking charge," I say, lifting my cup.

Mia smiles. "To fences." As she sips her drink, her eyes land on something past my shoulder. "Oh, look who's here."

I follow her line of sight and there's Wyatt, standing on the outskirts of a group of colleagues. His hands are shoved into the pockets of his dark jeans and the sleeves of his light blue shirt are rolled up to his elbows. When the group laughs, he doesn't, instead scanning the rooftop. His gaze skims past me but returns to settle firmly on mine. He offers a small smile, and I do the same, raising my glass.

"Didn't you tell me the other day you have no interest in men anymore?" Mia asks when she has my attention again.

"Yeah?"

"Then what was that?" She nudges her head in Wyatt's direction.

"What do you mean? It was nothing."

A few seconds go by, but then her face lights up as if she's just solved a decades-old mystery. "Oh my God, *that's* why you're wearing your sexy blouse."

"No." I adjust the pendant resting against the deep neckline of the thin floral fabric. "Stop it."

"I'll do no such thing. Admit it already. Your lady parts think he's hot."

"They do not."

"What's the big deal? You're human. Is it because he's older than you?"

I ignore her second question—he's probably in his midthirties, but that's hardly ancient—and decide to be as straight with her as I can. "The big deal is I don't want any part of me to have thoughts about him, or any other guy for that matter. I need to stay sharp. With the build progressing, shit's going to hit the fan soon. Sam will put two and two together, and I need to be prepared. Stay a step ahead."

"What do you think he'll do?"

"Oh, he can't do much. But I'm sure he'll try to come up with some legal obscurity to throw my way."

I'd always liked how well-read Sam is—a beast at any kind of trivia game—but it also means he doesn't like to be wrong. Now that I'm no longer on his team, not to mention I'm actively sabotaging him, it would be foolish of me to forget this. I plan to have copies of all my permits, contracts, and other supporting documents on me at all times should he start making a fuss.

"You should go say hi." Mia coaxes me with her shoulder as if she hasn't heard a thing I just said. "Otherwise, those heels are a complete waste."

"I don't know, he might be busy."

"Busy coming over here." She winks at me. "I think I need a refill."

"Mia, no, I don't—"

"Hey." Wyatt's only a few feet away. The fairy lights strung above us reflect in his eyes. Fireflies and shadows.

"Hi. You're out. Among people." I cringe. Might as well call him a recluse to his face.

"Just stopping in to say hi."

Ah, so he doesn't really *want* to be here. "Showing goodwill to the peasant masses?"

The question triggers a full grin that illuminates his face. One of his cheeks bunches more than the other when he smiles. "You'd think, but no. It is a little crowded for me, to be honest. But it's a nice evening, and everyone was going…"

Mia sidles up to me out of nowhere. "Hi there," she says to Wyatt, offering her hand. "I'm Mia, Dani's cousin and business associate."

He squints briefly, but then nods. "Ah, because of the house." He shakes her hand. "Wyatt Montego."

I've heard him say his name before, of course, but I don't know that I've paid attention to what he does with the letters. The way he pronounces it—a more open *E* before a plosive *G*—makes me want to repeat it to know what it would feel like on my tongue.

He turns back to me, and a whiff of citrus and wood trickles into my space. I inhale discreetly.

"I meant to ask you about the fence, actually," he says. "I drove past this morning and noticed they're only putting it up between the lots and not on the street sides? Is that what you wanted?"

I pretend not to see Mia on my left, staring me down. She thinks I should tell Wyatt that Sam is the neighbor. I disagree. The shortage of available architects makes him irreplaceable, so the longer I can pass this off as a normal job, the better.

"It'll be easier to access for the construction crew." I arrange my features into what I hope is a blasé smile. "We can always add the other sides later."

If he suspects I'm not being entirely truthful, he doesn't say anything.

One of the guys in the engineering group calls Wyatt's name, but he doesn't acknowledge it. "That's true," he says, instead. "Good thinking."

"Hey, Wyatt!" the same guy as before hollers. Chase or Chance or something like that.

I point. "I think they need you."

"Huh?" He looks the way I'm indicating.

Chase/Chance takes a few steps closer. "Wyatt, come here for a sec. We're trying to figure something out."

He holds up a finger to me and Mia as he backs away. "Sorry, I'll be just a moment."

"The Wyman build—was that 2013 or 2014?" the guy says, before they close ranks in their little circle again, taking Wyatt with them.

"And you've been going on and on about him being a jerk," Mia says when we're alone again. "He seems all right to me."

"Yeah, he's been a bit of a surprise outside of work."

"Maybe work's the jerk, then." She hooks her arm through mine and tows me farther away. "Either way, he's totally into you."

I roll my eyes. One-track mind. "Yeah, right. He's made very clear he doesn't date."

"Who said anything about dating? I'm telling you. You've been off the market for too long to pick up on the obvious."

"You're high."

"Not yet." She laughs.

Wyatt has his back to me, towering inches above the guys next to him, his shirt stretched tightly across his shoulders.

"Even if he was into me—and he's *not*—I don't have time for that right now. Like I said. The foundation is curing as we speak and—" Before I have a chance to finish my sentence, Wyatt's voice carries across the roof, but it's his work voice, not the one he uses in private. Not the one that follows loaded silences and accidental touches in a weekend-empty office. The memory is enough for me to forget the point I was making.

Mia tips her head to the side. "Huh. Interesting," she says.

I think he's had a haircut. He wears it long on top, shaved in the back and on the sides, and tonight it's short enough that the movement of muscle is visible beneath the velveteen stubble of his neck when the light hits it right.

"What's interesting?" I ask.

"Your face is all red."

There's no use in attempting even a half-hearted protest. A blush of this magnitude is impossible to deny, and my only option is to hide behind my drink. "Fuck," I whisper.

"Oh yeah, I see a lot of *that* in your future." She laughs and rubs her palms together. "It's rebound time, baby."

"Shh, he's coming back. What do I do?"

"Whatever you want to do." She mimes for me to take a breath. "I'll be inside."

My heart pounding, I swipe a thumb beneath my mouth to fix any runaway gloss just in time for Wyatt to reach me. "Everything good?" I ask, too high-pitched.

He nods. "Can I get you another drink?"

I'd kill for a margarita right about now, and yet... "Can't. Designated driver."

"Gotcha." He adjusts the wristwatch on his arm, looks off at the cityscape.

"Nice view, right?" I say. *Nice view... You're an embarrassment, Porter.*

We make our way to the edge of the roof.

"I've always had a soft spot for skyscrapers at night," he says. "They're like a human imitation of the starry sky."

I take in his profile and smile. "Aren't you the poet."

He laughs quietly and turns his face my way. Pauses. "Maybe I just like what I see."

Behind us the party continues, but somehow, we've vortexed far away. It's just him and me. The tick of his jaw, the blink of my eye, the scratch of his nails against his stubble, the parting of my lips...

Our hands rest on the railing an inch apart. I don't know

if he moves his first or if I do. All I know is that the skin on the side of his pinky is cool against mine and that I've failed hopelessly. I meant it when I made a toast to celibacy. My body clearly didn't.

I look away but brave the smallest lift of my finger to let it brush across his knuckle. Might be an accident, might not. Who can really say...

He does the same to mine.

"You can almost see my building from here," he says, leaning forward. His neck taunts me with its flawless slope.

"Oh yeah? Where?"

"Behind that mirrored one. Here, I'll show you." He steps back, but just as the absence of his pinky pings through me, his palm makes contact with my lower back as he passes behind me.

I'm not prepared for it, and I'm certain he must notice the quick tremble beneath his touch. It takes everything I have to stay still.

"Over there," he says. His arm extends past my shoulder, and I see exactly nothing. His building could be the freaking Taj Mahal for all I care.

"Mmm-hmm, yeah."

Don't move, I tell myself. As if he's a rare bird and I'm the living statue he's decided to perch on.

"Woo!" someone shouts from the overhang near the door where a poor piñata is no more.

Wyatt flinches and withdraws his hand.

Another second and we've both done a ninety-degree twirl apart.

"I should probably find Mia," I say awkwardly. "She doesn't even know these people."

He surveys the crowd and nods in greeting to a strolling couple. "Sure, no problem."

I hesitate. "Can I get you anything from inside?"

"I'm good." He finally looks at me again. "But I'll be here."

I locate Mia in the kitchen where she's helping Alaina pour bags of chips into bowls.

Alaina stops to hug me. "Can you believe all these people showed up?" she asks. "Without the roof I'd have been screwed. Even Wyatt and a few others who never usually come out."

"Yeah, we met him upstairs," Mia says. "Nice guy, right, Dani?" She grins at me, an eager slant to her chin.

I return a mock version of her expression, ignoring the unspoken question.

"Not talking about it," I say as we mingle, pausing here and there to say hi. "There's nothing *to* talk about."

"Yet. The night is young."

At one point, Mia gets sucked into a long conversation about the merits of social media with someone from our marketing team, but eventually I manage to drag her back up to the roof. In case Wyatt's been waiting.

The temperature has dropped, and people are huddled closer to the doorway now. Mia's phone chimes and while she reads the message, I scan the faces, without any luck. I wasn't gone that long. What happened to *I'll be here*? Did he go home? At that thought, the strung-up lights above transform from fairy magic into the Christmas remnants they really are. A few aren't working at all.

I press a palm to my stomach to quell the pang and pull my jean jacket tighter around me.

"Hey, Matt and his friends are around the corner. Would you mind if I skipped out?" Mia scrunches up her nose. "I totally won't if you want me to stay. Or you can come with?"

I suppose there's nothing keeping me here anymore. "We

can go but let me run to the restroom first. Meet you out front?"

"Yay." She takes out her phone—to respond to Matt, I assume—while I jog down the stairs.

The hallway by the bathroom is full of sweaters and light jackets people dumped there on their way in, and I step around them as best as I can. There's one person ahead of me in line— I think she's an administrative assistant on the engineering team. We exchange greetings, then focus on our phones. As you do.

"Are you sure someone's in there?" I ask when five minutes pass without a sound from the other side of the door.

"I've tried the handle twice."

"May I?" I lean past her and do the same. Locked.

She sighs. "Whatever, I give up. I've been here at least ten minutes. All yours."

Once she's gone, I turn back to the door. There's light coming from underneath it, but no signs of life. After a moment's hesitation, I knock. "Anyone in there?"

Nothing.

I put my ear to the door. "Hello?"

This time there's some shuffling. A groan.

I knock again. "Everything okay?" I ask, more insistently.

The person curses under their breath. A beat, then, "Not really."

I know that voice.

19

"WYATT?" I GO for the knob again, but no luck. "What's going on? Can you open the door?"

"Uh-uh."

"Should I get help?"

"No." Firmer this time.

"Okay." My hand rests against the wood. *Think, Porter.* I start rifling in my purse, hoping to find some kind of tool that will allow me to get inside. *Aha!* "Okay, I'm going to unlock the door."

No answer. I take that as approval. With a quick push of the bobby pin, the lock disengages. "I'm coming in now." I inch the door open little by little until my whole face fits in the gap, and there he is, leaning against the toilet.

I close the door behind me and lock it.

His skin is a greenish white and the front of his hair is stuck to his forehead. His eyes are shut.

"Hey, what's wrong? Did you have too much to drink?"

"I don't drink." He breathes slowly, methodically, as if he's counting his breaths. Whatever is going on, he's trying hard not to be sick. "I have…" Inhale. "Vertigo." Exhale. "It comes…" Inhale. "Out of nowhere." Exhale. He groans again, angles deeper into the bowl, and I cover my ears. If there's one thing I can't handle it's that sound.

When he's done, I offer him a tissue from the counter and my water bottle. He drinks, then rests his head on his arm on the seat again.

"Is there anything I can do? Someone I should call? Do you need a doctor?" My cell beeps in my pocket. Crap, I've completely forgotten about Mia. I text her back that I've decided to stay after all and I'll call her in the morning.

"No, I just… I need to get home. My medicine…"

"Okay. Are you able to walk?"

A bitter scoff. "Probably not."

"Can you try?" I place a hand on his shoulder. "I'll help."

He shifts back and immediately starts toppling sideways into me. I have to wrap my arm around him to prop him up. Considering the size of him and the size of me, this is not going to work.

"I'm sorry," he mumbles against my shoulder. "I don't want…" Inhale. "Anyone to know." Exhale.

By *anyone*, I assume he means people at work. But there are others here, people who don't know him.

"Okay, I have an idea," I say. "I'm going to go get some guys to help you down to the street while I pull up my car. I'll tell them you're drunk if they ask. Sound good?"

"Bring a garbage bag."

"Good idea."

"And would you happen to have any mints?"

I hand him a stick of peppermint gum, then leave with what I hope is a reassuring "Be right back."

The hallway is empty, but a group is gathered in the living room around a guy strumming "Despacito." Alaina's brother, Marcus, is among them, and while perhaps not the most subtle choice, he's someone I've been introduced to, unlike many others here. I tap him on the shoulder and gesture for him to follow.

"Does Alaina need something?" he asks.

I shake my head and explain the situation without getting into the details. "Would you be able to grab a couple guys and help me get him to my car?"

To his credit, Marcus doesn't ask questions, and it isn't long before he and two friends hoist Wyatt up off the bathroom floor and start maneuvering him downstairs. His face is even paler by the time they get him buckled in.

I slide in on my side of the car. "Do you need a minute?" I ask, not knowing how this works.

"No, please drive," he whispers. "Tenth to Bellevue Way, then left."

We do so in silence. Every few minutes, I steal a glance his way, but his posture is the same: head pitched back, hands gripping his legs, mouth in a tight line. The sight makes me step harder on the gas pedal.

It's not until we enter the underground garage of his building that I realize my mistake: I'll never be able to get him inside on my own.

"We're here," I say, softly. "But there's a problem."

"I know." Wyatt doesn't move, doesn't open his eyes. "My keys are in my pocket, sixth floor, apartment 630. There's a yellow pill bottle in the top left drawer in the bathroom. Meclizine."

When he doesn't say more, I reach over, tug at his jacket. He lifts his arm to give me access, and as my fingers slide into his pocket, his body tenses. Heat radiates off him.

LOVE AT FIRST SPITE

"I'll be right back," I say. "Don't go anywhere."

The corner of his mouth twitches at my attempt at a joke. Good—there's still some life in him after all.

Cool air hits my face as I swing open the door to Wyatt's apartment. The place is tinged with his scent, and an involuntary shiver races up my spine. There's something forbidden about entering another's space in the dark. I flick on the hallway light and allow myself only a cursory look around. I don't know what I had expected—glass and steel and monochromatic tones, perhaps—but instead the apartment is lived-in and inviting. Bookcases line one side of the living room, and a large leather couch the other. A well-used lacrosse stick hangs on the wall above one of the end tables. I both wish I had more time, and already feel like I'm snooping.

"Bathroom," I mutter to myself. It doesn't take long to find the medicine and a fresh bottle of water, and, on impulse, I snatch a blanket from the couch, too.

Wyatt is still in the same pose, but his chin quirks when I get back into my seat and open the pill container.

"How many?" I ask.

"Two."

I set them in his palm and pass him the water. His neck pulses as he drinks, the reflex replicating down his arm. With a minimal turn of the wrist, he hands me back the bottle.

"Thanks." He pauses. "I'm…really sorry. It's not how…" He swallows the rest of the sentence, his profile immobile, dark lashes splayed across pale cheeks.

I resist an urge to smooth back his hair.

"Are you cold?" I ask instead. "I brought a blanket." As I spread it over his lap, my knuckles brush his abs by accident. Neither of us acknowledges it. "So, what now?"

"I wish I had better news, but now I sit still like this until I fall asleep, and hopefully when I wake up, I can move again. It will be a couple of hours at least. Aren't you glad you helped?"

Before I can stop myself, I squeeze his arm lightly. "It's fine. I don't mind. What else can I do?"

His forearm stiffens then relaxes beneath my fingers. "Talk. If you don't mind. Tell me something that'll distract me."

I sit back at the same time the cabin light goes off above us. The interior of the car is in shadow, the only sound Wyatt's slow breathing. The clock on the dash is almost at midnight.

"Where are you from?" he asks. "Start there?"

I fold my right leg underneath me to face him. "I grew up in Coeur d'Alene. It's a small town in Idaho across the border from Spokane."

"I've been there. It's gorgeous."

I smile. "It has its moments."

His mouth curves slightly.

"Only child," I continue. "But nine cousins. Mia was kind of like an annoying little sister to me growing up.

"My dad's a financial planner, and my mom was a teacher before they had me." Images of her reading *Little House on the Prairie* to me and my cousins at family get-togethers flash before me. She'd wanted to go back to work, but the timing was never right according to my dad.

"Are you close?" Wyatt asks, his eyes still shut.

"Not really. My dad's older, extremely conservative."

"And your mom?"

I pluck at a rip in my jeans, my nail scratching the skin below. The thing is, I could have been close with my mom if it wasn't for the fact that she always takes Dad's side. For as long as I can remember, I've known she wants more. It's in the scrapbooks she keeps of places in the world she'd like to visit "one day," in her volunteer engagement in every class I ever took, in the way she's grayed and faded into the wallpaper since I left. What I've never understood is the resignation. Why does she let him hold her back? Make choices for her? The one time I asked, she told me I had no idea what I was talking about. Then she put salmon in the oven for him even though she's allergic to seafood.

"It's complicated," I say. "I mostly see them over the holidays." No need to delve further into that. Not everyone has to be tight with their parents. "What about you?"

He adjusts his position before responding. "Yeah, I'm close with my dad. And his mom, my nan."

"The one I'm doing drapes for?"

"Um, yeah. Right. Dad's retired, but he's got a small farm to keep him busy outside Burlington—chickens, a couple of sheep and alpacas, a vegetable garden. I have one older sister who lives near him, too."

No mention of a mother, and I don't ask. "Is your grandma also up in Burlington?"

"No, she's in Monroe."

Thank goodness. Burlington would have been a hike. I lean my temple into the headrest, cataloging in turn the creased plane of his forehead, the straight bridge of his nose, the rounded shell of his ear.

"Is the medicine starting to kick in at all?"

"Maybe. Think so." His Adam's apple rises and falls. "Why did you become a designer?"

We're back to me. I tell him my origin story, from middle school art class to the professor who tried to make me drop out of the design program in college, and sprinkle it with anecdotes about moving to the Seattle area. The one topic I leave out is Sam.

At some point I must doze off, because when my eyes flutter open again, the roles are reversed and Wyatt is watching me. I immediately jerk upright and rub at my neck. That's a kink that'll last for days.

"Sorry, I didn't mean to fall asleep. Do you need anything?" I cover a yawn with the back of my hand. The clock says it's 3:15 in the morning. Hopefully I didn't snore.

"You're fine." His pupils are inscrutable pools of dark, sucking me in, and a hint of color has returned to his cheeks.

"You look like you're doing better."

"Yeah, I should be able to go upstairs now. You still have the keys, though, and I didn't want to wake you."

"Oh." I reach into my pocket. "Sorry."

A tired smile. "I don't know why you keep apologizing. You didn't have to do any of this. I'm the one who should apologize for ruining your evening."

"Nah, I—"

"Dani, I'm serious." His hand traverses the center console and comes to rest on mine. "I don't know what I would have done."

His palm is warm and dry, his fingers arching so that only the tips graze my skin. I stare at the point of contact as if the sight might explain the fireworks that have gone off inside me.

"Does it happen a lot?" I ask, regretting it instantly when he pulls away.

After a brief stall, he answers. "It comes and goes. It's this thing called Ménière's that affects my inner ear, so…" He gathers the blanket from his lap and bundles it into a ball. "No big deal. You know what? I should head up and you should get home. Thank God it's Saturday, right? I'll be in bed until noon."

It's funny—up until this moment, I haven't thought of him as someone even capable of sleeping in. I had him sized up as the kind of control freak who brings weights on vacation and touts the hours between 5:00 and 7:00 a.m. as their most productive.

I blink at his broad back as he exits the car. The atmosphere shift is a slap in the face, a ten-degree gale after hot chocolate by an open fire.

"Will you be okay?" I ask, leaning across the passenger seat. "I could…" Go with him upstairs? Tuck him in?

"What?" He bends down to my level.

"Never mind."

"Are you…?" An amused crease forms between his brows. "You're worried about me?"

"Well, yeah… You were in pretty bad shape earlier."

A turbulent ocean roils behind the blue of his irises, waves of contradicting arguments. But "I'll be fine" is all he says, straightening. "I'll see you Monday, Dani. Get some sleep."

The door closes, leaving me alone in muffled silence.

He walks away slowly, as if testing whether his legs will carry him. Before he enters the elevator vestibule, he stops and turns my way.

It's not much, but he turns.

20

WHEN I WAS in eighth grade, I had a dream that one of my best guy friends saved me from an ice floe on a dark lake. A threat of death and a knight in shining armor. A romantic reunion kiss. I carried that feeling with me from class to class the next day—of him being something more than I'd previously thought—and, briefly, it was hard to separate dream from reality. The dream had planted ideas in my head that could have ruined our friendship had I acted on them.

This thing with Wyatt reminds me of that; Mia's suggestion that he's into me must be messing with my head. When I wake up Saturday morning, I text to check in, and he doesn't respond, which seems to confirm my cousin has read too many fairy tales.

By Monday morning, however, the foundation is ready for inspection, and Wyatt and I have a meeting early with Loel and the city inspector at the lot. It has taken longer than usual to choose my outfit, but I feel cute in a navy-striped pencil skirt and off-white slouchy knit top. I also did a clay-mask last night for a *fresh and dewy complexion*. But my efforts are not for Wyatt, no sirree—it's a big day, the starting gun for the actual build, and I'm trying to make it an occasion.

There are no cars in Sam's driveway as I switch off my ignition. It's gorgeous out, which means he's likely squeezing in an early tee time before work. Fine by me. The fence towers perfectly unsightly between the two lots.

Wyatt and Loel are already there. I've only spoken to my contractor on the phone so far, and given his and Wyatt's friendship I'm surprised to find he's a bearded giant with a waxed moustache that could win prizes. His jeans and reflective vest make for a striking clash with Wyatt's work attire and sunglasses, straight out of a *Men in Black* movie. Rough wood versus polished jade.

I run a hand through my hair before getting out of the car.

"Good morning," I call on approach, nerves trilling.

"It sure is," Loel responds with a grin. "You must be Dani. It's good to finally meet you."

"Hey." Wyatt barely awards me a glance.

Loel pulls off his cap, smooths down his strawberry mop of hair, puts it back on again. "He's almost done already." He indicates the inspector. "Everything's looking good so far."

"Great." I peek at Wyatt, but he's absorbed by his phone. I might as well not be here.

The inspector and one other guy, who were busy on the far side of the lot when I arrived, join us, and Loel introduces me to his foreman. "Joe, this is the owner, Dani Porter."

Joe's hand engulfs mine. "Looks like we're good to rock 'n' roll," he says. "We'll have a house here in no time."

I smile at him. "Fantastic."

While we're talking, Wyatt and the inspector wrap up their conversation in my periphery. There are handshakes and signed papers, and that's that. We're officially on to the next phase—things are finally moving! Without my coconspirators here, it's oddly anticlimactic. It's not like I can high-five Wyatt.

"I've got to take off," he says, as if driving home how right I am in that assumption.

Why is he treating me like I'm invisible?

"Yeah, yeah. I'll keep you posted." Loel pats him on the back and he tromps away.

"Hey," I call after Wyatt, but he still ignores me. I tell Loel I'll check in tonight, then hurry after the straight-backed iceberg I'd vainly thought might have melted further this weekend. He's already reached his car, moose-legged as he is, but I make a valiant effort to catch up that might have succeeded had the curb not taken me by surprise. Before I know what's happened, I'm up close and personal with the concrete instead, and the rear bumper of Wyatt's car is shrinking away.

"You okay?" Loel hollers.

I brush off my palms. "Fine," I call back. Mad as hell, but intact.

I jump in my car and get going, but I'm not paying attention, and just as I pass Sam's driveway, his Tesla zooms into the street, reversing lights like angry slits. So, he was home after all. I slam on the brakes and lay on the horn, and it's only by a hair that we avoid collision. I am so not in the mood for this.

Sam leaps out and comes around to inspect his trunk. He's in a suit and tie, his wavy brown hair parted and brushed back, just long enough on top to hint at playful. Not until he looks up does he recognize it's me.

I lower my window as he approaches. "Backup camera broken?" I ask, putting on my game face.

"Sorry, sorry, I was in a hurry. Didn't see you there." He leans forward, eager. "So, what can I do you for?"

"What do you mean?"

"I assume you're here for me?"

Oh shit. "Right…" I scan my surroundings for an official reason. A question to ask, something I need from the house… "Oh yeah, I forgot to, ah…" My brain rattles like a slot machine. "To get some…insurance papers. For my car. I think I left them in the office somewhere." They're in my glove compartment. Also, that reminds me I still need to send in the paperwork for The Spite House. I would write myself a note if Sam wasn't right up in my business.

He scratches his head. "I don't remember seeing any. But I can look when I get home later."

Phew. "That works."

Just then, the truck belonging to one of Joe's guys backfires at the curb near the fence. Sam whips his head that way and mutters a profanity under his breath.

"Have you seen this shit?" he asks.

My heart leaps in my chest. I sure have!

"I don't know if the city is marking boundaries or what's going on, but they didn't give a heads-up or ask permission or anything. You work in construction—maybe you know. Don't they need to say something before putting something like that up?"

I resist the urge to correct him about my job. It's close enough, I guess. "Wow, yeah," I say. "That must be pretty annoying."

"Catrina wants me to 'do something about it,' but, like, what's there to do?"

"Hmm." I lay a finger to my cheek as if this is indeed a conundrum. "If only we'd bought that lot while we could."

"I know, right?"

The sarcasm is wasted on him. He's mad about the fence, and Catrina is mad at him for not dealing with the fence. My glee is threatening to bubble over.

"At least the lot is too small for anything substantial," he says. "Whatever they're doing, no one's going to want to put a house there."

Oh, precious lamb chop.

"Small blessings." I smile. "Okay, I'll let you get going then."

I speed off and allow the triumph to settle in as I navigate the traffic lights along Eighth Street. Sam hates it. He's getting his due. The fates are being balanced.

But the closer I get to the office, the more the feeling dissipates, overshadowed by Wyatt's coldness earlier. Because who does he think he is? Friday night aside, we've worked together for almost a month now and are, if not friends, per se, then at least friend*ly*. Now this is how he's going to act? No, nope, nuh-uh. If he thinks I'll put up with that, he's in for a surprise. Civility is a bare minimum.

And I intend to let him know.

21

I TRY TO get Wyatt's attention in our north-side team meeting, but apparently, I've turned into a solar eclipse that can't be looked at directly, and he's the first one out the door when we wrap up.

I text him later that day. No answer.

Tuesday morning, I find an excuse to go down to his floor but catch only the back of his head as he rounds the corner into someone else's office. He's as elusive as Nessie of the Scottish Loch, and with each act of evasion, my temperature rises.

I return from lunch, late and frazzled from having attempted to squeeze in too many errands during my break. The all-hands meeting looms, and this time I'm determined not to let him get away. A thousand and one arguments run through my mind as I elbow open the elevator vestibule and wait for the ding of arrival.

I'm going to block his path in the hallway, force him to—

Before I can finish my thought, the doors slide open, and there he is, in the flesh.

He startles, a flinch of the chin more than a full body recoil, but it's obvious I'm unexpected. A surprise of the unwanted kind. "Uh, hi."

Today, his gray shirt has violet undertones that match the storm brewing inside me. Slate sport coat, purple tie. The impeccable facade further stokes my anger as I swing my arm out to hold the elevator and flatten him with the iciest glare I can muster.

"That's it? *Hi?* That's all you have to say to me?"

I enter and press the button to my floor. The doors take forever to close.

He remains immobile, no words uttered in defense.

"Are you upset about something?" I go on. "Is there a reason you've been avoiding me?" The sound takes up more of the small space than I intended. "After this weekend, I thought..." What did I think? "I thought we were becoming friends."

"Friends," he repeats, but on his tongue the word sounds like an insult.

We reach the second floor and freeze as the doors open. No one gets on.

"No, I'm not mad," he continues in a low voice. "But honestly, it's just... The whole thing makes me a bit uncomfortable—"

"I make you uncomfortable?"

"Let me finish," he snaps. "What happened—the vertigo—only a couple of people here know about that." The bell signals we're approaching the third floor. "Fuck."

The way the expletive bursts forth makes my stomach flip.

"I know you have friends here, and I don't want..." He huffs and shifts his weight from one foot to the other as the elevator climbs. "I don't want it to be held against me."

As he struggles to get the words out, the roaring in my head quiets, and the fight in me fades. "Are you worried I'm going to tell them? Because I would never."

His jaw clenches. "I don't want anyone's pity."

The mechanical whir above us intensifies, and I'm suddenly aware of his proximity, that we're almost at his floor.

"For what it's worth, I don't think they'd feel that way. I know I don't." I take a deep breath to relieve a quickening in my chest. Step closer.

He stares at the ceiling. "Dani, I… We really shouldn't…"

Before he can finish either sentence, the fourth-floor bell chimes and the elevator officially stops.

Shouldn't what? *Shouldn't what?*

He rubs his neck, disengages. "Look, I'll talk to you later, okay?"

The doors open and close, the objection sticking unformed in my throat, and I'm alone again. My head is a jumble, and the startling thought I return to over and over is—*This is hard for him.* Not that I'm letting him off the hook.

The only seat available in the meeting ten minutes later is directly across from Wyatt. He doesn't acknowledge my presence at first, but when Eve, one of the VPs, eventually kicks off the agenda, he puts his pencil down with meticulous care, leans back, and looks straight into my eyes.

The voices around me fall away as I dangle at the precipice of his gaze. My mouth is so dry I struggle to swallow. It's like he's asking me questions and drawing out the answers all at once. Begging forgiveness and making promises with the lift of a brow, the widening of pupils. Eons go by, or milliseconds, each more intense than the next.

"Wyatt?"

I blink as the room returns to focus, but somehow, he knows what they're asking, and without missing a beat, he mirrors his screen to the whiteboard to share updates on whatever project they're talking about. I don't listen; I'm too preoccupied trying to subdue the electrified critters running amok beneath my skin. I don't care about bids or prospective clients or trade show features. I want to go hide in my office and replay that whole conversation we didn't just have.

"And while you're in Chicago, Vera will field any requests your way," Eve says.

Wait, what?

"Sounds good." Wyatt nods. "I get in tonight and should still be available for meetings in the afternoons the rest of the week."

He's leaving?

"No." The word forces its way up my throat and hangs in the air, a flashing red light impossible to ignore.

The whole room turns. Alaina frowns at me from the end of the table.

Please kill me now.

"Um…" I venture a glance at Wyatt. A surprised smile teases the corner of his mouth. "I mean, no…um…remember you have that show…" My eyes flicker across blank faces. "That showing. On Thursday." *Come on. Help me.* I send him the message wordlessly, hoping the channel is still open. "So, you're not actually available that day."

Finally, he bobs his head, first slowly, then faster. "Oh right. The showing. I forgot."

"What showing?" Eve leafs through her papers. "I don't remember anything about that."

"Yeah." Wyatt squares his shoulders. "It's a recent addition to the itinerary. Danielle has a contact at the Vista Tower build. I'm going to check it out."

He's a master of deceit. With my history, this is probably not something that should impress me, and yet it does.

Eve moves on to her next item, and I sink deeper into my chair.

I'm the first one out of the room when we're done, taking off down the hallway to the elevator, where I stab the button five times. The others are starting to mill out, so when it doesn't come, I grunt an expletive and wrench open the door to the stairwell instead. Up or down? I hesitate. I have work to do at my desk, but facing my coworkers right now would be worse than a visit to the DMV. What I need is some air. Some space. Down it is.

I jog all the way to the garage, but as I'm unlocking my car, Wyatt exits the elevator vestibule calling my name. I wasn't fast enough. He may have saved my behind in that meeting, but he and I both know there's no contact at the Vista Tower. This is about to get messy.

I turn and his approach slows.

"You're leaving?" he asks.

I cross my arms. "*You're* leaving?"

"It's a work trip. It's been scheduled since February. I didn't think…" He's only a few feet away now. "Maybe I should have mentioned it."

"Maybe." I raise my chin. "You know, since we're working together on the house."

"Right." He points upward. "So that's what that was about in the meeting? You're worried about the build?"

He steps closer so that I could reach out and touch him if I wanted. My fingers tingle.

"Sure."

"And not for any other reason?"

I shake my head, but inches lower, my heart is trying to force its way out of my rib cage, threatening to betray me.

"Dani, come on."

He knows. It must be written in bold across my face by

now. "Does it matter? You've made it pretty clear how you feel about the possibility of me as even a friend."

"Friends wouldn't work."

"Why? Because *Wyatt Montego* doesn't socialize? Or because I specifically am not worthy of that title?"

His hands fist at his sides. "Because..." The word echoes in the cavernous space. He takes a breath, eyes like obsidian. "Because...what I want to do with you, you don't do with your friends."

A rush of heat pools low in my belly. *What he wants to do with me...*

The tightness in his voice gives me the courage I need. "And what if I feel the same way? Would that change anything?"

Wyatt's gaze sweeps across me as he draws nearer, only inches away now. "Maybe."

I lick my lips. This close, his face is a sepia portrait rendered in light and shadow, and there's a glint in the dark beneath his brow. *He's got me alone now*, it whispers. Or I've got him.

What are we going to do about it?

He pauses, then his head swoops down, his breath tickling my skin. "Quite possibly."

My pulse thunders in my ears as the heat of his body hits me, and without thinking, I let my hand come to rest just below his clavicle, where it idles before traveling north to his jaw.

"I'm sorry about this week," he says, the cadence thick. "I didn't know what to say or how to be after the other night, but ignoring you was wrong. Will you forgive me?"

His palm has found my hip, the pad of his thumb slowly caressing. It makes it hard to concentrate on his apology, but I manage a breathy "Yes."

He leans into my hand, his cheek rough beneath my fingertips. "Also, I'd really, really like to ki—"

I nod quickly and close the last bit of space between us.

We come together hard—lips first, then bodies—and his solid chest is home. Have I been longing for this since that night at the bar? His hands go to my hair, mine grasp his waist, panted breaths, hungry tongues. He tastes of peppermint and something sweet—strawberry, perhaps.

It lasts four seconds, maybe five, then voices emerge from the vestibule, and, as if on cue, we jump apart.

Wyatt straightens his jacket. "Yeah, about that project," he says, lifting a hand in greeting as two guys from the fifth floor enter the garage.

"Ah, Montego," one of them says. "Gina was looking for you upstairs. Something about a signature."

"Got it," Wyatt says. "Thanks."

They get into a car across from us and speed away, the tires screeching against the concrete as they disappear around the corner. But before we can pick up where we left off, the elevator dings again and a cluster of people from one of the other businesses in the building trickles out. More greetings, more inane pleasantries.

Wyatt rubs his forehead like he's trying to create wrinkles, not smooth them out, and I kick the toe of my ankle boot into the floor.

"I'm sorry I have to go to Chicago," he says, quietly. "I'll be back Saturday, and, if you *were* worried about the house, I promise I'll be in touch with Loel daily."

"Quick thinking about the Vista. I don't know what came over me," I say. "Or I do, but—"

"Yeah, I'm pretty proud of myself. Especially since I was quite distracted by the realization you didn't want me to go." He looks off into the distance where two cars are turning onto the exit ramp. "You're not the easiest to read, you know."

"I could say the same about you." He's at a safe two-yard

distance now. Reality is coming back into focus. Reality and Mr. Archer, who exits the elevator with his phone held out in front of him on speaker. Wyatt and I both wave and nod.

"We should probably head up," Wyatt says when the boss man is out of earshot.

There's no way I can make it through an elevator ride with him right now, so I tell him to go ahead. "I left some paperwork in my car. I'll take the next one."

We both know there's no paperwork, but he doesn't object.

It's not until I'm back on my floor that it dawns on me we left things unsettled. And now he's off to Chicago for four days. I sit down at my desk, my face reflecting in the dark monitor. Maybe it's a good thing. Neither of us is dating anyway, and I have a spite house to build.

My phone buzzes in my purse.

Later, is all the text says, but the letters light up my spine like a billboard sign.

22

LOEL AND HIS crew make quick progress on the framing, and I bring Mia and Iris to the site one evening to show them. At least that's one reason for our visit. The other is for some "decorating"—Iris's idea.

"How does Sam feel about garden gnomes?" she'd asked a few evenings ago, knocking on the door to my room. Turns out Ellen left Iris a mighty fine collection.

We exit the car, each with a bag of figurines. Since Sam's usually home this hour, we've parked under the cover of the huge elm.

"Oh, this is going to be fun!" Mia says. She could barely contain herself when we told her she could pick her favorites.

"Yes, thanks again." I smile at Iris.

"She'd enjoy this," Iris says, more to herself than to me. I don't need to ask who she's referring to.

We make our way up the sloped part of the lot to the fence and proceed to unload our ceramic friends. I've brought hula-hoop gnome, sunflower gnome, and mankini gnome. The latter has a boom box on his shoulder and his outfit doesn't leave much to the imagination. Ellen must have been one heck of a lady.

Mia chose a traditional gnome holding a mushroom, a meditating gnome, and a couple of kissing gnomes, and Iris has one riding a tractor, and a larger one carrying a lantern. It's a great start, but knowing we barely made a dent in the collection, I suspect these eight will soon be joined by many more. I snicker to myself at the thought.

"Where do you want them?" Iris asks me.

"If he's going to see them, they'll have to be over there where the fence ends." I point. We have limited options for where to stage our scene since the workers need access, but they have no reason to be that close to the property line.

"What if he takes them?" Mia asks.

I dismiss that outright. Sam may be a cheating asshat, but he's not a thief.

"Let's put them here." I pull out a few tufts of tall grass near the street. "I think they're having a party. Hula gnome and mankini gnome are bound to know how to get down."

"Poor meditation gnome. No zen to be had here." Mia giggles as she helps me put our cone-headed friends in place.

When we're done, we take a step back to admire our work. In the distance, the sun is setting above Lake Washington, the scattered clouds in the sky glowing with apricot edges.

"It is a wonderful location for a house," Iris says.

"Yeah, and from the sketches, I think it'll be great, but…" Mia sucks in the side of her cheek.

"But what?" Iris and I ask in chorus.

"Aside from blocking Sam's view, and these garden gnomes, how else is it going to be anything more than another cute tiny house?"

"Oh, I totally forgot." I draw out my phone, where I've started a list of things Sam can't stand. I've crossed off the fence and boats now that the house is shaping up to resemble one, but there are many others still available. I show them the screen. "My spite house to-do list."

"He hates flags?" Iris asks.

"Not just any flag—what could be more offensive to a Washington State alum than University of Washington Husky colors flying outside his window?"

"That's genius." Mia high-fives me.

"But first I want to name the place with a big old sign over there, next to where the mailbox will go. It's a pet peeve of his—kind of like how you feel about people dressing up their cars as Rudolph during the holidays."

"Oh yeah, I hate that." Mia shudders. "So tacky."

"What are you naming it?" Iris asks.

I've had to think of something less literal than *The Spite House*. We'll still call it that when advertising it as a rental, but the yard sign needs to be friendlier. I pause for dramatic effect. "*Gnome Sweet Gnome*. Thanks to Ellen for the inspiration. If that's okay with you, of course," I say to Iris.

She beams. "Like I said—she'd enjoy this. Thank you."

I tuck my phone away. "I'll let you know if I think of anything else for the list."

"We can help," Mia says. "Three heads are better than one. I'm going to noodle on it and come up with something good."

I don't doubt that she will.

23

I'VE TEXTED BACK and forth with Wyatt twice since he arrived in Chicago—short check-ins, nothing more. I keep waiting for him to make good on his promise of "later," but the more hours that pass without either of us mentioning it, the better I get at convincing myself the kiss was a temporary glitch in judgment, nothing else.

Unfortunately, that thought also makes me want to alternately stab a fork into the back of my hand and hide under a blanket, so come Thursday night, I'm a real joy to be around. That evening I curl up on the couch with Cairo stretched out next to me in front of whatever moody French show Iris is watching, until the credits scroll and she turns it off.

"I kissed Wyatt," I say into the silence.

"The architect?" Iris reaches for a wasabi pea from a bowl on the table. She keeps a party-sized bag in her pantry at all times.

"Yeah."

She pats the side of the chair and Cesar goes to her for an ear scratch. "Was he any good?"

That's the understatement of the day. I can't help the smile that grows on my face.

"I'll take that as a yes." She gets up from her chair, walks over to the bookcase, and scans the spines. "Then what's the problem?"

"Who says there is one?"

"Honey, why would you blurt something like that out to your elderly landlady unless it was weighing on you in some way?" She stops and picks out one of the books. "Ah, there it is."

"Well, I can't tell Mia. She'd pee herself with glee." I sigh. "But I have no business kissing anyone right now. I've sworn off guys for a good reason."

"You're breaking your own rules."

"So to speak."

"Isn't that what rules are for?"

"But I'm not sure what to do next. Do I pretend it never happened?"

She squints shrewdly at me as she sits back down. "What makes you think you get to decide that on your own? Last I checked you still need two people for a good smooch."

I let that sink in. She's right. "Do I wait for him to say something, then?"

"Wait for the man? I think you're mistaking me for someone who's not an old lesbian." She opens the book. "You'll figure it out. I'm going to read now. Cairo, say good-night."

Cairo lifts his head and licks me across the cheek.

Back in my room, I stare at my phone, Iris's words ringing in my ears. It's past eleven in Chicago, but you never know.

You awake? I text.

It takes less than a minute for him to respond. I am.

My thumbs perch above the screen. Now that I have his attention, I'm not sure what exactly I want to say.

I saw the Vista today, he writes first. Thanks for coordinating the meeting.

Smart-ass. Happy to be of service.

My phone rings, and a swarm of butterflies takes flight in my chest as I accept his call. "Isn't it a cardinal sin to call someone in the middle of a text conversation?"

"Add that to my list of vices?" he says, voice warm and sleepy. "You good?"

Better now. "I'm good."

"You know, I actually did go to the Vista. I called up an old classmate of mine who knew someone who got me a tour. It was pretty cool. Figured the boss might need proof."

"You did not."

"True story."

"You could have pretended it fell through."

He's quiet, then, "Damn, I didn't think of that."

I fluff a pillow behind me and lean back. "But you're having a good time?"

"It's been productive. Let's leave it at that."

"Not your idea of fun?" The question sounds more suggestive than I intended. I wince as I wait for his response.

"No. I can think of plenty of other things I'd rather be doing."

"Such as?"

"Hmm…"

"What?"

A low chuckle. "Nothing. Trying to figure out if it's a friendly question about my hobbies or something else."

I twist a strand of my hair around my finger. "Can it be both?"

Rustling comes through the line. I picture him getting

comfortable, wherever he is. "How about we stick to the former for now?"

I swallow away my disappointment. "Sure."

"But only because I'd rather address the *something else* part when I get back," he continues. "Okay, Dani?"

The fine hairs on my arms stand up. "Yes." His loaded promise has made me breathless, and I'm thankful he can't see me smothering a smile into my pillow.

"Good. So, hobbies, then," he says, slightly restrained. "Let's see. I run and go to the gym whenever possible, and I have a boat I spend a lot of time on in the summer. I used to play lacrosse, but I've had to step away from the league the past few years, and...oh, I paint from time to time—acrylics mostly. That's about it. Not very interesting. How about you?"

I remember the lacrosse stick on his wall. "Why don't you play anymore?"

"It's...um...it's a bit of a story. Not an interesting one. Your turn. What do you do when you're not at work?"

What *do* I do? Ever since I moved here, my free time has been spent on Sam and his friends. I did theater in high school, but I don't think that counts.

"Hello, you still there?"

"Sorry, yeah. I guess...some occasional yoga classes, hanging out with Mia, mostly. I like to read, and I used to do textile printing and the yarn crafts I told you about. I know it sounds super boring, but last year I spent a lot of time on wedding stuff. There wasn't much room for actual hobbies. And now it's the house."

Wyatt lets out a low "hmm." Then, "Can I ask why you called off the wedding?"

It was only a matter of time. "Will you tell me about the lacrosse?"

He laughs. "Touché."

"Well?"

"Fair enough," he agrees.

"And you're not going to walk that back once I'm done?"

"I'd never."

"Okay." I blow out a breath. "Okay, here goes." I start at the beginning—getting engaged, relocating out here, making plans for a future—and tell him everything about our house search and my conditions for buying one together (everything except exactly which house we ended up buying, that is).

He emits a pained grunt when I get to how those wishes were ignored. "How is it a wedding present if your name isn't on it?"

Thank you. "My sentiments exactly."

"Yeah, I don't blame you for getting cold feet after that."

"Except, there's more." I add the final paragraph in Sam's and my story, then sit back and wait for Wyatt's reaction.

"Man," he says. "How long did you say you were together again?"

"Three years."

"Goes to show, you never really know people. I'm sorry."

Something in his voice has me regretting I didn't save the lacrosse question and ask about Madeline Archer instead. Did he have his heart broken, too? Did she cheat on him?

"It's okay. Karma's a bitch. Now your turn. Why aren't you in the league anymore? Were you any good?"

"I was okay. No star player by any means, but I've played since I was eleven off and on. Started in middle school, continued through high school. I did not play at MIT, but when I came here after college, I found an amateur league, and it was a lot of fun. Made some friends, etcetera. When I saw you that night at the rec center, that's who I was with. We catch up every couple of months. They still play weekly…" He trails off.

"But not you."

"It's the vertigo. The Ménière's." He says it as if the word tastes bad.

"Playing brings it on?"

"Not necessarily. It's more that it's unpredictable. I tried to stick with it back when I was diagnosed around two years ago, but then I'd miss practices, not be able to show up for games. It wasn't fair to the team, so I quit. Nice little sob story, huh?" He chuckles but the sound lacks depth.

"You miss it."

"I do," he says eventually. "A lot."

"I'm sorry."

"Yeah, well. It is what it is. And it might not be forever. I have fewer attacks now than in the beginning. It's kind of up and down with this thing."

I wish he was here. I picture him massaging the furrow that sometimes forms at the base of his nose as if trying to erase it, like he does in meetings at work. I always thought it stemmed from contempt or irritation because of his general airs, but listening to him now it's like I've turned the kaleidoscope of him ninety degrees and the image is changing. It's not clear— not yet—but more colors are crystallizing.

"You know," I say. "Come to think of it, I believe I do have one other hobby."

"Oh yeah? What's that?"

My stomach rolls like I'm at the top of the high dive looking down. Should I? "Yeah, it's a new interest. Recently, I've really enjoyed exploring the city's underground architectural features."

"Oh?"

"Specifically, parking garages." I press the phone to my ear.

When he finally speaks, his voice is closer. "Small world— that's one of my hobbies, too."

We both go silent. A minute ticks by. I straighten a crease on my comforter.

"I wish we hadn't been interrupted," I say. *Not waiting for the man.*

A sharp exhale in my ear. "So do I."

I smile up at the ceiling.

"I wanted to kiss you in my office the other weekend, actually. As long as we're being honest."

A breathy laugh escapes out my nose. "You've been patient, then."

"*So* patient."

"And then to have it cut short. What a bummer."

It is going to be so distracting working with him on The Spite House over the next couple of months with this hanging over us. Unless... An idea begins to take shape...

"It definitely didn't end the way *I've* pictured it," he says.

I flush from my toes to my hairline. "No?"

"No. But..." He hesitates. "Was it for the best maybe? What do you think?"

There's no way he believes that with everything he just said, so here's my chance. If you don't ask for what you want you don't get it, and right now that's for him to draw me the full picture. Screw caution. Literally.

"I think we'll be seeing each other outside of work anyway, right? I also think we both want to...you know..."

"Definitely."

"And we've already established neither of us are in the dating game."

"Mmm-hmm."

"So what if we—" I cover my eyes as if that will make the words come easier "—you know—scratch the itch?" I wrinkle my nose. It sounded better in my head.

"As in...?"

"A fling or whatever you want to call it. Just while we're working on the house. Unless you think that's a bad idea?"

Wyatt makes a noise suspiciously close to a purr. "I'm going to go with *not* a bad idea. If you're sure," he adds.

"I'm sure." My conviction is ironclad. This may not be something Old Dani would have considered, but *she* doesn't live here anymore.

"You know," Wyatt says, "Loel tells me he's making good progress already, and we never celebrated the launch of your project in the first place. Dinner Saturday? My place. I'll cook."

Everything about that sentence is right. "So, a business meeting?"

"We could call it that."

"But with perks."

His heavy breath in my ear threatens my equilibrium. Saturday can't come soon enough.

"I'm looking forward to it," he says. "It'll be *something else*."

24

"OKAY, I'M HEADING OUT," I tell Iris around five on Saturday. "Need anything before I go?"

"I'm all right, hon. I like your skirt."

It's my lucky boho one. "Thanks."

"I hope it gets you some."

I almost choke on a gulp of air. "Iris!"

"Oh please. Have a lovely evening, then. Is that better?"

I pause in my car before turning the key. Am I really doing this? Thursday's phone call feels ages ago and my nerves are frayed. I no longer know if I'm thinking straight. What I need is a reality check.

Mia answers after the second ring. "I only have a minute," she says. "We're doing an evening hike."

"Who are you and where's my cousin?"

She laughs. "I know, right? What's up?"

I shouldn't have called her. With her being all gooey-eyed

about Matt these days, she's not exactly trustworthy with relationship advice.

"You know how I've sworn off guys and am putting myself first right now? Well, I'm on my way to Wyatt's and I need you to tell me it would be a terrible mistake to kiss him." I clear my throat. "Again." I scrunch my face together, waiting for her response.

"Dani, what the hell? Hold on." She says something off the line and then comes back. "Holy shit. Was it after I left the party? Why am I only hearing about this now?"

"Seriously, let's talk about this later. You're in a hurry. All I need you to do is remind me. Men, bad. Celibacy, good. Right?"

"But I have questions!"

"Nope, no can do. Look, I get confused when I'm with him. Lady parts and all that... Make the call for me. Working relationship only, right? No funny business. No fling. It's what's best for me. For our build."

She groans. "Fine. But we'll talk about this later. I expect details." She sighs. "You don't like men."

"Right."

"You're done with them and their egos."

"Preach."

"As a woman in the twenty-first century, you don't need male chromosomes cramping your style. Without them you can do what you want, when you want it, how you want it— No, I'm sorry. I can't do this." Her tone changes.

"What?"

"Yeah, you should definitely get yours. Forget the rest."

"Really?" And here I was just warming up.

"You said a fling, right? You're both grown-ups. Get it out of your system. I'm for it. Less thinking, more doing. Anything else I can help you with?"

"You suck."

"Aw, I love you, too. And I *will* call you later," Mia says. "You'd better pick up."

"Yeah, yeah. Enjoy your hike. Say hi to Matt."

We hang up.

"Less thinking, more doing," I say, gripping the steering wheel.

I drive the ten minutes to Wyatt's apartment, park, and ride the elevator, my mind in a haze. I haven't been with anyone other than Sam in a long time and the prospect is both daunting and exhilarating. At his door, I give a small shimmy to shake off the nerves.

I knock, and there he is, his presence alone making me silently congratulate myself for the daring proposal that's led me here.

"Aw, no taco pants tonight?" is the first thing he says once I enter.

I still can't believe I let him see me in those. "Got to mix it up."

Neither of us goes for a hug—a relief and a disappointment—but I can be patient. We have time.

His apartment smells amazing from butter, sautéed garlic, and something else sharp—ginger root, maybe. Last time I was here, I was only passing through with a mission, but now I take everything in.

"Make yourself at home. I'm going to check on the chicken. Can I get you a drink?"

"Whatever you're having."

He scratches at his temple. "Lemon seltzer?"

Oh, that's right, no alcohol for him. "Sure."

He disappears behind the island into the open-plan kitchen, leaving me to browse the spines in his bookcase. I wouldn't say he's a prolific reader based on its contents, but I find a few favorites.

"How was the rest of your week?" he asks, closing the fridge.

My pulse is still elevated from merely being here, so I gratefully latch onto the safe topic. "Yesterday was a bit rough actually. Apparently, we lost the Renton bid *and* had issues with a foundation at a site in Redmond, so everyone was scrambling to come up with fixes and silver linings before the weekend."

"Sounds like I should be glad I wasn't there."

Family pictures adorn the shelves—in one, Wyatt and his dad are toasting beers next to an alpaca (I'm going to need the story behind that), and in another, baby Wyatt sits in a stroller in front of his parents. I pick it up and try to make out the suave man in the round-cheeked child.

He joins me, and I return the photo. "Sorry, I'm snooping."

"Snoop away." His fingertips brush my arm, triggering a current of electricity beneath my skin. At first, I think it's an accident, but when he lingers, I'm forced to reconsider. His touch wanders to the small of my back, applying gentle pressure. *Relax*, it seems to say. *Breathe.*

I lower my shoulders and allow the goose bumps to subside. "You look a lot like your mom." I nod to the baby photo.

"Sorry, hold on." He reaches up and fiddles with something in his ear. "I'm trying out a hearing aid," he says. "I'm at twenty percent and dropping of my hearing in this ear—another wonderful part of Ménière's disease. Figured it was time to do something about it." He takes out his phone and taps the screen.

"You control it with an app?"

"High-tech, huh? There." He puts away his phone. "Sorry you were saying?"

"That you look like your mom."

He lights up. "It's been a while since someone's said that. I never really knew her, though. She died when I was three."

Oh no. That's why he didn't mention her before. *Way to go, Porter.* "I'm so sorry."

He shrugs. "My dad did great on his own. It was harder for my sister. But we don't have to talk about that right now. Dinner is ready." He gestures to the island where two plates wait on the counter. "You don't mind eating here, do you? I never use the dining room—it's become a bit of a catchall." He pulls out a stool for me, then sits down to my left.

I don't mind. It allows me to see more of his living space while we eat.

I sample a first bite and flavors explode across my palate. "Oh my gosh, this is incredible."

"I don't cook a ton, but I have a few favorites. This stir-fry is one of them. Glad you like it." He lifts his glass. "To your build."

"To a productive collaboration," I say. "With…benefits?"

Wyatt stills, surveying me above the rim of his glass. A Cheshire grin blooms behind it.

That effectively ends the business part of the evening. Over the next hour, we eat and talk and laugh. He asks about Iris's car, about Mia, about work. I learn the beer picture was a joke because his dad's first alpaca was named Budweiser (Bud for short), and that if he wasn't an architect, he'd be an art teacher.

"I can't picture you in a school, guiding impressionable minds day after day," I say. "Wouldn't it drive you nuts? Dealing with classrooms full of kids?"

"You think I couldn't handle it?" He folds his arms across his chest.

I squint, pretending to appraise his academic suitability. "Hmm…"

"Oh come on." He laughs. "I could totally do it. Here, tell me you forgot to do your homework."

I swivel my chair until I'm facing him completely, and then I raise my hand as if I'm at school. "Mr. Montego, my dogs ate my homework so I can't turn it in."

It's like a switch flips, and his expression becomes impenetrable. Even his voice drops into a more percussive cadence. "Unfortunately, the deadline was today. What do you propose we do about it, Ms. Porter?"

Ms. Porter... A quiver prickles the back of my legs. This is some primo role-playing goodness. Clearly, he has enough authority to manage a roomful of brats.

"Mmm-hmm, yeah. I see it now," I croak. *You can be my teacher any day.*

He smiles. "No, you might be onto something—it wouldn't be right for me in the long run. I like producing things, starting a project from scratch and seeing it take shape. Teaching wouldn't be the same."

I push my plate away, muster up bravery, and say casually, "If it helps, I can keep calling you *Mr. Montego.*"

His pupils dilate, almost indiscernibly. He's not immune to this game either.

"Does it bother you how other people pronounce it?" I ask. "I mean at work. It's not the way you say it."

He turns his legs so our knees meet. "And how do I say it?"

The touching point sends a trickle of heat up my thighs. "Montego." Soft *T*, open *E*. I know it's a decent imitation by the glimmer in his eyes.

He leans forward, and the air transforms between us into something alive and sparking. "Again."

A gasp slips out of me when he runs his hand up the side of my leg. I swallow. "Montego."

His hand skims my hip and tightens on my waist. "One more time."

He's a fascinating mix of work and play, and I don't know where one ends and the other begins. But I like it. It helps me meld the two versions of him together into someone real. Gentle and firm. Safe and dangerous. Nice and—

"*Ms.* Porter?"

The way he savors the syllables draws me to him like a magnet, and when I speak his name next, it's on a breath against his lips. He waits for me to deepen the kiss, and I do, my hand tracing his cheek, then around to the nape of his neck. I want to map out every part of him. All this uncharted territory.

"I don't care how they say it," he whispers when we separate, his stubble scraping against me. His fingers have found their way underneath my tank top and are sketching lines along my sides and back. "I like your version." He nibbles lightly along my jaw. "But I prefer…when you…call me… Wyatt." He demarcates each phrasing with another graze.

"I can do that." I put my mouth to his ear. *"Wyatt."*

He groans and takes command of the kiss with new urgency, his grip mimicking the firm demand of his lips. Now there's only mouths, and palms, and goose flesh, and drumming hearts. His hunger is obvious, setting off a firestorm in me—a highway of nerve endings ablaze straight to my abdomen.

It's okay, I tell myself. A *want* is not the same as a *need*.

"You never showed me around," I murmur near his ear. "Where do you sleep?"

He retreats an inch to scrutinize me, eyebrow arched. "Yeah?"

I nod. "Yeah."

25

WYATT TAKES MY hand and leads me down the short hallway behind the kitchen into his bedroom, where we stop in
the sphere of light created by the nightstand lamp. He slants
his lips over mine in another kindling kiss, and I yank at his
T-shirt, tugging it over his head. He does the same with my
tank top, then skims into the waistline of my skirt and slides
it off my hips. His eyes roam my body.

"Fucking hell."

It's the encouragement I need to tackle his belt and jeans.
He helps me get them off, and I'm immediately tempted by
the way his boxers bulge. I go to feel him, but he intercepts
me and links our fingers.

"Not yet."

He places a soft kiss beneath my ear, then my throat, my
clavicle, and lower. He follows with his fingertips, running
one into the top of my bra.

"You're teasing me," I whisper.

He looks up, gaze hot on mine, and runs the same finger slowly in reverse, then hooks it into the cup and pulls down.

I shiver from the unexpected air against my breast.

"Better?" His knuckle skims the puckered tip, back and forth, before he leans in and takes it into his mouth. His tongue tears a burning trail through me, making it impossible to produce any response but a whimper.

"Good," he says roughly, moving to my other breast. "I've been wanting to do this for a long time."

A long time? I always assumed he barely knew my name, much less that he was having daydreams about his tongue on my flesh. But Lord above, I'm not complaining.

When I can't handle it anymore, I maneuver him to the bed, grab the elastic of his boxers, and stare up at his gorgeous face. "Now?" I ask.

He steps closer, curves his hand to my cheek. I lean into it. Kiss it. Teeth to palm.

He sucks in a sharp breath. "Scoot back."

I do and he follows, planting more kisses that, one by one, ignite my skin from my belly to the hollow at the base of my throat. He lingers there as he lowers himself onto me, his thighs on mine, his hips, his chest. There's no doubt in my mind he wants me as much as I want him, but there are still too many layers of fabric in the way.

He sits back to fully undress me, but it's taking too long. My fingers dig into his forearms, tugging him to me. I'm too far gone to guard myself anymore.

"Hold on," he says, voice thick. He gets a condom from the nightstand and makes swift parting with his underwear, then hovers over me, brushing his hand up the inside of my thigh. It stops frustratingly short of its goal.

"You good?" he whispers.

"Yeah." I wiggle until his fingers make contact with my most sensitive parts, but after that all effort is his.

When I get too close, I ask him to pause. I want to drag this out.

He withdraws to let me catch my breath, even though I can feel him against my leg, ready and impatient.

I don't make him wait long.

As soon as I trust myself again, I reach down and let my hand encircle him, guiding him to where I want him most.

"Look at me," he murmurs, one arm on either side of my shoulders to prop himself up.

I do. Everything about him is mouthwatering in this moment—the strained tendons in his neck, the way his hair flops forward, his swollen lips. Even the way he has me pinned. A frustrated grunt escapes me, and he smiles.

"Is this what you want?" He makes a small circle with his hips, but it's still only a promise, nothing more. The audacity.

Well, two can play at that game.

I bring his face down and kiss him deeply, ending with a cheeky nip. My eyes throw down the gauntlet: *Your move.*

He doesn't wait. He covers my mouth with his again, and finally, *finally*, he shifts so I can wrap my legs around him. The pressure is exquisite as he sinks in inch by inch. Every nerve ending in my body is connected by a thousand electric pulses, and I can't get near enough even when there's no more distance to travel. We stay there for a suspended beat, both breathing heavily, our bodies slick and trembling.

Then he starts moving, and I die a little.

One of us groans, but there's no telling who.

I claw at his neck, his back, the rounding of his ass, my hands roaming, urging on, but whenever I'm about to lose it, he holds back just enough to leave me trembling but not yet at rapture. It's infuriating in the best of ways.

The climb lasts forever, but still not long enough. Peaks and valleys, valleys and peaks, and I'm lost to everything but the two of us and the sensation of him.

When I plummet over the edge, I'm loud and he's right there with me.

Thunderous fanfare, a crescendo to bliss.

Then silence.

Once the echoes of our voices fade, there's only our slowing breaths. His face in the crook of my neck, my cheek against his forehead. And that's no less of an event.

Consciousness returns gradually, the air cools, and our hearts reclaim their pacing. I expect him to roll off me, but he doesn't, just angles to the side to save me from carrying the bulk of his weight.

That just happened, I think.

Ignoring his protests, I extract myself from his embrace and sit up. I want to watch him come back together knowing I made him fall apart. He observes me as I study him, six and a quarter feet of languorous male stretched out before me. He's all defined muscle, of course—not bulky, but athletic, a poster boy for healthy lifestyles. Sculpted thighs, washboard abs in that V shape that points directly to—

"You'll get me hard again if you keep that up," he says, lids hooded.

I curb a smile. "I'm not doing anything."

"Right..."

I know what he means; he does the same thing to me.

My exploration stops at the red marks across his pecs inflicted by my nails. "Sorry about that." I lean forward to soothe them with my lips.

"I'm not." He buries his hands in my hair and rewards me with a leisurely kiss—a stroke of his tongue, a gentle tug, a shared breath. "That was...worth the wait."

A clenching low in my stomach reverberates through me. My body wants more, but my mind needs time to catch up.

"Oh, it's true. Patience wins the day," I say, sitting back up. "I'm going to get us some water. Want anything else?"

He stretches his arms above his head. "There's ice cream in the freezer."

Twist my arm. I retrieve my underwear and pad across the carpet, wiggling my butt for his benefit.

The sound he makes suggests appreciation.

When I return, he's in shorts, reclining against the headboard like some kind of tousled Adonis. It's an odd impulse, but I kind of want to bite him just a little.

"What side do you sleep on?" I ask instead. "Or do you splay out in the middle? Master of your domain?"

He takes the pint of ice cream and one of the spoons. "I always fall asleep on the left. But now that you ask, I suppose I do wake up in the middle."

"Unless you're sharing the bed with someone."

His eyes flicker to mine. "Depends on who I'm sharing it with."

"That's fair." I sit back and spoon out some cookies and cream, feel the cold sweetness on my tongue. I'm getting tired. Will he expect me to stay or leave? What exactly is the protocol for this type of arrangement?

"You're welcome to find out for yourself," he says as if reading my mind. "Unless your *itch* is done being *scratched*." He smirks.

In response, I toss the ice cream aside and press my lips to his sternum. Let them wander to his ribs, down his side, across his abs. When he doesn't object, I dare to steal a glance at his face. The light cast from the nightstand lamp draws a sharp line along his jaw.

"Don't stop," he says.

I don't.

I wake from gray light sifting through the curtains. The empty ice-cream carton lies overturned directly in my line of sight, a reminder of the fun we had with its melted contents well past the midnight hours. I should be tired, but I'm not. I'm well-kneaded dough, soft and supple, ready to spring back under Wyatt's touch. Except he's still asleep.

As quietly as I can, I get out of bed and tiptoe to the kitchen. Our leftovers sit forgotten in the pan and I grab a few noodles with my fingers. Still delicious. I find a chunk of baguette, too, and a can of seltzer in the fridge, and bring my loot back with me to the bedroom.

"You left," he mumbles against the pillow.

I deposit the food on the nightstand and crawl on top of him. "I was starving."

He wraps his arms around me with a sigh. "Did you find anything?"

"Mmm-hmm."

"You smell good."

I laugh. "I smell like you."

He flips me over and raises my arms above my head, then makes a show of sniffing my hair, my neck, down the side of my breast. I giggle, setting off a loud gurgling in my stomach that makes me laugh harder.

He resurfaces from beneath the covers, a bemused expression on his face. "Was that you?"

"Told you I was hungry."

"Good lord, then let's get some food in you before the cave troll gets even angrier. Here, have some bread. I'll be right back."

I take a bite and chew slowly while admiring his retreating behind.

"I'd like to go see how far Loel's come at the site sometime today," he calls from the bathroom. "Want to join me?"

As flattering as it is that he's open to keeping me around, it might be better not to allow him too much too soon. Anyway, I have plans. "I'm meeting Mia in a bit," I call back. "We have some stuff to do for the house."

"What kind of stuff?"

"We're finishing a sign that we're putting up. Like to name it."

"Gotcha."

I scroll through my emails. There's one from Mr. Archer, and I open that first. New project, exploratory meeting Tuesday, personal friends of his, great visibility. *I know you all will make me proud.* The plural pronoun automatically makes me check the address line to see who else is on the team, and my heart stutters as Wyatt's name comes into view. How about that for timing?

I have to add speed showers to his superpowers because he returns a few minutes later, drying his hair with a towel. He picks something up from the floor and presents it to me with a flourish. "Your undergarments, Ms. Porter," he says with an adorably bashful grin.

My stomach does a somersault, but I chalk it up to indigestion from the food I just gobbled down.

"Much obliged, Mr. Montego." I jump out of bed and gather the rest of my clothes.

"Hey, did you see this?" He holds up his phone. He looks half amused, half troubled.

I pull on my skirt and adjust the waistband. "Just did. But it won't be a problem, right? We can handle it."

"Yeah." He scans the screen once more. "Yeah," he says

again with more conviction this time. "We're both adults. This—" he points between us "—is separate from work."

I'm suddenly eager not to prolong this morning-after hassle. We got it out of our system. No need to dawdle. "As it should be."

He nods to himself.

Once I'm dressed, he walks me to the door, but before I can go, he grabs hold of my hand and spins me toward him for one last kiss, a light depression of his warm, soft mouth that's so decadent, it's like he's letting me in on a dirty secret. He makes a gruff noise and pulls me into him with his other arm, his hand splaying against that area of my lower back he laid claim to earlier. Any thoughts of Mr. Archer and work fly out the window.

"Glad we finally got a chance to...*celebrate* our progress," he says into my hair.

I lick my lips to savor his minty morning flavor. "It was certainly an enjoyable occasion."

He releases me with a playful pat on my behind. "I'll see you tomorrow, Dani."

Right before the elevator doors close, I flutter my eyelashes and give him a flippant "Not if I see you first."

26

IRIS SMIRKS WHEN I show up in yesterday's clothes, but she keeps her thoughts to herself.

"What are you up to today?" I ask, passing through the living room.

"Oh, big plans. Sun, patio, book. You?"

I tell her Mia is on her way and just then, the sound of my cousin's squeaky brakes reaches us from the street. "Can you do me a favor and let her know I'll be right out? The sign is in the garage if she wants to get started. I need to change."

She touches her forehead with two fingers in an affirmatory salute.

Ten minutes later, I wrap my wet hair into a knot on top of my head and enter the garage. Mia is busy drilling a hole through a wooden, 2D garden gnome that we're going to screw onto the sign.

"Walk of shame this morning I hear," she says with a fiendish grin. "Finally. Good for you."

I take a bow, but don't address her comment beyond that. This fling is between me and Wyatt.

"Did you want me to do the lettering?" I ask. The background coat in bright green has dried, so the words—*Gnome Sweet Gnome*—are all that's left.

"You know it."

I grab the white paint from the bench and place my first careful brushstroke. One eye-catching spite house sign coming right up.

"You should be done with that by tonight, right?"

The *N* gets a curl at the end. "Are you questioning my skills?"

"I'd never," she says. "What I mean is—you're free tonight? I have a surprise for you at the house."

I lift the brush off the wood and squint at her. "What kind of surprise?"

She zips her lips. "I'll need you there at seven."

❧

I get there thirty minutes early. The sign is dry, the gnome attached. If I can get the post in the ground before Mia arrives, this won't be such a one-sided surprise.

Loel and his crew must have gotten a lot done yesterday, because suddenly the skeleton has some meat on it, and the whole structure is looking more like a house. I take a turn around the property to gauge the best spot, before retrieving the sign and a sledgehammer from my trunk. There's a patch of undisturbed soil near the fence where it shouldn't be in the way of the construction.

Balancing the post and hammering at the same time requires more effort than I expected, but after a few false starts due to hidden rocks, I finally have success. A couple more hits and it should be steady enough. I'm too preoccupied keeping my fingers un-smashed to notice I've got company.

"What the hell are you doing?"

I whirl around to find Sam in front of me, barefoot and huffing.

"I saw you from the window. Why are you..." He reads the sign. I can practically hear the wheels turning.

After weeks of subterfuge, the moment has come; we're only a few seconds away. The plan was always to have him connect the dots himself, and, honestly, it's been a longer time coming than I thought. I'm ready to roll with it. Have a little fun.

"It's shaping up to be a nice place, don't you think?" I clutch the signpost and smile my sweetest smile.

"You know who's building here?"

Okay, maybe more than a few seconds. "I do."

"Who? It's been a fucking nuisance so far, but the foreman doesn't give anything up."

Good man. "You know them," I say. "Pretty well."

"What?" His top lip draws up like he's reciting the alphabet backward in his head.

"Yeah. In fact, you almost married one of them."

His gaze snaps to my face. "No."

I nod.

"*You're* building this house?"

"Mia and I figured it's the perfect location for an Airbnb. I mean, look at this view." I extend my arm toward the distant waters.

He takes a step closer but remains on the sidewalk. "What the fuck, Dani? Why? Do you realize that this...thing...is—I can't see anything but your ugly-ass fence out the kitchen window now." He startles as if something's snuck up on him in the dark. "Wait, I complained to you about it last week. You didn't say anything about this."

I lift a shoulder. "It's not like I owe you an explanation. I happened to know this lot was still available—you know, on account of you not buying it in the first place. And I had some money in my savings—you know, on account of you neglecting to make me co-owner of that house." I gesture to his place. "I struck a deal. It's as simple as that."

"The hell it is!" His face turns red. "You need to stop."

"I don't think so. I was just admiring the progress the guys made this weekend. I hope they didn't start working too early in the morning for you?"

"Dani, I swear…"

I cross half the remaining distance between us. "You swear what? I have building permits, zoning permits, and a long memory, *Samuel*. Why don't you go complain to Catrina instead? She seems to enjoy comforting you."

"Is that what this is about? You're jealous?"

"Ha! You wish."

"Because I've moved on and you haven't? I'm telling you right now, you won't get away with this."

"And I'm telling you, I already am."

Sam lets out a frustrated groan, his arms flailing in the air. That's when Mia comes around the house-in-progress from the back of the lot. "I thought I heard voices. Hello, Sam."

"You…" He points at Mia.

"Yes me." She sidles up to my elbow. "Isn't it coming along great?"

"You two are in over your heads. I have connections."

I snicker. "Sam, come on."

"No." He recoils a couple of steps. "Fuck you, Dani!"

"That's nice," Mia says. "Do you kiss your mom with that mouth?"

"It's fine." I walk back over to the sign and pretend to adjust an imagined lean, then train a dagger-laden glare directly on my ex. "Fuck you, too."

27

"I GUESS NOW he knows," Mia says, after Sam slinks back to his house.

"Sure does. Thanks for backing me up."

She puts her arm around me. "Always. And now we can celebrate. Come on, we're over there. The sign looks great, by the way."

"Who's 'we'?"

"Matt, Iris, the dogs…"

"I hope there's food."

She laughs. "There's food."

The sky has turned overcast by the time we reach the others in the far corner of the lot. They're near the fence by the elm tree and the giant boulder, seated around a smoking grill.

"Hi, guys." I pet Cesar and Cairo, who crowd me in greeting. "What have we got here?"

Mia motions at the setup. "It's a barbecue."

"I see that."

"Take a load off." She indicates the empty camping chair. "We're going to eat, and then you can open your present."

Matt gives me a wine cooler and I have a swig. "A present, too? It's not my birthday."

"Just for fun," Mia says, giving me a one-armed hug.

I start to protest, but Iris interrupts, "Humor the girl. I for one think this is the most exciting thing since Ellen and I accidentally got caught in the Fremont Solstice Parade one year."

"Naked bicyclists," Mia clarifies, seeing the question on my face.

"Ah." I reach my palms toward the fire to test its heat. There's a tinfoil package resting on the ground next to the grill. "What are we eating?"

Mia folds back the cover of the basket she's brought as if she's some kind of Austrian milkmaid. "Salmon burgers with all the fixings."

I thought it smelled fishy. "Yum."

"Uh-huh. And here's the best part." She hands me something from her bag.

"An empty binder?"

"That's not what it's for." She and Matt exchange a smug glance. "Wave it in front of the grill."

I do. At first, nothing happens, but then a smoky pillar rises up and over the fence. Sam's patio is maybe fifteen yards from where we're sitting.

"Some fish on the grill and that will smell awesome," Mia says. "Aren't we sharing in such a good, neighborly way?"

"Yes, who doesn't like the fumes of cooking seafood?" Iris grins.

Cesar and Cairo bark their agreement.

"Amazing." I laugh. "Couldn't have done it better myself."

"This is temporary, of course, but I thought I'd show you

the potential. Firepit, right here." She marks the space. "A few Adirondack chairs, some fairy lights."

"Oh, I like that."

The food is surprisingly tasty given Mia is normally kitchen-adverse. When we're done, she passes me a wrapped box.

"You weren't kidding."

She beams. "Did you bring a flashlight?"

"I have my phone."

"Good enough."

I tear off the paper to a chorus of melodic jingles.

Mia can barely contain herself, and when I finally extract the contraption inside, she claps her hands together.

Iris leans closer. "What is it?"

"Wind chimes," Mia exclaims. "With mirrors. I got it on Etsy."

I stand up and hold it out. It resembles a small chandelier, and the flute parts are indeed surrounded by decoratively cut mirror shards.

"Matt, can you take it and go stand over there?" Mia points to a spot closer to the house and he complies. "Flashlights out," she tells me and Iris.

The three of us shine our lights at Matt, and instantly light patterns flutter against the tree, the boulder, the fence, and beyond.

Cesar goes wild and tries to catch the reflections on the ground like a kitten on catnip.

"Again, that's brilliant," I tell Mia. Two in one. This wind chime should keep Sam sufficiently annoyed on a sunny day. I especially like how the play of light evokes water on the ground. It suits the boat theme.

We toast to Mia's ingenuity while Matt ties the chime to a low branch near the fence. It's darker now, but with another log on the fire, ours is a bright enough spot. There's much talking and much laughing, and Iris is in the middle of a story about her childhood neighbor's escape-artist goat when there's movement behind Mia, and I jump. Cairo and Cesar start growling.

"Still here, huh?" Sam says, stepping into the light. His hair is mussed up and he's in his robe—the maroon terry one his mom had monogrammed for him last Christmas. He looks like a Hugh Hefner wannabe. Cesar lets out a sharp bark, stopping him in his tracks.

"There, boy," Iris says, holding his collar.

Sam clears his throat. "Can I talk to you?" he says to me.

"Go ahead."

"I mean over there?" He nods away.

I plant myself more firmly into the chair. "Whatever you have to say to me, you can say in front of my friends."

"Fine." He puts his hands on his hips, then lets them fall to his sides. "I just wanted you to know I've contacted a lawyer about all this." He gestures toward the house. "It's a freaking circus."

"It's a building site. What do you expect?"

"And I suppose the builders brought in their own garden gnomes?"

"Those belong to me," Iris says. "Aren't they fabulous?"

Sam scoffs. "Dani, please."

He sounds so miserable, the thought occurs that I should feel bad for him, but I quickly come to my senses. "I don't think so. Everything is on schedule with the build. A lawyer isn't going to help you. If it bothers you this much, maybe you should move."

"You know I can't do that."

I do. I studied up on building equity when I still thought we'd be co-owners. I shrug. "Then I guess we're done here?"

"Unless you want a marshmallow?" Mia asks, offering up

one of the small fluffy pillows. "The embers should be ready about now."

Sam's eyes narrow like he's about to curse her out, but Cairo has now joined his brother in a two-part snarling chorus that encourages him to retreat instead. "You haven't heard the last from me, Dani. Expect a call from my lawyer this week. I'll see you in court."

"Looking forward to it," I call after him.

Mia scrunches her nose at me.

"I know, I know—not my finest retort."

"Does he have a case?" Matt asks.

"Nah, Dani has things under control, right, cuz?" Mia pops one of the marshmallows in her mouth.

I grin wide. "You know I do."

28

I TAKE MY seat at the creative all-hands meeting, one eye on the North Creek budget I'm about to defend, and the other on the door. Wyatt should be here by now, but every time someone enters, I'm disappointed. I need to know what happens next in this arrangement. If anything.

Alaina sits down beside me with three minutes to spare and gets her pen and notepad out of her bag. "How was your weekend?" she asks, flipping to a blank page.

"Oh fine," I tell her. If she only knew.

I concentrate on the door again, and there he is, walking in with Mr. Archer. In the middle of a sentence, he glances my way, a pointed smile on his lips. It's quick, but enough to assure me I didn't imagine Saturday. And Sunday morning. *I see you*, it says. *We know something the others don't.*

Regina kicks off the meeting with an update on the Kirkland project, followed by a celebratory round of applause for the team who just had their Magnolia property featured in *Dwell* magazine.

"Well done," Wyatt says across from me, shaking the hand of the lead designer, Lars, who's next to him. "Good feature."

Lars sputters an "Oh wow, thank you" that speaks volumes about the rarity of such praise.

When it's my turn, I answer every question thrown my way about North Creek, and I'm about to wrap up when, in my peripheral vision, I see Wyatt lean forward, reach for his travel mug—it's new, not his usual silver one—and slowly spin it 180 degrees. As he does, a black "up" arrow becomes visible to me against the white stainless steel. He reclines and keeps his focus on me. A sign?

Somehow, I manage to finish my report, and as soon as the meeting's over, I stack my things, preparing to go find out.

"That was a fine summary," Mr. Archer says to me as people file out. "The clients have been happy, too. Would you be able to send over what you just shared?"

Wyatt leaves the room and doesn't look back.

"Uh, yes. Of course."

"The sooner the better. I have a lunch meeting where they will come in handy."

As much as I'm itching to know if I read Wyatt right, the boss's request triggers a return-to-work mode. Something I've created used to solicit new clients? "I'll do it right now, how's that?" I smile at Mr. Archer.

"Splendid. Thanks, Danielle."

I sink back down and open my laptop, my email churning like it's been programmed to raise blood pressure. I tap my fingers on the table as it loads and compulsively check the time. The seconds drag. Finally, I navigate to all the right attachments, compose something brief, polite, and grateful, snap the laptop shut, and shove it into my bag.

The stairs will be faster than the elevator.

I'm out of breath when I reach the eighth-floor landing, so I take a moment to collect myself. Close my eyes. Clear my lungs. I push the door open, and it swishes against the carpet, the muffled sound amplified by the silence of the empty floor.

Wyatt's facing the window when I enter the conference room.

"What I want to know is if you bought that mug specifically for this purpose?" I say, from the doorway.

He turns and rests against the windowsill, amusement playing across his features. "You took your time. I was starting to think you missed it."

I approach him slowly. "A big black arrow? Not super-subtle."

He shrugs. "I didn't have much time."

"Mr. Archer needed something. Glad you're still here." I drop my bag onto the floor.

He pushes off the sill and steps closer. "Yeah?"

I bridge the final foot between us, and then my hands are on his chest, his arms around my waist. The doorway gapes in my periphery. It would be bad in so many ways if people knew about this.

"Don't worry. No one ever comes up here."

"You're sure?"

"If I wasn't, I wouldn't do this." His firm stroke up my back stops below my ponytail, then his mouth finds mine, eager, hungry.

My body is quick to respond, yielding to his expert plying of my lips, my tongue, my skin, and matching it with famished bites and licks of my own. The danger of discovery adds a new flavor, as does the knowledge this is all we can have. I want to yank his tie off, make the buttons on his shirt fly, undo him, but I can't. Not here. I suspect he feels the same, because his hands stay in chaste places.

Eventually, he angles his face away, allowing me access to his throat. He exhales deeply and says my name.

I plant a kiss beneath his ear. "Yeah?" My voice is hoarse, but if he can control himself, so can I.

His grip moves to my shoulders. "I have another meeting in five. I wish I didn't, but…"

I nip him. "And here I was about to ravage you."

"Ravage, even?" A quick intake of breath. His lips are satin plush, infinitely edible, and his chest rises and falls in time with mine. "Shit, you're going to make me lose it."

I want him to lose it. In fact, it's currently at the top of the list of things I want. But we've already agreed we're responsible adults. "Fine. If you'd rather work…" I pretend to pout.

"I'm pretty sure you know what I'd rather do." He slowly grinds against me, and yes, yes I do know.

I smile and step back. "There. You're welcome. Or you'll never get *that* under control before your meeting."

He laughs. "So generous."

I take the clip out of my hair and smooth the mess back into a new ponytail. He adjusts the cuffs of his shirt and straightens his tie.

"Do I look okay?" I ask.

He doesn't reply, but the way he ogles me is answer enough. If I don't leave now, I will shortly be too disheveled to return downstairs at all.

29

IT'S AMAZING HOW many reasons I find to visit the fourth floor over the next few days. There's the new client meeting we're on together, of course—a fifteen-minute consultation where Mr. Archer clarifies the client's objectives, and Wyatt and I do our best impression of two people who definitely have not seen each other naked. I also drop off coffee for Alaina in the mornings, decide to ask the architect on the North Creek project questions in person instead of emailing, and offer to bring internal mail down when another designer gets misdelivered materials. Even though we can't do anything more than observe each other through the glass walls of Wyatt's office, it still feels like wading through the rapids back home. A dangerous thrill.

He seeks me out in similar ways, taking his lunches in the communal cafeteria at the same time I'm there. On Thursday, we end up next to each other in line at the salad bar. It's the closest we've been since Monday. Everyone's working long hours, and I've been reluctant to invite myself over for another sleepover midweek, as much as I'd like to.

"Dani," he says in greeting, all business.

"Wyatt." I nod at him, matching my tone to his.

"Busy week?"

"As always." I reach for a piece of baguette at the same time he does, and for a moment, our fingers touch beneath the towel, triggering a charge up my arm. I pull my hand away and glance at the person behind me, but he's busy in conversation with someone else.

We load our plates in silence until Wyatt heaps a big spoonful of pickled gherkins onto his. I wrinkle my nose.

"What, you don't like gherkins?" he asks.

"Any pickles really."

"No olives? Cocktail onions? Artichokes?"

"On pizza, maybe."

"Wow. Noted."

"They're cute, though. I've never seen such tiny cucumbers."

Wyatt peeks at the people in line and lowers his voice. "You know what they say—tiny cucumber, big..."

I bite my cheek to stifle a smile. "Zucchini?"

His composure breaks into a sputter that he tries to camouflage as a coughing fit.

"You okay, Montego?" the guy behind me asks.

Wyatt nods, patting his chest to clear his throat.

I lean in under the guise of grabbing a napkin. "Maybe you should try softer foods in your salad," I say for his ears only. "I hear the *peaches* here are really good." Then I walk away with my tray, his gaze burning at my back.

I join Alaina's table, and fifteen minutes later, as I'm finishing my plate, Wyatt bumps into my chair on his way to the exit. No apology. Alaina looks up after him, but I look down. Drifting to the floor at my feet is a scrap of paper with an arrow on it. I only wait a minute before excusing myself, then race to the elevator.

This time, he's waiting for me right inside the doors of the conference room, and I'm up against the wall before I can say *sizable produce.*

His hands are in my hair, on my neck, on my ass. "Do you have…any idea…what you do…to me?" he asks between licks and nips.

I stroke my hand down the front of his pants. "I do." I flatten my chest to his and kiss him deeply, savoring even the tang of pickles left on his tongue. I might have to reevaluate my flavor preferences after this.

"I can't wait to be inside you again," he groans. "You're so…" His fingers find their way into my waistband where they tease the bare skin below my belly button. "I just want to feel you."

I'm about to nod when a door opens somewhere on the floor and we both freeze. Two muffled voices approach, a bucket of ice water dumped on our heads.

"Fuck," Wyatt whispers, letting go.

I search for a place to hide and spot a coffee cart draped in a floor-length tablecloth in the corner. "Over there."

The conversation outside grows louder as we crouch behind the cart, Wyatt frantically trying to straighten his clothes.

"I thought you said no one ever comes up here?" I hiss.

He covers my mouth with his hand and peers around the cart, then points toward the hallway and mimes "Right there."

The tip of my tongue slips out to touch his palm because I can't help myself. I know this is serious, and I definitely don't want to get caught, but hunkering down behind a coffee cart with Wyatt Montego is also the best thing I've done all week.

His eyes go wide as they bore into mine, but the way his

lips stretch and quiver betrays the same kind of thrill that bubbles inside me. He removes his hand but doesn't look away.

"If we move HR to this floor, it will free up space for marketing to expand over the next year," Mr. Archer says to someone. "It should be an easy enough transition. Get facilities to move desks up from storage."

"How soon do you want it done?"

"End of the month enough time?"

They continue down the hallway to the open area that soon will be filled with people and cubicles.

"Did you hear that?" I ask Wyatt.

"Something about HR?"

"He's moving them up here."

Wyatt sits and extends one of his legs. "But this is *my* space," he says with a crooked smile, echoing our very first conversation in this room.

"Apparently Archer doesn't see your name on the door either."

"Damn."

Damn indeed. I peek above the top of the cart but duck back down right away. "Hold on, they're coming back."

This time the two men pass the conference room, and soon the ding of the elevator announces we're once again alone. Wyatt stands first and helps me up.

"Close call," I say.

"A little too close." He rubs at his neck. "I think maybe it's in our best interest to not...you know..."

My stomach sinks. "At all?" I can't help it—the words just tumble out.

Alarm crosses his face. "What? No. I mean at work. I definitely want... I mean, if you want..."

"Yeah, I definitely want."

He grabs me by the waist. "Believe me—you do not want

to be the topic of sordid office gossip. Been there, done that, never want to do it again."

This might be my chance. "Are you talking about you and Madeline Archer?"

He blinks. "How do you know about Maddie?"

"Like you said, people talk. I don't know any details, though."

His jaw tenses as if he's going to refuse the topic, but then his face smooths out again. "Yeah we dated for a couple of years." He releases me. "But it's been a while now."

"Was it serious?"

"I thought so."

Ouch. Then again, I almost got married two months ago. "What happened?"

When he doesn't respond right away, I lean forward and touch my fingers to his. "You don't have to answer if you don't want to."

"No, it's fine. I guess long story short is that Maddie had a hard time with my Ménière's diagnosis. We were pretty active before it started—lots of boating and skiing. Going out. But you know the vertigo comes out of nowhere, and suddenly I couldn't do a lot of the things we were used to doing. I had to bail on stuff and I'm also supposed to stay away from alcohol, sodium, caffeine, stress… I just wasn't in a good place."

Alaina's words ring in my mind—something about one of them getting sick. She must have been referring to Wyatt. "Wait, did she leave you over it?"

He shrugs. "I had to make changes to my daily life, and she didn't, so I was holding her back. Guess she got tired of asking how I was doing all the time."

What the actual hell? "Wow, that's the worst. I'm really sorry."

"Don't be." He seems confident, but it's not lost on me that he's now several steps away, his elbows tucked at his sides, hands in his pockets.

"Thanks for telling me."

"Yeah, well…"

"I take it that's why you don't date?"

His shoulders flex forward and back. "Let's just say it's a lot less complicated this way."

He must have really gotten hurt. And the boss's daughter of all people? That's not easy to recover from.

"What?" he asks. "What are you thinking?" He comes closer again and it's a relief. Wherever he was a moment ago, he's broken free.

"Nothing." I rest against him, my forehead against his clavicle. "That's a lot to deal with."

"It's fine. We don't have to talk about it anymore. Just… let's keep things away from work."

"As in, I'll see you this weekend, then?"

He kisses me one more time. "Can't wait."

30

IT'S A RAINY Saturday and Wyatt's out of town. He texted me yesterday that he was driving up to see his dad after work and wouldn't be back until late tonight, so I have no plans today. I scroll through our exchange and smile at how we ended things.

Free Sunday? he asked. I have a surprise for you.

In response I sent him an eggplant emoji (which was the closest I could find to a zucchini) and a winky face to keep things casual.

He seemed to like that. (LOL. Someone's mind is in the gutter today...) But then he clarified it's something to do with the house. We're meeting there tomorrow at two.

Fortunately for me, Mia is equally bored, so she comes over after noon and, with Iris making it a trio, we sit around the kitchen table with an ancient deck of UNO.

"Ellen and I used to play all the time," Iris says, tenderly. "If there are any dog-eared cards, it's her doing. Such a cheater. Okay, who's dealing?"

"I will," I volunteer. I'll deal all day if I have to. Anything to make time go faster.

We play round after round to the pitter-patter of a steady May rain. I win one, Mia wins one, then Iris wins three in a row.

"Read 'em and weep," she says, placing her last card on the discard pile with a giant grin.

Mia laughs. "I think you have the wrong card game."

She waves Mia off and reaches for the deck to prepare another shuffle.

"Does anyone want tea?" I ask, forcing my leg to stop bouncing up and down. "I can make some. Oh, and maybe we can pick up takeout later. Watch a movie?"

"No tea for me," Mia says, collecting her new cards as Iris deals.

Iris peers at me over the black frames of her glasses. "You're unusually excitable today. Is it because the plan is working and Sam is miserable?"

"Maybe."

"Yeah, that explains the look."

"What look?" I add a yellow two on top of her green one.

"That glow. You've been bright-eyed and bushy-tailed since you got up this morning." She sorts the cards in her hand.

"Yes, because there are no *other* recent activities that could have the same effect..." Mia prods me with her elbow. "If you know what I mean."

"Draw four. Take that!" Iris gloats.

I pick up my penalty. "I've got him exactly where I want him. Sam that is," I hurry to clarify, before Mia can get another word in. "The house is going up, he's freaking out, Catrina is pissed... She called me yesterday to plead Sam's case because he's *such a good guy* and asked me to stop the build *for old times' sake.* No self-awareness about how weird that is. So yeah, things are great."

"Not to mention you have fun plans for tomorrow."

"Sure, but that's neither here nor there."

"I think it's somewhere," Iris says, wryly. She and Mia share a silent exchange.

I choose between two blue cards. "I ordered the Husky flag by the way. The big one. It should get here in a couple of weeks."

"That reminds me." Mia takes an extra card. "I had another idea for the house, and no, you do not have permission to make fun of me for dating the nerdiest of nerds."

"What are you talking about?"

"Matt's into live-action role play." A good-humored eye roll. "Because what twentysomething doesn't want to run around the woods dressed as an elf on the weekends?"

"Oh God, remember that time we went to the Renaissance faire?" I ask. "And that wench tried to bring Sam up onstage."

"He could have murdered you." Mia laughs. "Which is exactly why I think we should do a gathering at the lot. Apparently, the only thing LARPers love more than getting into character are pictures of themselves as their alter egos, so we can set it up like a photo shoot."

"That's perfect."

Iris plays a draw two, but this time Mia is on the receiving end. "UNO."

"Again?" Mia groans.

I consider my remaining cards and slap down a yellow eight. "UNO."

"You, too?" Mia shuffles through hers. "How?"

"Sounds like you've found another fun way to poke the bear," Iris says, before playing her last card, thereby winning a fourth game. "Now, I don't know about you, but I need some cookies to celebrate all these wins." She stands, and from the folds of her tunic, several cards fall to the floor. She stills, her eyes rounding. "Oh my. How did those get there?"

Mia collects them and spreads them out on the table one by one. All general number cards. "And you called Ellen a cheater," she says with a shake of her head.

"I don't know what you're talking about." Iris gestures to the dogs next to the table. "Maybe Cesar got into the deck earlier."

Mia and I look at each other.

"Tell you what," I say. "If you share those cookies, we'll agree that's what happened."

31

WYATT IS SNAPPING photos when I arrive at the lot the following day. He meets me at my car.

"I think we're a couple of weeks from electrical and plumbing," he says. "You're still cool with using Loel's people, right?"

I tell him I am. "Is it safe to go inside?"

"Should be, but I brought hard hats, just in case."

He takes the lead as we walk up the slope to what will become the main entry, where the yellow helmets wait for us.

"Very attractive," I say, tapping my knuckles at the hard plastic.

"You'd look good in anything and you know it." He brushes a strand of hair off my cheek. "Come on. Let's check it out."

I follow, eyes on his sun-kissed neck, his solid shoulders, that star-shaped freckle on his right ear.

"Oh wow," he says once inside. "It really is coming together."

The first floor is still only plywood, and the walls have visible framing, but it's easy to see our drawings come to life. Hallway, kitchen, living space. A small bathroom. There's a makeshift staircase to the second floor, but I don't want to risk it. This is good enough for now. Proof it's real.

And the view...

I beeline to one of the window openings and rest my hands on the coarse edge. In front of me, the green trees weave a lattice framework over Lake Washington's glittering waters in the distance. People will want to stay here, I know it.

Wyatt comes up and places his hands on my hips. "What are you thinking?" he asks.

I lean back against him. "I'm thinking I picked a good spot."

He kisses my temple. "It's beautiful."

We stand there quietly among sawdust and sunlight, an unexpected calm at the center of great turbulence. The Spite House is the storm, but in this moment also a respite from the world. I take a deep breath—fir and concrete, fresh-cut grass. Wyatt is solid behind me, warm and strong.

Eventually he lets go. "I'm going to get your surprise from the car. Be right back."

I amble around the bare-bones floor, picturing the kitchen with cabinets, the windows with drapes, maybe a plant in the corner, until Wyatt enters carrying several sample tile boards. His muscles strain and swell at the weight—a fine sight. He props the boards against the far wall and steps back with a wide grin.

"What's this?" I move closer.

"Surprise! I thought we'd get a head start on materials for in here. If we order sooner rather than later, we'll minimize any risk of delays." He holds up one of the boards to the wall where the vent hood will go. "Something like this maybe?"

"And here I was thinking you didn't care for interior design," I say dryly.

"I've never said that." He picks up a different board. "Or like this?"

"No, subway tile is too predictable." I scan the other samples, not seeing any I like. "I was thinking more along the lines of natural stone." I found a tumbled Carrara last year at the trade show that I was planning on using for my own kitchen before everything went south—a gorgeous chevron mosaic that I still dream about.

"How about this, then?" He holds up a large gray granite tile.

"Too formal."

"Okay…" He joins me and bumps my shoulder with his. "You're really hating this, aren't you?"

"What? No."

"Don't worry." He's in front of me now, blocking the tiles from view. "I haven't forgotten—you're the boss. Just thought I'd help."

I grasp his shirt and peer up. "It's…very nice of you."

"But?"

"But nothing. Thank you."

A scrutinizing squint. "I knew it. You do hate it." He spins away, his right cheek puckering gleefully as he feigns dejection.

My hands chase in protest, but he just smirks and evades my grip.

"Oh, I've stepped in it now," he says. "But lucky for you, with the way things are progressing here, I should be out of your hair before long."

"What do you mean?" I laugh. Then my stomach drops and the elation dims. "Oh, because of the house and…" I wag a finger between us. "Yes, thank goodness. Ha ha."

"Time's a-flyin'…" He stills, finally letting me catch him. His waist is firm beneath my palms.

"I'll still have to help your grandma with her curtains,

though," I say. "After the house, I mean. Unless she's in a hurry? Maybe I should get started sooner?"

He collars my shoulders with his arms. "No, no, that's not necessary."

Good. I lean into him. "It *was* nice of you to try to help."

"Yeah?" He trails one hand down and past my elbow, uses the other to lift my chin.

"Mmm-hmm, yeah," I murmur against him before a soft stroke of his tongue cuts me off.

My body remembers faster than my mind and it's like a spell sweeps over me, loosening every joint. His kisses reach my neck, and his breath alone is enough for desire to flare.

"Maybe we should get out of here," I say.

His traveling hands pause, and his eyes find mine again. "My place?"

"I'll race you there."

Afterward, we lie tangled in the bed, half-covered by the comforter he's managed to fold over us. I'm drifting, but his fingertips against my shoulder blade tether me to consciousness. He blows a cool breath across my forehead.

"You have forty-seven freckles on your nose," he says, kissing it. "I've counted."

"You have one by your ear. Right here." I brush it with my lips.

"Mmm, you're giving me goose bumps."

"Like this?" I do it again and let my teeth graze the lobe.

He exhales with force. "You're killing me."

I giggle and reach under the comforter, but he maneuvers away and sits up. The sight of his back should be discouraging, but it isn't. At least in bed, I understand him.

"I actually have something else for you," he says, glancing at me. "I'll be right back."

Another surprise? Considering how the last one went, I'm not sure how I feel about this. I try to cover my trepidation with a meek whistle as he crosses the room in nothing but his birthday suit.

"Is that all you can muster?" He turns to give me full frontal. He's still semihard, and as much as I've already enjoyed him, I reserve the right to remain impressed.

"Don't take it personally. You're extremely sexy."

He winks and disappears into the hallway before returning with a large bag tied with a ribbon.

"What is it?" I expect it to be heavy, but it's no weightier than a beach ball.

"Open it."

I untie the ribbon and the familiar scent of raw wool reaches my nostrils. I pull out a handful of the soft fluff.

"From Dad's alpacas," he says. "I thought maybe you could use it for your shop. *Wool Is Cool?*"

My rib cage is suddenly several sizes too small to contain what's going on inside. I hug the bag in my arms and kiss Wyatt. "This is awesome. Thank you."

"Are you sure? It's not too corny?"

"Not at all. I'll be able to make a lot of stuff with this. Oh, I should felt some decorations for the house. Maybe gnomes for the windows."

His smile falters. "More things for the house? Not your Etsy shop?"

"One doesn't exclude the other."

"True, but I guess I was hoping this could be something that takes your mind *off* the stress of the house."

"I'm not stressed. You're the one daydreaming about finishing it."

"Only because— Never mind, forget about it. Maybe this was a bad idea."

He goes for the bag, but I get to it first.

"Hold on, let me get this straight. Do I only get to keep it if I use it for something you approve of?" Dad's annual Costco gift cards on Mother's Day come to mind. *She shops there all the time anyway...*

"What? No."

"Then don't take it back."

He raises his hands, palms forward. With each breath, he retreats behind that old wall of his a little more. How do I get him to stay?

"It's a nice gift," I say in a softer voice. "The best, actually." I mean it.

"I'm sorry," he says with a sigh. "Maybe I'm the one who's stressed. Busy times, you know. My ear's been ringing like mad."

"If it would help, I guess I could stop being such a distraction at work... Leave you to your pickles," I deadpan.

It takes him a second to process that I'm joking, but when he does, the tension drains from his face. He grabs me and lifts me into his lap. "No way," he says, seeking out my mouth. "My pickle lives for your distractions, and if you come with me to the shower, I'll prove it to you."

"Only if we get some food after. A girl can't survive on condiments alone."

He digs his fingers into my sides in a relentless tickle attack that leaves me howling with laughter and panting for air.

32

"I THOUGHT WE were going out to eat," Mia whines from the passenger seat as I park in front of a new hardware store I've been meaning to check out. "Me hungry." She pouts.

"It's just a quick stop. Faucets first, *then* shrimp tempura rolls."

Wyatt's tile surprise a few days ago may have been misguided, but it at least made me realize I need to get my ducks in a row. With everything else I have on my plate—work projects, permits and paperwork for The Spite House, keeping Sam at bay, settling in at Iris's—I have been neglecting this next step in the build.

"Wouldn't it be easier to just order something online?" Mia asks. "This place looks fancy."

As if to underscore her assessment, a sales guy in a suit approaches as soon as we enter. "Welcome, welcome. What kind of project brings you in today?"

"Not dinner unfortunately," Mia says, despondent. "We're building a house."

The guy lights up, pupils morphing into dollar signs. "Is that so?"

I push by Mia and hush her with a glare. "Where are your kitchen faucets? Let's start there."

"Right this way."

He walks us through flooring, gas inserts, and paint at impressive speed, but slows when we reach the tile department.

Mia sighs behind me as we dawdle past painted ceramic, limestone, and travertine. One of the displays is a gray marble in an interlocked pattern reminiscent of my dream one. "Do you happen to carry a tumbled Carrara similar to that one?" I ask on impulse.

He stops as if he'd been expecting my question. "Oh, you're in the market for tile, too?" His tone is a little too innocent.

"A specific one." I describe it to him, and he tells us to follow him to a sales counter so he can look it up.

"What happened to *just a quick stop*?" Mia hisses. *"Faucets."*

I dig through my purse and find a stick of gum. "Here." I hand it to her and start leafing through a catalog.

Mia chews demonstratively. "I like that one." She points to a subway tile similar to what Wyatt brought to the house.

"No."

"What about that one?"

And she wonders why I don't like to delegate more. "Definitely not."

The guy swivels the computer screen toward us. "Good news." His fingers click against the keyboard. "This one, correct? Gorgeous."

There it is. *My* marble.

"If we place a custom order today, we should get it in—" he scrolls down the page "—ten to twelve weeks."

I should be out of your hair before long...

"That's too bad," Mia says to me. "It's really nice."

I can almost feel the sleek chevron pattern against my fingertips. "No, cows are *nice*. This tile is...a nonpareil. And what do you mean 'too bad'?"

"We can't wait twelve weeks."

"Why not? We're not in a hurry."

"But there must be something that's available right here in store."

"Nothing like this."

Mia stares at me a long while, then turns to the guy. "Will you excuse us for a moment?"

"Of course." He disappears.

"Okay." Mia takes my hand. "Level with me. What's this really about?"

"What do you mean?"

"You know we'll only recover our money once we finish the house and start renting it out. Waiting twelve weeks for tile doesn't seem excessive to you?"

I pull away. *Time's a-flyin'...* "No, whatever it takes. I'm building the perfect revenge. That requires the perfect house, which requires the perfect materials. You and Iris told me I could do it my way."

Mia taps a finger against the counter, seemingly considering this. Then she shrugs. "You're right."

"Okay?"

She nods. "Sorry."

"Do we have any more questions over here?" The sales guy is back.

I smile at him. "No, let's do it."

"And did we want to include faucets in this order, as well?"

"Ha!" Mia holds her hand out to me, palm up. "Keys, please. My hangry self will be waiting in the car. I think I saw a protein bar wrapper under the seat—with any luck there's a crumb or two left that'll save me from perishing."

"Not today," I tell the guy. Faucets will have to wait.

33

OUR WEEKLY CHECK-IN for the Rose project—Mr. Archer's personal friends—throws the whole team a slight curve ball. The client meeting where we're supposed to present schematics and design concepts has been moved to Monday instead of Thursday next week, which means I know what I'll be doing this weekend. Normally preparing artwork and graphics to bring a proposed build to life is my favorite part of the job, but I typically have more time to do it. It's going to be tight.

Wyatt's pinched expression tells me he's doing workload versus hours math in his head, too. I try to get his attention, but he's Mr. Professional today. As per our agreement.

"Wyatt, Danielle, could I see you two in my office?" Mr. Archer says once everyone begins dispersing.

"Right now?" Wyatt asks.

"If you will." Mr. Archer gathers his things and nods at us. When he's gone, Wyatt and I stare at each other across the table until the honking paper jam alarm from the copier next door goes off and knocks us out of our stupor.

"It's probably about this presentation, right?" I say, tucking my laptop into its sleeve.

"It would have to be."

"You don't think—"

"No," he says quickly. "No way."

"Okay."

He rounds the table. "Don't worry. I'm sure it's nothing."

I walk three steps behind him to the boss man's office. We've been discreet, haven't we? No shenanigans here since that close call—in fact, we barely even talk at Archer unless a meeting requires it. We've only seen each other at The Spite House or his apartment, never in public, and the one time we had to get from one to the other, we drove separately. I know we're only two weeks in, but so far, I'd say we're rocking this secret fling thing.

"I'll cut right to the chase," Mr. Archer says after I close the door behind me. "You two are some of my best creatives, which is why I put you on my good friends' project. I have full confidence that they'll be happy with what you come up with."

Wyatt and I glance at each other. So far so good.

"Thank you," I say.

"Appreciate the confidence," Wyatt says.

"I pride myself on running a tight ship here," Mr. Archer continues. "Quality output, congenial atmosphere, no nonsense, and I believe clients sense that. That's how we've grown."

I nod, but this time, Wyatt remains immobile.

"So, when there are, ahem…stirrings in the pot, I think it a mistake not to address them head-on."

"I'm afraid you've lost me now, sir." Wyatt's voice is a steel vault, all emotion safely locked away.

"A rumor is going around. About the two of you." Mr. Archer's eyes are kind, but the scrutiny in them is peeling back my skin layer by layer.

I swallow and try to imitate Wyatt's tone. "What kind of rumor?"

His focus travels from me to Wyatt. "Relationships in the workplace have the potential to complicate things, something I know you know, Wyatt. Normally I'd put no stock to water-cooler talk, but the Rose project is important to me personally, so I thought it prudent to get to the bottom of things."

"Of course, but I assure you, there is no relationship," Wyatt says. "Danielle and I work well together—in a professional way. You have nothing to worry about."

"So, whoever claims they saw you two *together* Sunday night was mistaken?"

Sunday night? My brain churns. What was Sunday night?

"I only speak for myself, but I was home all evening," Wyatt says.

It dawns on me. We went out to pick up pho near his place after a particularly invigorating shower. "Yes, me, too. I... played cards with my landlady." I dig my nails into my palm. *Too much detail, Porter.*

"Well, then." Mr. Archer stands. "I'll take you at your word and say nothing more about it. Keep up the good work."

Wyatt holds the door for me, and I give him a polite nod that he returns with a tight smile. His face is drained of color.

"Talk later?" I ask under my breath as we head down the hallway.

"Yes," he says in a clipped tone before he stalks off in the direction of his office and closes the door.

34

WYATT DOESN'T ANSWER when I call that night and he's not in the office Thursday. The only response I get to my texts is that he's swamped.

On Friday, I have lunch with Alaina to distract myself from obsessing about Wyatt being MIA. Work is ramping up to our busiest season and we're commiserating about our respective workloads over cups of the soup du jour.

"I was here until ten last night, and today doesn't look any better," she says, ripping a roll in half. "The Carter job is worth it, of course, but I wish they'd put someone else on the parking garage in Kirkland."

Out of the corner of my eye, I register Wyatt entering the cafeteria. He walks slower than usual, as if he's weighed down by invisible stones. "Yeah, that's not super...sexy," I say to Alaina. "That job, I mean. But they can't all be exciting."

I follow his movements while blowing on a spoonful of soup. He sits down in a sunbeam by the window, spotlighted just for me. The fact that we haven't talked about what Mr. Archer said is making my stomach churn.

"What projects are you working on?" Alaina asks, bringing me back to her.

I swallow the forgotten spoonful. "North Creek is the big one, and the Rose project, but I'm also helping in Queen Anne and Ballard. I had 186 unread emails in my inbox when I left for lunch. I'm sure it will have passed two hundred by the time I get back to my desk."

"Oh yeah, I don't do email during the day anymore. That's what evenings are for, right?" Alaina smirks.

"Right," I say, even though it's more likely I just won't get to them at all. Eve, my VP, wants me on-site at the Bellingham office next week, and the working drawing sets for Queen Anne need to be reviewed and revised before I leave. Also, let's tell it like it is—some people ought to be more prudent about who they include in email chains. No, Bob, I don't need to know that the leveling in Tacoma is complete.

Two project managers join Wyatt's table and the three of them strike up a conversation. They're too far away for me to hear what it's about, but suddenly the sound of Wyatt's warm laugh floats over, making me smile. I rush to stuff a piece of bread in my mouth to hide it.

Alaina looks toward their table and rests her chin against her knuckles.

"I wonder what's going on with him," she says.

The bread gets stuck in my throat, and I cough. "What do you mean?"

"Come on." She cocks a brow. "When was the last time you heard Wyatt Montego laugh? Jenya must be right."

"About…"

"That he's met someone. I didn't believe it at first, but he *has* been more relaxed lately. He didn't even have an opinion on the projects he's not assigned to in our floor meeting last week, just listened and nodded. That never happens."

So Jenya is the culprit. "Maybe it's the weather? Or he… I don't know…got a dog?" I take a long swig of my water bottle. *Relaxed, huh? Glad I can be of service, Mr. Montego…*

Alaina titters. "Someone suggested it's you, actually." She says it offhand, but the underlying curiosity is obvious.

I sputter a protest and gather my garbage onto the tray. Time to go. "*Someone* has a vivid imagination."

To my relief, she nods. "Yeah, that's what I said. Well, who-ever she is, I'd like to shake her hand. When he's happy, our jobs are so much more pleasant." She puts the lid back on her cup. "You taking off? Diving into those emails?"

I tap my nose in a "you got it" kind of way and hightail it out of there.

Her words reverberate in my head. Her words and his laughter. It never occurred to me others might benefit from our arrangement, too.

Seeing the button for the eighth floor in the elevator gives me an idea, and I text Wyatt an upward-pointing arrow and a question mark. I still have twenty minutes left of my lunch hour…

I'm at my desk before he texts back.

I wish, but I can't. Too much going on and I was out yesterday. Rain check? Sorry.

The lightness from before dissipates. Sure thing. Let me know if I can help in any way.

Don't worry about it. Then another text: How are you com-ing along on the Rose project presentation btw? Pretty tight deadline. Good times.

Not the words I'd use to describe it. I don't want to work

all weekend. I want to see him, want to make sure he's okay. That we're okay.

My fingers fly across the screen. Want to prep together this weekend? It'll make for a more cohesive presentation. Oh, screw it—Plus I really want to see you.

The dots move right away, then stop. No message appears.

"Come on," I whisper. The ghostly white of his complexion after the meeting with Mr. Archer comes to mind. I know that got to him, but surely—

The dots again. Sorry, got a phone call. Yeah, for sure. I take it you have some "color samples" to show me? ;)

Phew. I grin. I'm reading that in the naughtiest of ways...

As you should.

I start a saucy reply but erase it halfway. There's no knowing how long this could go on. Head in the game.

My turn to surprise you, I text instead. Bring your laptop and meet me at the house Saturday at two thirty.

I'm going to make him forget Mr. Archer, make us shine professionally, *and* help him relax—all in one fell swoop.

Like he said—I am the boss.

35

"YOU'RE FLUTTERIER THAN Ellen before our wedding," Iris remarks as I rush through the house gathering everything I need for an epic picnic. She's wearing yellow-framed glasses and a black turtleneck today, a combo that makes her look like a stylish bumblebee. "There's a basket with a lid on the top shelf in the garage, and I have several gingham tablecloths if you're interested."

"That'd be great," I say, on my way to my room to grab another blanket. I throw in a couple pillows for good measure. "Let's see, I have sandwiches, cookies, cheese, gherkins, fruit." I count on my hand. "I'll pick up our coffees on the way, the water bottles are in the car, blankets... What am I forgetting?"

"To breathe?" Iris snickers.

"Funny. Oh, I should probably bring my notes for the meeting in case we actually want to get some work done."

"What about the birdbath? It's heavy, but he can help you get it out of the trunk."

I pause, a finger pointed her way. "Good idea."

She follows me to the storage room in the garage, and to-gether we drag out the three-foot-tall birdbath, complete with frolicking gnomes in various states of undress, from its rest-ing place amid Ellen's collection. It's extremely kitsch, and therefore perfect for The Spite House. Hopefully, it will also attract birds that'll poop all over Sam's car. Once it's in my trunk, I run through my list one more time and decide I've got everything.

I arrive well ahead of Wyatt and make a vain attempt at lift-ing the concrete birdbath out of my car before giving up. Loel and his guys have started on the siding and roof, and later this week, we're getting pipes and wires, but the inside is still much the same as the last time we were here when I lug the rest of the stuff into the house.

I stand back to admire my handiwork just in time for Wyatt to pull up outside. I head out to meet him.

"Hi there, stranger," I say, shading my eyes from the sun that's temporarily peeked out from behind heavy clouds.

Wyatt closes the passenger side door after retrieving his portfolio and straightens to his full height. "You're looking very pleased with yourself. What are you up to?"

No kiss? It's been almost a week, but I guess we're saving that for later. "You'll find out in a minute, but first, I need your muscles."

He flexes an impressive bicep. "You mean these?"

I can't resist gripping it, and with one hand locked on his upper arm, I drag him to my car and pop open the trunk.

"What on earth?" He peers down at the birdbath.

"An addition to the collection. Help me get it out?"

He does, and together we maneuver it to the other gnomes.

"You guys have strange tastes in lawn decor," he says, scratching his head.

I shrug. "Yeah, I guess it's not for everyone. Want to see your surprise?"

He squints at me. "Should I be worried?"

"No, come on." I lead him inside to my blanketed haven and throw my arms out. "Ta-da!"

"Wow." He blinks at the setup. "When did you do all of this?"

"You like? I figured if we have to work, we might as well make it enjoyable." I toe my shoes off and step onto the soft mat of woven fabrics. He does the same. "I have food and drinks. Here." I pick up his coffee. "A decaf mocha with caramel drizzle."

He stares at me. "You remembered."

"Well, I…" I hand him the beverage. "Good memory I guess." I open the cooler of food to hide how self-conscious I suddenly feel. "Make yourself comfortable. Are you hungry?"

"I could eat." There's rustling among the pillows as he sits. "Need me to do anything?"

I gather an armful of my fare and spread it on the blankets. Wyatt reclines on one arm, dark-jeaned legs stretched out before him, in a navy blue Henley, matching leather belt and watch strap. His shoes are neatly placed at the edge of the blanket with his portfolio.

Panic rises up. This is too juvenile, too tree-house club meeting, too—

"I love this," Wyatt says, surveying the goods. "I can't remember the last time I had a picnic. And you brought gherkins!"

I let a small smile slip. "You don't think it's too much?"

"Best work meeting I've ever attended. Do you want to go over the presentation plan while we eat?"

Is he really only thinking about work?

I crawl toward him and position myself astride his legs. "Sure," I say, my hands on either side of his jaw.

"Dani, I…" He sighs, looking down.

"Yeah?" My fingertips depress the tight muscles at the nape of his neck.

His eyes fall closed but when he opens them again, they're squarely on me as if a decision has been made. "Nothing." He runs his hands up my torso. "I missed you."

My heart pounds a double beat. "I missed you, too." The air around us has stilled and the only movement I'm aware of is the brush of his lashes when he blinks, the inky swirl in his pupils. I want to kiss him then—remind him that this is our spot, the center of our alliance. Ask him to forget about work. "Office gossip, am I right?" is all that comes out.

He flinches, and the moment is gone. "Right." A pause, then he maneuvers around me for a sandwich.

I slide off him in confusion. "What just happened?"

"What?" He unwraps the turkey and cheese. "The presentation—isn't that what we're doing?" A perfunctory smile my way.

"Why are you being so weird?"

He's about to take a bite but hesitates. "I'm not. We have stuff to get done. Archer is relying on us." His teeth sink into the bread. "This is really good."

My throat aches, but I grab my tablet from my bag and pop a grape in my mouth even though I'm no longer in the mood for eating.

We compare notes for Monday, sitting side by side without touching. Strictly business.

Not until I get to the color palette page does he lean into me, his chin on my shoulder. His warm breath against my skin is the olive branch I need.

"Done with work?" I ask, powering off my tablet.

He lifts his head. "Yeah, I'm spent. And I'm sorry. This week was…complicated. Thank you again for this." He organizes his paperwork and piles it next to his portfolio. For one scary second, I think he's going to get up and leave, but he sits back and puts one of the pillows behind his head. "One of these days we should do a real picnic," he says. "Maybe a hike."

I keep a neutral expression even though my insides are anything but. "As long as you promise to protect me from bears and cougars."

He grins. "Naturally. And you'll stomp away any snakes?"

"Deal. Though I don't much care for danger noodles myself."

"Ah, the sacrifices one makes for— I mean, that's very big of you."

I set Spotify to a random radio channel on my phone. Outside, it's now raining and large droplets smatter against the Tyvek wrapping. When Wyatt brings my feet to his lap, I'm a goner. An actual moan escapes me when his thumbs work the arch of my left foot.

"That good?" He probes my heel with small circular movements, then continues down the sides to my toes.

"Mmm-hmm. You should switch careers and become a massage therapist."

"You'd like that." He trades the left for the right and repeats his ministrations. For a while there's nothing but the rain, the music, his fingers, my feet. Then he slowly rubs his hands up my calves, sparking fire elsewhere. I stretch like a cat and use my legs to hook him toward me. Together we slide lower until we're lying down on our makeshift picnic bed.

He kisses my neck first, then my cheek, my mouth. It's jeans on jeans, but the friction is still good, and I'm already half melted when a remix of Elvis's "Can't Help Falling in Love" starts playing. It's the song Sam and I were supposed to dance our first dance to—not because we loved it, but because that was his parents' song. How I missed these red flags along the way, I have no idea.

I wiggle away. "Sorry, I have to change this."

While I fiddle with the phone, he rests against the blankets, one hand slung above his head.

"I'm surprised Loel and them aren't here," he says as if the thought just occurred to him. "I thought they typically worked Saturdays."

I select a playlist that seems promising and scan the titles. "I told them not to come today so we could have the house. Oh, I love this song." I hit Play, and the discordant guitar intro to Chris Isaak's "Wicked Game" vibrates through the air. I return to Wyatt, but now a frown mars the bridge of his nose.

"Won't that delay the build?" he asks.

"Not really." I keep my tone light as if I'm oblivious to his clear disapproval, but it doesn't help. He pushes himself up, his shoulders rolling in like he's closing up shop, and I'm faced with the expanse of his back.

I get up on my knees and place a soft kiss behind his right ear. "I typically find that people work better if you cut them some slack," I say. "Are you telling me you regret this afternoon?"

"No, that's not…" He exhales, then takes my hands to wrap my arms around him. "Of course not. I'm sorry. Again. I'm stuck in my head."

"It's okay." I kiss his neck. "Just be here with me. Forget about everything else."

"You're right." He lets out a gruff noise, then stretches behind him for my leg, and before I know what's happened, he's spun me around to straddle his lap again.

That's more like it.

"Some trick," I say, pressing up against him.

The glint is back in his eyes, as warm fingers caress the skin up my back. "This is the best surprise I've had in a very long time, and there's nothing else I'd rather be doing." He swallows. "I really like—" I hold my breath as he struggles to find the right word "—hanging out with you." He peers up at me as if unsure of how I'll interpret that, and it's the insecurity that lands the sentiment for me. He's saying more than he thinks he is.

I can't contain my smile. "I like hanging out with you, too."

His thumbs dig into the flesh above my hip bone, massaging firmly. "As much as you like tricks?" he asks, lips curving into a dangerous smile.

I pretend to think about it. "Almost."

"So, you're saying you want to see another one?"

I dive for him in response, and my bra clasp snaps open.

"One hand," he whispers. "How about that?"

I smile against his mouth. "Impressive. Now do my shirt."

He doesn't delay and I'm bare before his weighty gaze a moment later. He drags a palm from my throat to my belly as if he needs to feel my skin to believe it. I don't mind. He can prod and stroke to his heart's content.

My phone rings, but I tune it out. "Your turn."

His Henley comes off, and the relief of contact overwhelms my senses. Is there anything better than being skin to skin, all those nerve endings dancing together, all that *surface*? We're practically clawing at each other already and we're not even naked yet.

He wrestles me horizontal to remedy that situation. The button on my jeans comes undone with a *pop*, followed by a tug of the zipper. He places a kiss below my belly button before peeling the fabric off my legs.

"Cute." He smiles, his finger tracing the elastic of my underwear.

I look down at the cartoon kitten with a speech bubble that says *Purrrrr.* "I thought you'd appreciate them."

"Mmm-hmm," he says, emphatically. "Looks like a happy pussycat…"

I rack my brain for an equally cheeky response, but he steals my ability to speak with a hot breath beneath said kitty.

My head falls back onto a throw pillow. "Again, please."

He nuzzles the crevice where my leg meets my hip and teases the sensitive skin with the stubble on his cheek. His fingers travel up my other hip, across my stomach and down, then ease the flimsy undergarment off me. He skims his hands back up my shins, and I shamelessly let one leg fall open, which he correctly interprets as an invitation.

"Fucking A," I murmur on an exhale.

He's not satisfied until I'm in tatters beneath him, and only then does he not object when I reach for him.

His pants are halfway to his ankles when he tenses up, prompting me to stop undressing him. "Damn it," he whispers. "I didn't bring condoms."

My phone rings again. Someone is being really disrespectful of our canoodling time. "Are you sure?"

"Yeah, I didn't think…" He scrubs a hand over his face and swears again with more fervor.

"I might have one in my wallet." I scramble for my purse, but my wallet isn't there. I left it in the mid-console when I got the coffees.

"My car," I say. "I'll be right back." I pull on my shirt and my jeans sans underpants, and half walk, half jump to the door, shoes in hand. It's a miracle I don't trip. My phone rings a third time. I see just enough of the screen to catch a big *M*.

"It's Mia," I say, shoving my feet into my shoes. "Can you

get it and find out what she wants. Or just tell her to stop calling."

I hurry down the stairs, across the muddy dirt in front of the house, and almost skid into my car. The rain is only a drizzle now, but still uncomfortable enough that I don't waste any time yanking the door open and snatching up my wallet. I retrace my steps with the same kind of triumphant feeling of winning the 100-yard dash in elementary school.

"I got it!" I exclaim once back indoors, thrusting it up like a trophy.

Wyatt looks up at me from the floor, my phone still stuck to his ear. "Uh-huh. Yeah, I totally understand," he says, an odd expression on his face.

"What is it?" I mime to him, but he ignores me.

"I wish I could help, but like I said, I don't work in finance… Yeah. That's right. You know what, here's Dani now." He holds the phone out. "Not Mia, your mom," he says to me in a flat voice.

"What?" I take it and turn my back to Wyatt. "Hi, Mom, everything okay?"

"Finally," she says. "I've been calling and calling."

"What's going on?"

"Well, I spoke to your aunt again, and now Aaron is searching for summer internships. I thought maybe Sam could help."

At the mention of my ex, I spin around, and sure enough, Wyatt's throwing his shirt back on.

Mom giggles. "I thought I got lucky and he was the one answering. I might have confused your coworker with my rambling, but we figured it out eventually. Why are you working on a Saturday anyway?"

"We're really busy. Um, Mom, now is actually not a good time. Can I call you back later?"

"But Aaron needs—"

"Okay, bye." I hang up and toss the phone onto a pillow. "Hey." I sit back down on the blankets. When I do, Wyatt stands.

"I forgot I have another meeting to prep for," he says. "I think I need to head out."

"No, come on."

He bends down for his portfolio, and when he straightens again his features are stone. "Why does your mom think Sam's answering your phone? Have you not told them you broke up with him?"

"You know I have. And even if I hadn't, don't you think the canceled wedding would have tipped them off?"

The joke flops and now he's putting on his shoes. The Wyatt from minutes ago is gone, hidden somewhere deep below the surface.

"Like I've said before, they're not the most understanding about what happened," I say. "Maybe they're hoping we'll patch it up. I don't know. Can we at least talk about it?"

"There's nothing to talk about. It's a bit of a cold shower that's all. And like I said, I still have a lot of work to do."

"So now you're going. All of a sudden."

"Yeah, I think that's best."

His tone makes clear it doesn't matter what I think, and I'm not about to pick a fight. "Okay, I guess."

"Okay." He's all rigid and stilted. "I'll see you Monday, okay?"

He's out the door, and I'm left with a picnic to clean up and an unused prophylactic in my hand.

36

THE BAG OF wool stares at me from the corner of my room as I pack for Bellingham and get ready for work Monday. It's been over a year since I last did any crafts. With the move out here and starting a new job, I haven't had the time. Now it beckons to me, and once my duffle is zipped shut, I stick my hand into the bag and rip off a wad.

Wyatt may be running hot and cold, but I can't help but feel that gifting the wool, the level of thoughtfulness it required, must stem from genuine care. And he did say he missed me. We *both* said it.

On the other hand, even if he really left Saturday because he had to get more work done, that doesn't explain why he didn't respond to my texts yesterday.

The uncertainty unsettles me, and I bring the wool to my nose and inhale the comforting organic scent as I sit down on my bed. The smell takes me back to the time my mom taught me how to knit, when I was eleven. That particular skill never stuck, but the satisfaction of creating did.

Mom...

As much as I've left Coeur d'Alene behind and made peace with not having the kind of relationship with my parents that Mia has with hers, there's still a pang at the memory of Mom holding my hands to show me how to hook the yarn onto the knitting needles. Before I grew up and started to ask questions she couldn't answer. Started to question her.

In the midst of this rumination, my fingers still remember what to do, and I begin pulling and stacking the fibers, then rolling and compacting them. With the wad of wool firmly in one hand, I search my closet for the craft tote that holds my felting needles.

I've long since stopped trying to get Mom to see her relationship with my dad differently. Maybe she doesn't want to. Maybe it's just easier to pretend she has everything she wants.

Isn't that what I might have done, had Sam not cheated?

I pause, my hand deep in the tote. I was about to overlook his steamrolling about the house, wasn't I? And while I'd like to think down the road I would have put my foot down, I can also visualize the blurry lines of compromise that might follow after you tie yourself to another for life. Not wanting to rock the boat. Too bad understanding this doesn't set things right. For my mom or for me.

I find what I'm looking for and, before I know it, I'm on the floor, prodding the fibers into an oval shape. Any thoughts of my parents, Sam, Wyatt, and the real world disappear, and I am lost in the movement of the needle. I go slowly at first but soon pick up speed. No thinking necessary. There's such freedom in relying on muscle memory alone.

When it's time to go, I tuck the wool and the needle back in the tote and, after brief consideration, throw the whole thing in my Bellingham suitcase. I don't know what I'm making yet, but whatever it is, I do know it'll be my choice, no one else's.

I enter the conference room thirty minutes before the client meeting and set up my mood boards on the easels near the window. Mr. Archer will be at the head of the table since the Roses are personal friends of his. No pressure.

It's just me until Wyatt arrives ten minutes later, portfolio over his shoulder as usual and a cup of something hot in his hand. "Good morning," he says, beelining straight for the table to set his things down. "The boards look nice."

As if nothing's amiss.

"Thanks." I watch him, but it's one-sided—he's already opened his laptop and is getting to work.

The hallway outside is quiet.

A deep breath and I walk over to him.

"So, did you have a good rest of your weekend?"

"It was fine." He still doesn't look up from his screen.

"Pretty relaxing?"

"I guess."

"Really?" Maybe I should have picked that fight Saturday after all. "I thought you were swamped with work." I sit down next to him.

Now his head jerks up. "What are you doing? We should keep our distance here."

I flinch. "We're alone, and I'm just sitting in a chair. What is up with you?"

"Nothing." His lips close, then part again. "I just think— we talked about this. Work has to be separate. But maybe it's too complicated."

"What?" My stomach roils uncomfortably.

Before I can say more, the lead engineer shows, followed by a few others on the account.

"Let's just concentrate on the meeting," Wyatt says to me under his breath, while the others help themselves to coffee from a cart. "Archer will start us off, then I'll run through the drawings and timeline, Mark will do his thing, and we'll end on your stuff. Sound good?"

"Yep." I don't know why he tells me this—this isn't my first rodeo. It pokes at a sore spot at the back of my mind, but I don't have time to address it, because here is Cal Archer and the Roses.

The presentation begins as planned. Wyatt explains his drawings on the smart screen, answering questions along the way. When he's done, Mr. Rose turns to Mr. Archer and asks if any efforts have been made to tie in the atrium-looking interior hallway with the exterior of the home, which will be set back on a three-acre lot amidst mature cedars and cottonwood.

"Danielle, if you wouldn't mind taking this one?" Mr. Archer says. "Then we'll get to Mark last."

"Of course." I push away from the table and start talking about how we'll implement the convergence of interior and exterior. "As you can see," I say when I get to my display boards, "we've kept the coloring simple—a natural palette that next to these windows brings to mind sunlight sifting through a canopy of trees." I position the board in front of them and keep going until halfway through the second board, when Wyatt clears his throat, forcing everyone's attention to shift.

"I'm just wondering," he says, forehead creased, "considering the size of the windows and the wide angle view they provide, if it would be better to center the color scheme on the sky, which is a constant, as opposed to the changing trees?"

What the hell is he doing? I force myself to suppress the flare of irritation at being interrupted. "An interesting idea, but not quite in line with the client requirements." *As you well know*, I try to telepathically convey. I put a smile in place for Mr. Rose. "Personally, I feel a sky palette would be too cold paired with the materials you've chosen. I am, of course, happy to discuss, should you feel differently."

"Not at all," Mr. Rose says. "Please continue."

I finish my part of the presentation without further take-over attempts from Wyatt, which is lucky for him. The more I think about his comment, the angrier I get. Where does he get off Old-Wyatting me? As if he hasn't already told me that's a role he plays to keep people at arm's length ever since Madeline. Don't I deserve better than to be lumped in with the others? With her?

Overall, the meeting is a success, and the clients greenlight almost everything we propose. It's a massive job, so the rest of the room is all handshakes and pats on the back as soon as they leave. I'm gathering my things, getting ready to head up to the Bellingham office, when Wyatt approaches.

"Can I talk to you?" he asks quietly as I'm grabbing my bag from my chair.

Mark and two others are still dallying around the table. "Now isn't the best time," I say through clenched teeth.

He follows my line of sight. "Yeah. I just…"

"What?" My phone buzzes and I fight the urge to check it. My PM has sent me five emails in the past half hour. "You knew what I was presenting. Don't you think it would have been better to question my choices literally any other time than in front of the clients?" I stare him down and he at least has the decency to appear bashful.

"I was concerned with the best business outcome, and I don't want Archer to think I'm playing favorites, but maybe I should have… Look, I'm sorry, okay? I didn't mean—"

I put up a hand to stop him. "I don't know what's going on with you," I say. "I don't know if that was a deliberate attempt at making me look bad or what, but it wasn't cool."

"If you let me, I can try to explain…"

"Not now, I have to run. I'll be in Bellingham until the end of the week, but I'll call you."

"Okay." His chin juts out, indicating it's anything but.

"You knew I was going up there this week."

"Nice job, Dani," Mark hollers at me as he passes.

I wave a thanks, before facing Wyatt again. Or I attempt to—he's now studying the sconce above me.

"It's fine," he says. "I have another meeting, so… You should go."

When it seems he has nothing else to add, I set course for the elevators.

Glad at least *that* we agree on.

The whole situation chafes like a pair of too-tight jeans the rest of the day, and as soon as I get to my hotel room late that night, I call Wyatt. He doesn't pick up. Same thing Tuesday morning. I send him a text, but still nothing. Not until midafternoon does my phone ping with a message: Sorry I was sleeping. Wasn't feeling great yesterday.

Vertigo? I text back, but again he doesn't respond. Two hours pass, my heart sinking further each time I note the blank screen. Eventually, I type I'll call you @ 7 before necessity forces me to tuck the phone away—I have to finish research for a four-thousand-square-foot farmhouse before the end of the day.

That evening, I'm browsing spite house kitchen cabinets on the hotel bed, a healthy meal of fast-food hamburger and fries at my side. I thought I was set on this cabinetmaker I really like in Snohomish. He's usually booked far in advance, but now that the tile will take its sweet old time, that's no longer an issue. It's just that I'm not sure anymore. If I wanted,

I could change the tile order, and get a decent set of cabinets from a midlevel place with half the wait.

I check the clock—ten to seven—then click open a third tab for another quick search. Before the results fully load, a video call comes through. Wyatt's beaten me to it.

"How's it going up there?" he asks, a trace of apprehension in his voice. Good. I'm glad he hasn't moved on. We need to talk about what happened.

He's on his couch in a white fitted T-shirt. I wish I could see more of him, but the window is too small.

"Lots to do, but that's what we want, right?" I go for a smile, hoping it will bridge whatever distance is still between us.

"Mmm."

He falls quiet, and I fight the urge to apologize for my chewing. He's seen me eat before.

"Hey, about yesterday," he says, eventually. "I'm really sorry. I was out of line."

I swallow a mouthful of soda. "You were."

His dark eyes observe me through the screen. "Are you mad?"

"That's not the word I'd use."

"You seemed like you couldn't wait to get away."

I put my burger down. "I told you, I had to get to Bellingham. I obviously wasn't happy about being undermined in front of the boss *and* the clients. I'm just trying to understand."

"I feel really bad about it."

I look down at my lap. Does he? "So talk to me."

"And if I'm not sure what to say?"

I meet my gaze in the mirror across the room. "What about Saturday, then? Did you really leave because you had work to do?"

"Why else?"

"You tell me." I pick at the fries spread out on the bag in front of me. Arrange them in a star. Everything inside me is tight and the food in my stomach churns.

A minute goes by. Another. Ads glare behind the video window. Fifty percent off at the big-box store. *Kitchen extravaganza.* Maybe I *should* just go with quick and cheap and be done with it. Done with the house, done with the fling. If that's what he's angling for. He's clearly not interested in even attempting a conversation.

"You know, I have a pretty busy day tomorrow," I say, finally.

"Oh. Okay." A first sign of animation on his face. "Look, I'm just…" He brings his phone closer. "Will you let me know when you're back?"

"If you want me to."

"Of *course*, I do." He says it with sincerity, as if I should know this is a given. "And we're, you know… We're okay? I'll see you in a few days?"

I bite down on my cheek. "Sure. There's that happy hour on Friday with work, too."

He sighs. "Right. Yeah, I probably won't go. With office gossip going around we shouldn't be seen together anyway."

He has a point, but his comment still stings.

"You should go, though," he says. "Don't cancel on my behalf. How about Saturday instead?"

"I have that LARP thing at the house with Mia and Matt. You could join us?"

He wrinkles his nose. "Not really my scene. Maybe afterward? Dinner?"

"It'll probably go late."

"Huh. Okay." The tips of his fingers smooth his brow. "You know what—I think I'm going to let you go. You've got a lot on your plate, and I don't want to be the one keeping you from it. Guess I'll see you at work."

No, not like this. "Wyatt…"

He pauses, a finger perched to end the call. "What?"

I want to tell him we'll figure this out, but he's so far away. "Nothing. I'll talk to you later."

His chin dips toward his chest and then he's gone.

Slowly, the room around me takes shape again. This empty room. Is there anything more depressing than the cookie-cutter blandness of a business hotel? It feeds the gloom lingering from our call. Yes, he apologized, but I'm starting to feel like we're no longer on the same team. Like he's deliberately trying to misunderstand and find obstacles. Have I misread him?

Maybe this week away is for the best—a way to get some perspective. I'll be back in town soon enough and then I'll know.

I fall asleep that night willing him to prove me wrong.

37

"YOU'RE UP EARLY," Iris says, muting the TV. She's in the middle of one of her rainy noir movies again. There are a few that play on repeat, which means I now know the story lines by heart. I'm not sure whether she watches them for nostalgia or because she's convinced they're superior television. Not that it matters. They make her happy.

"Couldn't sleep." I pull my legs up under me in the beat-up recliner. Another wad of wool is in my hands and the needle is working.

The happy hour last night was a bust. For me, that is— everyone else seemed to have a good time. Mia and Matt rocked the house with their karaoke duets, but I couldn't stop thinking about Wyatt. Still can't stop thinking about him. I texted him when I got home from Bellingham and received a Good to know back. Nothing since, so I'm giving him space. The pit in my stomach is a lead orb, pushing me deeper into the cushions.

Iris peers at my moving fingers from one corner of the couch, her face flickering white and rainbow in the glow of the screen. "Want to talk about it?"

"Not really."

A brief pause, then, "Okay." She unmutes her movie.

To make matters even worse, I dreamed about Sam. Three weeks have gone by, and I haven't heard from him or his lawyer. I must have been right that he has no case, but it's still vaguely disconcerting not knowing what he's up to.

"Oh, there was a package for you," Iris says. "It's on the kitchen counter."

I put the felted wool down, pad across the floor and rip the thick envelope open. It's the UW Husky flag I ordered. My throat starts to burn at the sight of the purple-and-gold fabric in my hands. The house is coming along great, plumbing and electrical are in—I should be elated. The flag will be the crowning glory in sticking it to Sam. I press two fingers to my eyes until my vision blurs. I don't want to cry. This is ridiculous.

"Get it together," I mutter.

"What's that, hon?" Iris asks.

I return to the living room and sit back down. "I don't get what he wants."

"Ah." She turns off the TV as if she was waiting for this all along.

"He's sweet one moment and pushes me away the next. He says he wants to see me, but at the same time it's like he's trying to make up reasons why we shouldn't do what we're doing—like it's going to interfere with work, or there's something suspicious about my mom mistaking him for Sam. It won't and there's not."

"Yes, who doesn't like being confused with the ex...?"

"Not to mention he was a perfect jerk to me in a work

meeting." I tug a throw pillow into my lap and pick at its fringe. "It's like he's choosing not to get me, choosing to see only obstacles, and it makes me doubt he wants anything to do with me at all."

"If that was true, he could just call the whole thing off. Is that what you want him to do?"

An image of Wyatt running his fingers across my skin surfaces—his face filled with reverence. "No," I say.

She nods thoughtfully. "You really like him, don't you?"

"Don't tell me you disapprove."

"Quite the contrary." She nods at Cairo and Cesar, who are sound asleep on their beds. "He passed my most important test."

She must be referring to the dog park. "He did have a way with them," I agree. It was instant canine love. Night and day from how they reacted to Sam when he showed up at the barbecue.

Iris leans forward. "Then tell him what you *do* want. If you even know."

"What does that mean?"

She gives me a long look. "Friends with benefits never works."

"That's not true. It is. Or it was."

"Clearly."

"I don't…" I frown at her dry expression. "What do you…"

She turns the TV back on. In her usual fashion, I don't get a say in whether or not the conversation is done.

After a minute or two, I give Cairo a pat and head back to my room, where I shove the flag in my purse, out of sight. I need to reassure Wyatt, to let him know I want the house and the fling to stay a package deal. That I want to spend this time we have *together*. Last night would have been vastly better if he'd come out with us.

You should have been there yesterday, I type, hitting Send before I can change my mind.

❧

I get to The Spite House by two thirty to meet up with Matt and Mia for the photo shoot. Still no response from Wyatt. By now there's no chance he hasn't seen my text; clearly, he doesn't feel the same. I should have known better than to let my guard down with another guy. I should have stuck to my guns and not allowed him to get under my skin. The more I think about it, the angrier I become. Angry at myself for not being able to resist him. Angry at him for everything else. At least respond to my texts!

Matt has told people to show up at three, and we need to stage the lot first. He's brought props and camera equipment and wants three different "scenes" for the various costumed critters to pose in. It's gray out, but thankfully there's no rain in the forecast.

While he tweaks the setup, Mia and I sit on the ground eating sandwiches from a shop near her place. Loel's guys are finishing up behind us, and I think I saw the man himself through a window a minute ago.

"Looks like the house will be done pretty soon," Mia says, midchew.

She's right. The roof and siding are completely done, drywall and insulation should be next. What started as a wild idea over two months ago is now real. I dig deep for that excitement I know should be there. That bubbling glee. Where the hell is it?

"Things still rocky with Wyatt?" she asks. "You look like you've sucked on a lemon."

I nod.

"You'll figure it out, though, right?"

"I want to. I—"

"Hey, Dani." Loel comes up to us and tucks a pair of gloves into his pockets. His moustache is extra perky today, matching his squinty crow's feet.

"How's it going?"

"I'm about to take off, but if you'd like to see the progress, I can show you around first."

"That would be great." I get up and brush off my pants.

Loel leads the way.

I was wrong, they've already started on the insulation. The stairs leading both up and down are in place, there are light switch receptacles, HVAC ducts, and the bathroom shower unit has been installed.

"I'll show you my favorite spot," Loel says, heading upstairs.

It's the first time I've been on the second floor, and right away I know where he's going.

He opens the sliding door to the deck and spreads his arms wide. "Isn't this phenomenal? Heck, *I'd* pay money to stay here. Crack open a beer, watch the sunset."

I hum in agreement. "It was Wyatt's idea." Always a visionary.

"He has a good eye. Anyway, I thought you should see how things are coming together. We'll finish the insulation and get drywall up this coming week."

I skim the posts and wires, landing on the space where the loft was supposed to be. It's been closed off. "Where's the loft?" I ask, stepping sideways to get a better view.

"I asked Wyatt about it while you were out of town and he said not to do it."

I still, the sounds around me fading away. "He what?"

"Not worth the time or money, he said. I thought you guys had talked about it."

No, I want to shout. We'd done no such thing. "Miscommunication," I manage through clenched teeth.

"I would have called you, but he sounded so certain."

I bet he did...

"Not your fault." I flash him a quick smile and move toward the stairs. My whole body feels like it's vibrating like one of those heat mirages above summer asphalt. I need to get out of here before I explode. I offer a clipped "thanks for the tour" and excuse myself.

I look for Mia, but while I've been inside, she's been swept up in a sea of elves, goblins, tree people, sprites, ogres, and even a giant. A long line of people snakes off the property and up the sidewalk past Sam's house. Some are strumming oddly shaped string instruments and blowing on flutes, and spirits are high.

I kick at a hardened ball of dirt and it disintegrates into a heap.

Where is she?

I round the corner hoping she'll be there, but instead I come face-to-face with Sam rolling in at full speed like a thundercloud. Fucking great.

He flings out his hand to indicate a gathering of tree-nymph creatures. "This has got to stop," he says. "I get it. You don't like Catrina. But I've got to live my life here. I don't want trolls and whatever those are waltzing about my yard on the weekend."

Somewhere behind me a chorus of voices come together in a cheerful ditty about a maiden and a boar. Two fiddles and a lute join in.

"I thought you had a lawyer on the case?" I feign innocence.

His expression darkens further. "Come on, Dani. Let it go, will you? Enough is enough."

This is what I wanted. I wanted him losing his shit about this house, to share some of my pain, and that I have clearly achieved. High fives all around. Except, he still doesn't understand the most important thing: no one tells me what to do. I draw myself up to my full five feet six inches, hands on my hips.

"I don't know what you're upset about," I say. "It's a nice day and we're having a good time over here. There's music and laughter… If you have a costume, you're welcome to participate."

His fists curl at his side. "I want you to stop this whole vendetta. It's beneath you."

I raise my chin, sulfuric fury expanding inside me. "It's my property and I'll do what I want with it."

"Hey there." Mia sidles in between us. "Everything okay?" She gives me a pointed side-eye that I take to mean we're getting too loud.

"All good," I say with a huff, standing down. "Sam was about to leave."

"You sure you don't want in?" Mia asks him. "You'd make a great orc."

He glares at us, nostrils flaring before he stalks off.

"Ah, this brings back memories from the Renaissance faire," Mia says.

A wave of nausea washes over me, and I crouch down to rest my head in my hands. Wyatt's voice and Sam's face twist into a tangled mess that makes no sense. The two of them together is a labyrinth I can't think my way out of. The more I try, the more turned around I get. I should know how to get out. It should be easier than this.

Mia puts her hand on my back. "What's going on?"

The Spite House looms tall behind her. I've done it. I've built the thing. I've shown Sam—put a permanent cloud in his sky. This is when I celebrate, right? When I turn my face to the sun, ready to take on the world?

That's how it should be, but here I am much more inclined to hide beneath an old blanket.

"I'm tired," I say. "Or I need a drink. One of the two."

A look of concern. "The lawyer?"

"No, that seems to have fallen through." I push up to standing and she follows.

"Then what?"

I stare at the gaping windows on the second floor of The Spite House for a long moment before responding. "Wyatt pulled a Sam on me." I tell her about the loft. I still can't believe he went behind my back like that.

Mia frowns. "Maybe he thought that's what you wanted?"

"That's not the point. It wasn't his decision to make. And he probably did choose the quickest solution on purpose." Saying it out loud sheds new light on his helpfulness with the tile. I thought we were having fun. Why would he want to cut that short?

She puts her arm around me and leads me away from the house. "Okay," she says, her voice soft like when you comfort a small child. "I love you, but you need to go talk to Wyatt. You need to have the facts before you assume this was intentional. Wyatt and Sam are not the same."

Next, she'll tell me a Chihuahua and a German shepherd aren't both dogs.

I scan the line of cheery LARPers. "I don't know."

"I've got it covered," she says, before giving me a shove in the direction of my car. "Go. Get it done. You can meet us at Crow-Bar after. Or not."

I glance at the porch of Sam's house, but my ex is gone. "Fine."

38

I TRY TO clear my head while I drive the fifteen minutes to Wyatt's place. "Keep an open mind," I mumble to myself. "Get the facts." Easier said than done with snippets of the past few months running through my head. His little comments and pushbacks—the fence, the tile, the alpaca wool, the Rose meeting. Now the audacity Loel's just revealed. I'm done giving him space.

He opens the door with the tentative pace of someone who isn't expecting company. Black joggers and T-shirt. Five-o'clock shadow.

"Can I come in?"

"Um, sure."

While I take off my shoes, he scurries around the kitchen, from the sounds of it gathering things off the counter and tossing them in the garbage.

The light on the side table next to the couch is on and a book lies open on a cushion. I stop in the middle of the living room, searching for the right thread end to start unraveling this mess.

"It's good to see you," he says, pausing several arm's lengths away. He's pale, as if he hasn't been outside in a week, but other than that he looks every bit the same Wyatt who's found a way past my defenses over these past couple of months.

"I tried texting you," I say. "Maybe there's something wrong with the phones?" It's supposed to be a joke, but its sharp edges poke at my throat.

"No, I got it." His voice twists with a bitterness that doesn't suit him. "Sorry to be such a disappointment. What was it you said? *I should have been there.*" He sneers the words.

What?

"No, what I meant was, I *wished* you'd been there. The night could have been better."

A beat of silence. "Oh."

He must have read it completely wrong. "But that's not why I'm here." I steel myself. "I saw Loel at the lot. I know about the loft."

His jaw ticks. "And?"

"Come on. I think you know you should have asked me what I wanted to do with it."

"When we talked about it last, you were leaning toward not doing it. He needed an answer, so that's what I told him."

My chest constricts at his dismissive tone. "So, this has nothing to do with you wanting to be done with the build sooner?"

He looks away. "I don't see what the big deal is. Are you telling me you changed your mind?"

"Yes!" I want to stomp my foot. "But even if I hadn't, you don't get to make the call for me." Like I haven't told him the reasons Sam and I fell apart.

His eyes flash. "Loft, no loft—what does it matter? You're not going to live there anyway."

"It matters to me!" I breathe in through my nose and count to five. Force my features into something other than a scowl. "It's *my* build. *My* house. And I didn't hear you deny it, so why are you so eager to finish it up? Speed over quality isn't like you, and I thought—" My voice cracks. "I thought you liked spending time with me."

He grabs his neck and pitches his head to the side. "Damn it, Dani. I do."

"But?"

"But what?"

"What aren't you telling me?"

He crosses his arms. "What am *I* not telling *you*? Wow that's rich. Loel just informed me you ordered tile that will take three months to get here. *Three* months! Anything you want to say about that?"

I stare at him, tongue-tied.

"And what about all the little pranks—the garden gnomes, the birdbath, the wind chimes…"

"A bit of fun," I manage. "That's all." I can't tell him the truth now. Not when he's looking at me like I've been sprayed by a skunk.

"Well, fuck me." His hands land on the back of his head, and he paces a few steps toward the hallway before he spins on me, his face contorted with something not unlike pain. "I know," he says.

"What?"

"I have waited, patiently, thinking you needed time, needed to get to know me better first, and still, I get lies. Even now."

"Wyatt, what are you—"

"Were you just never planning on telling me we're building next to Sam's house?"

I stiffen. Somewhere in my brain a gong goes off, its din reverberating against the sides of my skull. He *knows*. "How long..." The question evaporates.

"I suspected it early on, and then I saw him come home one day when I was at the lot with Loel."

I don't even try to hide the heat in my cheeks. This is bad.

"So, what's the deal? You just can't let him go? That's why you're messing with the build?"

I blink as his words sink in. "Is that what you think? That I'm trying to stay in his life?"

"You tell me."

I take a step toward him. "But you know I'm not. I've told you about our breakup."

"Doesn't matter what you told me. You didn't tell me about *this*. How is that supposed to make me feel when even your mom doesn't think you're over him yet? So yeah, maybe I am tired of everything revolving around the house. Around *Sam*."

"*Revenge* on Sam," I clarify, willing him to look at me. "I'm building a *spite* house."

"That's some kind of vigilante justice."

"Maybe." I move another step closer, like he's a skittish animal I need to pacify. "But if you knew all along, you also knew what you were getting yourself into. You could have said something."

The tension in the air magnifies everything. One of his eyelashes sticks to his cheek and there's a soft swish when he brushes it off with a finger.

"Well, that was before..." He rakes a hand across his hair, messing up the sleek top.

"Before?"

He scratches his temple, his gaze stuck below my knees before it flickers toward the windows. "It wasn't my place to pry it out of you. And maybe I thought it wouldn't be a problem at first, but then I changed my mind." He wanders over to the couch and sits down, shoulders slumping forward.

My anger retreats at the sight, and I take a seat next to him on the leather, knee touching knee. "What changed? Help me understand."

His fingers flex against his thighs, their tips digging into the black fabric. "I don't know. Maybe I didn't expect—I thought we'd just…" He leans back against the cushions, faces the ceiling. "Ah, fuck." A deep sigh, then he falls quiet.

"What's going on?" I ask, gentler now. "Are you okay?"

He recoils as soon as the words are out, jerking away from me. "Don't do that," he snarls.

The muscles in my back wind tight. "Do what?"

"Act like you're waiting for me to break. I'm *fine*. Yeah, I can't go to happy hour because my ear is ringing, and I get dizzy sometimes. So what? You don't need to ask how I'm doing all the time."

I shift away, my chest cramping. "I'm not. You know your Ménière's doesn't bother me one bit. I'm expressing concern because I care about you. And I thought you stayed home because you were worried about office gossip. Why didn't you tell me it was the tinnitus?"

"I don't need anyone's pity."

This again. "When have I *ever* pitied you?" I fly off the couch and back toward the bookcase, wrapping my arms around me. "I know you were hurt before, but I'm not *her*. You're not being fair."

"And you are? I'm supposed to just be cool with your days being taken up by your ex and this revenge scheme?" His eyes harden. "Tell me, did he like your fun little display today? The one that took so much time to set up you had none left to see me?"

"Nice one. Really. And what the hell makes you think you

get to have an opinion on what I do and don't do? I make my own decisions, and I refuse to have them limited by other people anymore. Besides, I'm here now, aren't I?"

"Well, maybe you shouldn't be."

I back away another step. The clouds are gathering outside.

"Clearly, I had this all wrong in my head," Wyatt says, voice cold. "But don't worry—I can take a hint. I'll call Loel tomorrow and tell him to go directly through you from now on. I'm done."

With each word, the hope I've held on to wilts further. *So that's how it is.*

"'Kay," I mumble, grabbing my purse and shoes from the floor. "If that's how you really feel."

I slam the door shut behind me, my vision blurring with tears.

The elevator, the garage, the car, the road.

The heartbreak.

39

I STARE AT the dark surface of my phone as if there's something profound hidden beneath it. Four hours have passed since I left Wyatt's apartment, and not a word. I picture him in his bed, pillow propped up behind him, chest bare. The splintered wedge between us grates further. I don't know why I hoped he'd reach out. He doesn't care about me. He thinks I pity him, that I still want Sam. That I've been toying with him this whole time. As if I was in control and this is what I was aiming for. This was *never* the plan. Wyatt *made* me lose track of what I was supposed to do—stick it to Sam and come out on top. He confused everything.

I down my martini and order another where I sit perched on a barstool at Crow-Bar, a quirky University District hangout made even quirkier tonight by the fact that half the place is still in costume from the afternoon LARPing.

"Anything?" Mia asks over my shoulder.

"Nope," I say, cheerless.

"You could try him first."

"Do I look like a glutton for punishment?" I nod a thanks to the bartender as he sets my drink down on a napkin.

She hugs me from behind. "It was that bad, huh?"

I tip my glass back. "I think it's a sign I should be done with guys. For real this time. Screw 'em!"

"No, don't say that. You've been really happy this spring and I know Wyatt is a big reason. It's the circumstances that are complicating everything. Personally, I think you're perfect for each other, but terrible at owning up to it."

"Easy for you to say when you have Matt. Are you in *love* with him?" It comes out as a sneer, so I force my mouth into a smile to counteract it. I must be more buzzed than I thought. They've been dating for two and a half months now. I think he's the first boyfriend she's had who likes her without any caveats about her goofy humor, or her body, or her fashion sense. If she's Bridget Jones, he's her Mark Darcy; he likes her *just as she is*. Why can't I have that?

Mia pauses, lips pinched. "Maybe. And I think I'll go find him now if it's all right with you. I know you're hurting, but if I stay here, I might say something I regret tomorrow." She disappears into a group of elves doing shots of something electric blue.

My glass is empty again, but doesn't stay that way for long. Occasionally, someone from the group steps up to the bar next to me and we chat while they order, but mostly I'm left to my own devices. I'm lonely here in a room full of people, my mind stuck on Wyatt's eyes. How they lured me in with their soft caress only to cut deep when my guard was down. He said he missed me, that I could trust him, that he wasn't like Sam. Or no—he didn't say that.

I shake my head. The vision of the room is on delay, not

quite following where I go. Where was I? Right. Wyatt making promises he can't keep. Or no—that was me. My assumptions. It was implied, though, wasn't it? That he'd be different? Otherwise, I would have never let him close.

My elbow slips off the bar, and I jerk upright. The bartender gives me a long look, then hands me a bottle of water. Some drips on my shirt, but I'm past caring. I wipe my chin with my sleeve. Where's Mia?

I scoot off my chair and scan the room. It's a blur of colors and noise, but eventually I find her near the door, huddling with Matt.

She stands when I approach, her expression evolving into concern. "Dani, what's wrong?"

"I think I should go," I say. "I don't want to be here anymore." I stumble into her arms and try to rest my head there. "Why does he think he's not what I want?"

"She's pretty wasted," I hear Matt say. I want to object, but I don't have the energy.

"Okay, let's get you home." Mia holds me up by my shoulders. "Sorry," she adds to Matt.

Noooo. Now I'm ruining her night, too. Even through my cocktail fog, this seems like a shitty thing to do. "I can just take an Uber," I say on impulse. "No biggie. You stay."

Mia seems skeptical. "I don't know that I'm comfortable with that."

I fish out my phone and open the app. "There. Done." I give her an air kiss. "It'll be here in four minutes."

Thankfully, she doesn't argue further. "Okay, but at least let me make sure you get in the car."

"I'll wait here," Matt says. "Hope you feel better, Dani."

I offer him a noncommittal wave as Mia leads me outside by the hand.

The cool night air has the same effect as a snowball down

my shirt. Every muscle in my body contracts in protest, but when they relax again, the world is less hazy.

"Are you sure?" Mia asks.

"I'm fine. And there are like ten steps from the street to Iris's door. Don't worry." I shiver. Did I have a jacket when I got here?

Mia checks my phone. "One minute."

She's done so much for me. She's the only one who has. And here I am… "I'm sorry," I blurt. "About what I said about you and Matt. You know I'm happy for you, right?"

She squeezes my arm. "I know. What you need is a good night's sleep, and things will look better tomorrow. I'm sure you misunderstood Wyatt."

His voice echoes in my head, proof that she's wrong, but I don't tell her that. I don't want to think about it right now.

My car pulls up, and Mia opens the door. "Promise you'll text me when you get home."

I tell her I will, and then we're off.

The driver reads out the address to confirm.

"Uh-huh," I say, and close my eyes.

I swear no more than a minute has gone by when we come to a stop.

"Okay, have a good night."

I blink at the overhead light. "Thanks." As soon as I'm out, the driver speeds away.

The sidewalk wobbles beneath my feet like a fun-house illusion as I tuck my phone into my purse. I can't wait to get in bed; I'm going to sleep for a week. One step forward and I halt, confused. There's not supposed to be grass here. My head lurches up, and for a moment there's no comprehending what I'm seeing.

I'm not home. I'm at Sam's house. Because that's still the default address in the app.

Just perfect.

40

"OF COURSE," I say out loud, staring at what used to be my home. There's a light on upstairs, but otherwise no signs of life. No way am I ringing Sam's doorbell at this hour.

In the distance, the wind chimes at The Spite House play their eerie tune, drawing me in like the Pied Piper. I pause at the entrance, fingers tapping the makeshift handrail. Yes, Wyatt was mistaken about the loft, but I never actually let him know I'd changed my mind. That means it's possible, likely even, that he only told Loel not to do the loft because he honestly believed that's what I wanted—not to sabotage me.

I make my way to the basement through the thick plastic that still covers the window opening. Out of habit, I fumble against the closest wall for a light switch and flick it. Nothing. I flick it a few more times, until I realize there's no light fixture.

It's dark, but the flashlight on my phone leads the way—up to the first floor, through the kitchen, to the living room. I stand in the middle of the space and my arm falls to my side. The air is infused with the now familiar scents of wood, paint, and caulk, but my nose itches at some new, faint acridity. I rub at it with little relief—if anything, it stings more. Not long ago, Wyatt was with me here. I can picture us on the floor, feel his breath on my neck.

I startle as the first tear trickles down my cheek, quickly followed by another, then several more as I sink to the floor. "I don't need you anyway. I can do this on my own," I whisper between sobs, but even I hear the conviction is lacking. There's a Wyatt-shaped hole at my side, and here, in the house we built together, things could not be more wrong. I should have kept my distance, focused on the project like I set out to.

My eyes skirt the many textures of the room as another sob breaches the surface, paving the way for a pounding headache. If the floor wasn't so hard, I'd lie down and get some rest.

I reach for my purse and dump out its contents. Tissue, tissue, tissue… Ah, there's one. I blow hard then toss the crumpled paper into the corner. As I stuff everything back in, my fingertips find something soft and silky. I laugh out loud—a weird, strangled sound.

The fucking flag.

I run my sleeve across my face and get up. Might as well finish strong. I've put enough time between me and the martinis now that the world is once again steady beneath my feet, but the climb to the second floor is nevertheless a precarious one. I keep bumping my hip into the railing as I fumble my way up the spiral staircase.

My phone illuminates everything in bright circular flashes. That's where the loft would have been. Again, that drop in my stomach—I've messed up. Sam deliberately went against my wishes. Wyatt did what he *thought* I wanted. And I did lie to him. I struggle against another surge of sadness, this one accompanied by a burst of remorse. Why did I compare them?

A clang from outside breaks my reverie. A car door? Garbage can? Suddenly, the darkness is less friendly, and I push onward to the door leading to the deck. The moon peeks out from behind a cloud as I step onto the wood slats, wavy tree shadows rippling across my feet. The wind chime peals softly down below.

I shake out the flag and consider my options. If I had thumbtacks, I could put it up on the siding, but even I am not that prepared. Hang it from the roof? Yeah, if I'd like to be a heap of broken bones on the ground within the next half hour. In the end, I make do with tying it to the railing, facing Sam's house. *"Bow down to Washington,"* I hum while I work.

And then it's done.

I got the lot I wanted, secured money, planned a house, and got it built. Boo-yah!

"Take that!" I shout into the night.

A new wave of tears burst forth out of nowhere, knocking the breath out of me. I squat down, my head in my hands. If I got exactly what I wanted, why am I still miserable? I'm supposed to be fulfilled, zen, and here I am instead crying on a balcony like an aged *Juliet*.

Another couple of thuds, from directly below the house this time, and my sobs sputter to a stop.

"Who's there?" a voice calls out. "Dani, is that you?"

Sam? I stand up and lean over the railing. He's on the other side of the fence staring back at me, his face pale in the moonlight. "Yeah, it's me."

"What the hell are you doing here? Hold on." He runs off along the fence and returns on my side. "You can't be here in the middle of the night. You'll wake the whole neighborhood with your drunken rants."

I didn't think I was that loud. "That's your opinion," I say. My words are still slurred, but at least I'm aware. "Plus, it's not my fault. The Uber dropped me at the wrong place. Do you like my flag?" I gesture to it with exaggerated flourish.

"It's too dark. I'm sure it's great." He cuts a look toward the street. "But seriously, come down from there. It's still a construction site—that's not safe."

"It's a Husky flag," I clarify. "Your favorite."

He ignores me. "I'll drive you home, how's that? Can you walk okay, or do you need help?"

I pout. "You're no fun." Going home sounds good, though. My bed. My pillow. Sleep. *Fine.* I grab my purse and head back inside.

"Dani?" he calls, voice fainter.

My turn to ignore him. He should be asleep by now anyway. Being an early riser is a strange point of pride for him. I've never met anyone less nocturnal.

"Ouch!" My knee gets up close and personal with the stairs. Maybe I need to rethink this particular design feature or include a warning in the rental agreement. *No climbing when drunk.* I giggle at the thought.

"Are you okay?" Sam springs out of the shadows like an antsy ghost. "Come on, I'll help you." He takes me by the arm and proceeds to lead me down the steps at breakneck speed. I don't know why he doesn't toss me over his shoulder and be done with it.

"Slow down—I'm going to break things. Getting bruises everywhere," I mutter.

And then we're outside. I check my leg in the glow of the streetlights. It's banged up, that's for sure.

"Okay, let's get you home." Sam puts an arm around my shoulders.

I shake him off and bend down again. There's something in my shoe.

Then everything happens in slow motion.

"Come on," Sam says somewhere up ahead.

I straighten, ready to respond, but he's intent on something behind me now, his pupils suddenly a dancing red.

"Holy shit," he spits out through gritted teeth.

One moment I'm on the ground, the next I'm being hoisted into the air. Sam has one arm under my knees, one behind my back, and when he spins, one of my shoes flies off. I'm about to protest, but before I get a word out, there's a whoosh, followed by a sharp crack, and the world around us lights up in a blinding blaze. The force of the explosion thrusts us forward several feet and I don't have to look back to know what's happened.

The Spite House is on fire.

41

SAM AND I are alone behind a curtain in the ER. He's had his wrist x-rayed and judging by its size and color, it's broken. The results are taking forever. Me, I have a few Band-Aids and a mean headache, but in all honesty the latter is more likely due to the martinis than the fire. I think I called 911, or maybe the firefighters showed up before I could—time and the order of things are a blur. All I know is when the ambulance took off, we left behind a giant bonfire.

"How's your arm?" I ask Sam.

"Hurts like hell."

"Can I get you anything?"

"Nah." A small pause. "Thanks for coming with me."

"Of course." The paramedics wanted to check me out, too, but I doubt he remembers that. He was pretty out of it.

"Are you okay?" he asks.

I yawn and touch my fingers to my forehead. "Yeah, I mean, not great." A few cuts and bruises are one thing—at some point I'll have to start considering the actual losses. Not now, though. Not now.

"Could have been worse?"

I let out a sad chuckle. "Right."

"Damn lucky I was there." He looks away.

"Yeah." A question arises from somewhere deep below the surface. One that floated past when we were in the ambulance. "Why were you?"

"What do you mean? I heard you up on the deck. You were really loud."

"Not *that* loud."

"Loud enough."

We glare at each other. Whatever, I'm too tired for this shit. "Okay."

"Okay," he echoes.

"I need to make a few phone calls. Will you be all right for a bit?"

He nods.

It's a quiet night in the ER, a few muted voices, a phone ringing in the distance, a bleary-eyed couple at the front desk asking for the room number of a patient. The clock above the couches announces it's 1:47 in the morning. We've been here almost two hours already, prodded and interviewed at length, and all I want is sleep.

I try Wyatt first, but as expected it goes straight to voice mail, where his tone is curt and professional. Now I'll be back among those who only ever get that side of him. I'll have to pretend I don't know any better.

"Hey, it's me," I say after the beep. "So, I need to...wanted to let you know something's happened. At the house." I hesitate. "A fire." My chest constricts as the sparks of story-high flames crackle through my mind. The intensity of the heat made it feel like the fire's objective was to shove me away, like the house didn't want me there anymore. I clear my throat. "Anyway, call me. Please."

I hang up and wait a minute as if he's magically going to wake up, listen to my message, and call. But of course, he doesn't.

I leave the same message for Loel and then dial Mia. She'd texted asking if I got home okay, but that was over an hour ago.

"Hello?" She sounds unusually awake for this hour. Maybe since Matt is with her, they weren't sleeping.

I go to speak, but nothing comes out.

"Dani, are you okay? What's going on?"

"The house burned down," I whisper.

"What?"

I draw in a sniffling breath, then try again, louder. "I'm fine. But the house is gone."

She says something to Matt in the background, and the static grows as she puts me on speaker.

"Is Iris okay?" Matt asks.

I frown. Iris? *Oh.* "Not her house," I clarify. "The Spite House. I was there."

"You were there?" Mia half yells. "Why?"

"It's a long story. Can you come get me? I'm at Overlake."

"You were hurt?" Another frantic shout. "Oh my God, Dani. What the hell happened?"

"No, I'm fine." My chin drops to my chest. "Sam broke his wrist."

"Sam!?"

I guess this is how we communicate now—I make a statement, and she hollers back at me.

"Please, come get me. I want to go home."

She and Matt mumble to each other. "I'll be there in fifteen. Hold tight, everything will be okay."

"Okay." I hang up, unwilling and unable to move. I know I have to go tell Sam Mia's coming for me, but first I'll have to convince my legs to carry me there. I don't want to. I don't want to do anything, talk to anyone, be anywhere.

I want to be invisible. Vanish like smoke.

Sam is in the process of getting his arm put in a cast when I return, but he doesn't protest when I tell him I'm leaving.

"I'll call you tomorrow," he says. "Glad you're okay."

42

MIA TUCKS ME into her back seat, blanket and all, and hands me a snack bar from her glove compartment. The chocolate is partly melted, but it's the best thing I've eaten all day. With my forehead to the windowpane, the world outside blurs as we pass, making me dizzy, but at least that means I can still feel. The surrealism is fitting.

Iris's house is dark and quiet when we pull into the driveway. The dogs stir on their pillows when we enter, but Mia shushes them, and we reach my room without waking Iris up. Mia sits me down on my bed and takes off my shoes.

"You smell like hotdogs," she says, wrinkling her nose. "Sorry."

"It's okay." I keel over and, finally, my head meets soft down. I turn my face into the cool fabric and let out a long breath.

"Move over," Mia says, nudging me. "I'm staying."

A sleepover. I picture Mia's childhood bunk bed at her parents' house. And then I'm out.

When I wake an unknown number of hours later, Mia is at the table in my room scrolling her phone.

"Good morning, sunshine," she says without looking up. "Or good evening, rather—you've slept through the whole day. There's ibuprofen on the nightstand."

I swallow the red pills with a full glass of water. My mouth tastes like death and I don't smell much better. "Thanks. What time is it?"

"Five thirty. Figured you could use the rest." She puts her phone down. "I filled Iris in earlier. Oh, and I think Wyatt called."

That gets me out of bed. "You think?"

"Unless you have other WMs in your contacts."

I grab my phone and open it with shaky fingers. One missed call. No messages. "Should I call him back?"

"You'd better. We're going to need him to rebuild."

Yeah, I might have burned those bridges last night. No pun intended. What was it I told him—that he was limiting me? Exactly what a guy whose ex dumped him for not being able to keep up wants to hear. No wonder he ended things.

He doesn't pick up and my stomach roils at the possibility he doesn't want to talk. *Except, he called you back*, I remind myself.

Iris is in the kitchen baking when we join her. She takes one look at me then gives me a cursory hug. "How scary," she says. "Come, sit. The cookies are almost ready."

Her kindness makes me want to cry again, but my eyes are already so swollen from last night that I fight it.

After a few minutes, she sets out a plate with chocolate chip cookies and pours us each a glass of milk. Mia waits until I've had a few bites before she asks me to tell them exactly what happened after I left the bar.

When I'm done talking, Iris dunks another cookie in her glass, pops it in her mouth, and chews slowly. "And you didn't see how it started or anything out of the ordinary?"

I shake my head. "I wish I did, but the whole night is foggy. I'm trying to remember."

She pats my hand. "Don't worry, they'll figure it out. I'm just grateful no one got hurt. It could be worse—you could have still been inside."

That part still seems unreal. Maybe there was still too much liquid courage in my veins at the time for my brain to realize the danger I was in. But sure; I am alive. In the midst of losing the house and Wyatt on the same night, I suppose I should remember that.

"It's really gone?" Mia asks.

"I can't imagine they were able to save it."

Iris sits back. "Don't worry, girls, everything will be fine. Ellen and I had a house fire when we first lived together. It wasn't a big one, but we had to gut the kitchen completely." She taps the table. "What you're going to do is take tomorrow off, call your insurance company, and then make sure you get a copy of the fire report when it's done. We'll recover our losses, rebuild, and it will be like none of this happened. One step at a time."

I want to believe her. Let her lead. For the first time since calling off my engagement, the thought of doing anything on my own is exhausting. I want to defer, rely, follow. I *can't* do this alone.

"Wyatt might not want to be involved anymore," I say, glancing down. Not to mention, if he's gone, what's to say Loel will still be on board?

"Why are you mad at him again?" Mia asks. "I don't get it. Has he actually done anything bad?"

"Mia," Iris says, her tone cautionary.

"No, it's fine. Give it to me," I tell my cousin. Might as well get everything out now.

She studies me, splays her hands out in front of her. "You know I couldn't stand Sam from the beginning, and I know your dad is…a certain way, so this is not about defending all guys."

Her mom, my dad's sister, couldn't be more different as a parent and spouse, but we do share a grandfather. I know she knows.

"But I do think you kind of cast Wyatt in a villain role from the beginning. It was a self-fulfilling prophecy."

"Cairo and Cesar love him," Iris inserts. "They are the best character judges I know."

What do I say to that? He wants me to wrap up the project I lied to him about? To stop dwelling on my ex? He won't let me care about him? Hardly felonies—especially in light of how I feel when I'm with him. Deep inside, I know Mia and Iris are right. That Wyatt is not like Sam or my dad. But, but…

"It's just so complicated," I say. "Why can't I be like you, Iris—a strong, independent woman on my own? Get some dogs, live happily ever after…"

Iris takes a long moment to respond. "I was never stronger than when Ellen was by my side," she says eventually. "Being alone isn't something I'd recommend to anyone, and it's certainly not the same as being independent. Did we always want the same thing or have the same opinion? No, but I relied on her and she relied on me. It's not weakness to need another person."

I want to argue with her, tell her that it's too risky. After my close call with Sam, I don't know if I can trust my judgment with men, and I don't want to end up like my mom. I want more for me, and I'll never stop wishing more for her even if she herself has given up.

"Now, I don't know what's going on between you and Wyatt exactly," Iris continues, "but as much as you don't want to hear it, relationships are a two-way street. Don't let pride make you forget that." She strokes Cesar's head, her firm gaze on me. "And while life would be easier if things were either black or white, either exactly right or completely wrong, that's not how relationships work. Love exists in the vast gray to add color. With grace, most people eventually come around. If you give them a chance."

"Maybe you met him too soon—that's one thing," Mia fills in. "Maybe *he* met *you* too soon. But I see how you are when you talk about him, and I think you're making a huge mistake if you simply accept this being over." She nods once, having said her piece, then softens it with a curve of her lip. "Thank you for coming to my TED Talk." She stands. "And on that note, I need to head out, but I'll be back tomorrow after work. I'll bring pizza. And Matt, if that's okay?"

"Sure." Her words are trying to organize themselves in my mind. She's not wrong, but Wyatt is done. His words. Even if I talk to him, I don't think there's much chance of us picking up where we left off.

❦

Per Iris's advice, I call in sick, and after a decent night's sleep, I'm determined to tackle what needs to be tackled. Insurance claim, fire report, and onward. I've got this.

After breakfast, I find the filing box where I store all my important papers and leaf through the *insurance* tab. There's my health plan information, car insurance, renter's insurance, and 401(k) papers that should be elsewhere, but no sign of the insurance for The Spite House. Wondering if the retirement plan materials could have gotten swapped for the house insurance, I turn to the next tab, then the next, but come up empty-handed. This makes no sense. They have to be here somewhere. By the time I've gone through the whole box and my work bag, my pajama top clings to my back. *Think, think, think.*

I change into a clean T-shirt and tie on my runners. If the papers aren't in my car, I'm going to have to check my desk at Archer. That's the only other place they could be. I grab my phone from the charger on my nightstand and it lights up with Wyatt's initials. Another missed call. I'll have to try him from the car. Or maybe he's in his office. At that possibility, I start sweating again. No, I'll call. Or…

Gah! Stop it!

I give myself a mental slap.

"I'm heading out for a bit," I holler to Iris when I'm already halfway out the door. "I'll be back."

I've never been more annoyed at the red lights along Bel-Red Road, but at least I score a parking space by the elevators. Normally, I'm not wild about the fact that my office is near the vestibule—the noise is constant—but today it works to my advantage as I don't run into anyone on my way.

"Okay, if I were important paperwork, where would I be?" I sit down at my desk and pull out the drawers one by one, and there, at the bottom, is the white, letter-sized envelope with the blue logo.

My chest expands for a split second, but as soon as I touch the paper, it's as if the tactile memory of placing it there catches up with me. All my thoughts crystallize into one long *NO.* That can't be right. I open the flap, and there they are—my original forms, signed by me but never sent in or paid for. Everything inside me drops, and the papers fall to my desk.

There's no insurance. I've lost everything.

43

I TAKE THAT BACK. I've lost *more* than everything because Iris and Mia also have money in this.

I grab the papers and rush out to my car. There, in the dark, I rest my head against the steering wheel while the facts take hold. No house, no guy, no money, no friends, possibly no place to live if Iris kicks me out. Plenty of crushing debt and guilt, though.

I bang my forehead against the hard rubber and try to slow my breathing. How could I let this happen?

There's a knock on my window, and instinctually I think, *Wyatt*. But it's Alaina, gesturing for me to open it.

"I thought that was you in the hallway," she says. "You weren't at the meeting this morning. Apparently, we lost the bid in Kirkland."

"That bites." I keep my face straight to avoid her seeing the Band-Aid on my right eyebrow. "But yeah, I took a personal day. Ended up needing to get something from my desk."

She gives me a once-over, her frown deepening. "Are you all right? You look a bit…" She leans forward, her mouth a silent O as she notices my cut. "What happened?"

I sigh. "That house I was building? It burned down. The other night."

She gasps. "No. Is that why Wyatt's out, too?"

He is? "I don't know. Maybe."

"You don't know? Aren't you working on it together?"

"We were. It's complicated."

Her eyes narrow, then she crouches down next to me. "Oh my God, the rumors *were* true. You and Wyatt—"

"Shh!" I gesture for her to lower her voice. "You can't tell anyone. And either way they're not true anymore."

Her face falls. "No, no, no. On behalf of my whole floor, please tell me it's not over. He was getting much nicer. I want to know everything and I promise I won't tell a soul." She crosses her heart.

The urgency to talk to him increases tenfold. "Sorry, Alaina, I have to go."

"But I…"

"Let's do lunch soon," I holler through the window, speeding away.

If he's not at work, where can he be? He's not answering his damn phone. Maybe Loel has talked to him? I try him instead.

"Hey, it's Dani," I say. It occurs to me then that he never returned my call either.

"Hi." He sounds gruff, nothing like the cheery fixer I've come to know. "I meant to call you back, but when something like this happens, shit kind of hits the fan. I've got to talk to insurance, to my guys, figure out how we go from here, you know. I'm sorry about the house."

Why didn't I think of that? Of course, he's also insured.

I can't get the question out fast enough. "You're covered for this?"

His response is a reluctant "We'll see."

My driving has brought me within blocks of The Spite House. I need to make sure this hasn't all been a bad dream.

"What does that mean?" I ask, turning onto the street. To my surprise there are two cars parked across from the lot, and I recognize Wyatt's right away. The other one is an older model Corolla. "Hey, are you at the site?"

"Yeah?"

"Okay, hold on, I'm parking." I hang up, fighting back nausea at the prospect of seeing Wyatt again.

In the unforgiving daylight, the black remnants of the house rise out of the soggy ground like an exoskeleton left by some prehistoric creature. The concrete foundation is still there, as is part of the front wall, but anyone can see it's not salvageable. The name sign is leaning, and next to it lies a blownover figurine. I pick it up and brush off the kissing gnomes. They'll have to go back in Iris's garage for now.

"You should put this on," Loel says, handing me a face mask. "There's still stuff in the air."

"Thanks." I do as he says and walk with him the last few yards to where Wyatt is standing.

He's watchful above his mask but stirs when he spots my bandages.

"Hi," I say, with a small wave near my hip. "Guess we've been playing phone tag." *Brilliant opening, Porter.*

"What happened to your face?"

"It's only a scrape from the blast."

"Blast?" His eyebrows jump. "You were here?"

My message the other night must have been vaguer than I remember. "I didn't tell you?"

"No." He takes a step closer, but stops short, his arm falling to his side as if he was about to reach out but thought better of it.

"I'm okay." I shuffle my feet and dare myself to face his scrutiny. "It's not that bad."

"But why were you here at all? What happened?"

I grind my teeth behind the mask. I can't lie to him. Not anymore. "I had too much to drink and gave the driver the wrong address. And then I was dumb enough to go inside. Sorry," I add in Loel's direction. "I know I wasn't supposed to, but it seemed like a good idea at the time. I was...upset."

"And then what?" Loel asks.

"I was up on the deck, and I guess I was a bit loud. Sam came out and told me I was waking up the neighbors and to get out of there. We were in the front yard when it blew. He fractured his wrist breaking my fall."

"Sounds like you were lucky." Loel peers toward the wreck.

I do the same. As soon as I mentioned Sam, I could sense Wyatt shift away, and I want to avoid his look of disapproval.

"I wanted to ask," I say to Loel. "You mentioned your insurance over the phone. What did you mean?" I try not to sound too eager. Wyatt doesn't need any more ammunition against me.

"It's not clear-cut," he says. "If the fire started because of an electrical issue or an accident while the guys are on-site, it would be on us, but we had it inspected and it was all up to code. I'm convinced something else caused it."

"I think I flipped a light switch when I went inside. That wouldn't have messed things up, would it?"

"No." He adjusts the mask strap behind his head. "The other thing is—this looks like a real aggressive blaze. And you say there was a blast." He shakes his head. "We'll see what the fire investigator comes up with, but I don't think this was an electrical fire. So basically, you could make a claim against my insurance, but unless there's proof, I'll fight it. Don't take this the wrong way—I'm only protecting my business. And you should be fine—it'll just go on your insurance instead."

It's a good thing the mask is covering most of my face or I'm sure my shame would be written all over it. In thick black Sharpie. "Right."

"You'll figure it out," Wyatt says, flatly. "You always do."

We, I want him to say. *We* will figure it out. Together. I want us to be a team.

The insight brings forth a tremor across my skin. I want more than this fling, more than just-for-now. I want to hook my arm with his and parade down the street, through town. Kiss him at the top of the Space Needle for all to see.

"What?" Wyatt asks.

"Huh?"

"Were you about to say something?" His eyes are on mine, searching.

Every muscle in my body wants to go to him, but I can't. Not now. I need to make everything right first.

"No. Sorry." I emphasize the last word, hoping to deliver it directly into his brain, even though telepathy isn't a strength of mine. I don't think it's successful.

"Okay, well, I need to get going." He starts to leave but pivots back. "Oh, almost forgot—I found something. Hold on a sec." He hurries to his car and returns with a bundle of something purple. "It was stuck to a branch in that old tree when I got here." He hands me the Husky flag. It's singed in one corner, but otherwise intact. "For when you rebuild."

Rebuild… "Thanks," I say, my fingers pinching the silky material.

"Yeah, I'm going, too," Loel says. "Don't go any closer— it's not safe, okay?"

"'Kay."

They walk away together. Wyatt's broad shoulders pull back as he reaches the car. *Turn around*, I think. *Look at me.* But he doesn't. When they're gone, the tears come. I've been so fucking stupid. So fucking oblivious and selfish. Karma really is a bitch, but she's not nearly as satisfying when you're on the receiving end.

I rub the back of my hand across my cheek and step back onto the sidewalk.

"Dani, hey!"

There's Sam, traipsing across his lawn toward me. His arm is in a sling, and he's wearing glasses instead of his contacts. Nerdy cute. Part of why I fell for him.

"I thought that was you," he says with a smile. "How are you?"

I tug my mask down. "Okay. How's the arm?"

He lifts it. "They gave me some quality painkillers. Should be good as new in six to eight weeks."

"Sorry you got hurt."

"I'm just glad you're all right. You could have died."

Yeah, no shit. "Well, you saved me."

He beams. "Right place at the right time."

That still doesn't sit right with me. We were together for over three years and he always went to bed at ten like clockwork. And no way was I loud enough to have woken him up. On the other hand, maybe I'm just still looking for faults in him. Who knows? I haven't exactly been the most rational person lately.

"I was thinking," Sam says. "The other night kind of shook me. And you know how they say 'life looks different when death is touched upon'?"

"Do they?"

"Uh-huh." He shifts and cradles his cast in the opposite

arm. Shifts again. "How about we give it another go? I know I screwed up, but I miss you. I realize that now."

I sigh. *This is not happening.* "Sam."

"If there's any way—any way at all—you think you can forgive me..."

He does an uncanny impression of a lost puppy, standing there all banged up, and suddenly the animosity drains out of me and into the remainders of the hose water still wetting the curb. I'm spent. I don't want to do this anymore.

"If you're worried about Cat, don't be—that's done. She was a bit..." He spins a finger at his temple.

Charming. "I have no interest at all in Catrina."

"Fair enough." He kicks at a wayward blade of grass pushing up through a crack in the concrete. "Then how about it? We've both made mistakes. We can fix them, be better this time. I was always good at making you smile."

He's not wrong, but that seems so long ago now. "I think too much has happened."

His shoulders slump. "You really can't forgive me? How about I go first? I forgive you for the house. That's a pretty big thing, don't you think? That was bonkers."

"That's not..." I twist, my gaze landing on one of the blackened beams still reaching skyward. *Enough already.* I force myself to relax. "I do forgive you. For everything."

He lights up.

"But." I hold up a finger. "I don't have feelings for you anymore."

He huffs. "Because of Mr. Hotshot Architect?"

"Is that necessary?" I step back. "You know what? I'm going."

"No, I'm sorry, okay?" He carves his good hand through his hair. "I don't want this to be it. Like, the end."

I open my car door and pull off my mask. "And yet it is. See ya, Sam."

And there it is in my rearview mirror, wrapped up with a neat little bow, *Sam and Dani forever*. I should be elated that this pains him and not me, but I'm not. I'm empty. It doesn't matter anymore. Maybe he was right. Life really does look different when you've had mortal danger breathe down your neck.

44

THERE'S NOT MUCH pizza left when the conversation slows around Iris's table. Édith Piaf trills in the background as the already gray sky outside gets darker still. We're supposed to be heading for the lightest time of the year, but the world is way too gloomy for that to be true. Which is fine. I don't think I could handle sunshine at the moment anyway. I have to tell them I've lost their money. That we can't rebuild. The truth is simmering at my core, threatening to boil over.

"You're barely eating," Mia says, dipping her head at the nibbled slice on my plate. "Are you feeling okay?"

I push it away. "Yeah, I'm okay."

"Maybe you hit your head. Concussions make you nauseous," Matt says. "I speak from experience."

"No, it's nothing like that." I inhale all the way from my gut. "I actually need to talk to you guys about something."

Three faces turn to me.

"Something not great." I finally look up. Mia's concerned

frown only feeds the feeling inside. I have to get this out now. "I forgot to send in the insurance papers," I say in a rush. "We don't have insurance for the house." I tuck my hands under my legs to keep from fidgeting and force myself to make eye contact.

Mia's mouth opens, then closes. Iris leans forward.

"I'm so sorry," I say. "You have no idea... If I could go back and change things, I would. I feel terrible."

"How could you..." Mia covers her mouth with her fingers. "You forgot?"

"The builders are required to have insurance, too," Iris says, ever pragmatic. "Won't that cover it?"

"Only if they're at fault. Loel doesn't think they are."

"So, the money is gone? There's nothing left?" Mia falls back against her chair. "That was my savings."

"Yes, that's a doozy of a misstep, isn't it?" Iris gets up and goes to the sink.

"I know." If I could, I'd walk out of the house now, out of town to the middle of the woods where I'd dig a hole and bury myself with the dirt. "I'll figure something out, I promise. I'll find a way to repay you both even if it takes a while."

Mia scoffs. "I can't believe this," she says to the table, shaking her head. She homes in on me again. "Actually, I take that back. I told you you should have delegated more stuff. That whole thing about 'if you want things done right, do them yourself'—that's bullshit."

"I know."

"Do you?" She stands up. "I'm sorry, but I can't be here right now. Come on, Matt."

I do, I want to yell. I really do.

They leave in a hurry. Mia's disappointment breaks something within me, and for the umpteenth time in the past forty-eight hours, tears brim over in a steady stream down my cheeks.

I cry and cry until a sudden weight in my lap forces me to a sputtered stop. Cairo is resting his head on my thigh. Cesar soon follows, pressing up against my other side. Their steady warmth allows what's welling up from inside me to subside, and Iris, who's doing dishes in silence, turns. I'm sure I'm a mess, hunched over the table, strands of hair stuck to salt-watered skin. I'm also sure she's about to tell me I can't stay here anymore.

She gives Cesar a firm pat, then sits down at the table. "I was in my thirties when I bought my first new car," she says, eventually. "Up until then I drove my brother's crappy old Chevy that had taken a tumble or two. It made an awful grinding noise whenever I hit the brakes, but it was better than nothing."

I pull in a sniffled breath and rub at my nose.

"Oh, for Pete's sake," she exclaims, handing me a napkin.

"Thanks." I clean myself off as best I can.

"Like I was saying—crappy car etcetera. I'd finally saved up enough for a new one and it was a beauty. A midnight blue Ford Galaxie 500. It was more than a car—it was confirmation I could live my life the way I'd chosen to. It was freedom. I'd had it about a month when Ellen needed it for an interview downtown. She parked in a lot that had light posts with concrete bases, and for some reason she didn't pay attention to the closest one when she drove off. She scraped the paint off the whole passenger side. Wonderful woman, terrible driver." She chuckles softly, lost in the memory.

"What happened next?" I ask.

She looks up. "Oh, not much. I loved her. People make mistakes. I probably pouted for a while. As will Mia. But she's your cousin, and she loves you. Give her time."

New tears sting behind my lids, but this time I squeeze them shut to keep the deluge at bay. "I'm mortified," I say, heavily. "It's not like me."

"You've had a lot on your plate."

"I'll find somewhere else to live if you want me to."

"Pah, I don't think we have to take it that far." She reaches out and touches my hand. "This isn't great, I'll give you that, but it's also just money. No one died."

Stupid tears with a life of their own. I don't deserve her kindness and sympathy.

"Come on, now. Wipe your eyes."

I take a deep gulp from my water bottle and ask for another tissue. "Will this feeling go away?" I ask, rubbing Cairo's head. "Like I've ruined everything. There's nothing good left."

She smiles. "You young people. Everything is the end. I'll say it again. No one's dead. You're a self-sufficient woman. You start over."

Maybe not as self-sufficient as I've made myself out to be. "With what? I have no money, no friends, and Wyatt's…" My voice cracks. "I think I've been wrong about a lot of things."

"Then tell him that."

"I doubt he'll hear me out."

"Why? Because Sam didn't?" She tuts as if to underscore that I'm doing it again.

She's right—I have operated on the assumption that Wyatt would be a certain way based on previous experiences. Preconceived notions. And they need to go.

"All you can do is try. Try to set things right. Try to start over." She knocks twice on the table and stands. "Go get some rest. Take a moment to breathe. You'll work it out." She gives a sharp whistle, and the dogs scramble to their feet. "Come on, boys, let's go outside."

"Thanks, Iris."

"Anytime." The three of them disappear through the patio door and into the dusky evening.

I don't linger. My insides are a soggy blanket, good for nothing, so I curl up in bed with my clothes still on. Before I'm completely out, I'm already dreaming of shadows, and smoke, and sensations of falling.

45

I TAKE TUESDAY OFF, TOO. It's a coward's way out, I know that, but at least I don't have any clients scheduled. Wednesday, I'm not so lucky, with Mr. Archer's friends returning for another meeting. After a mirror pep talk I'd rather forget, I'm in the office early. The world keeps on turning.

Wyatt arrives last to conference room B, where Mr. Archer, the Roses, the engineer, and I are already seated.

"Morning," he says as a general greeting, not acknowledging me. He nods to Archer. "You received my email?"

"Yes, got it," the boss man says. "No problem."

Wyatt rolls his chair in, rests his hands on the table. If he moves fifteen degrees to the left, I'll be directly in his line of sight. But he doesn't.

Mr. Archer kicks off with a friendly exchange about the promising golf weather this coming weekend, complete with compliments on Mr. Rose's swing. I tune them out, aware of little but Wyatt's finger clicking the end of his pen, the way he subtly shifts his arm to check his watch, how the fabric of his shirt stretches across his upper arm, the tilt of his chin, and… My gaze snags on something in the midst of this nostalgic field trip. He's wearing his hearing aid. It must be working out, then. Good for him. As if he senses my discovery, he reaches up absentmindedly to adjust the tiny shell.

"We've had some time to consider your drawings and designs," Mr. Rose says, forcing my attention elsewhere. "And we're ready to sign."

"Excellent," Wyatt chimes in. He raises a questioning brow at Mr. Archer, who nods back. What's going on with the two of them? "But before we go further, I should let you know I'll be stepping back from the project. For personal reasons."

My heart sinks. Is it because he'd have to work with me?

"We'll of course find a replacement," he continues. "But I thought it prudent to be up-front about this change."

"Oh." The Roses address Mr. Archer, "And who will that be? We'd like to meet them as soon as possible."

"This was a last-minute change," Mr. Archer says. "I'll have to get back to you before the weekend, but I assure you you'll be in good hands with any of our architects."

I will Wyatt to look my way, but he's stubborn. If I want the room to notice me, I'll have to make them. My mind takes a moment to fire up, but then I push my shoulders back. "Alaina Santiago," I say with as much authority as I can. "She'd make a great replacement. Her style is similar to Wyatt's, and she's very detailed." I also happen to know she has room in her schedule since we lost the Kirkland bid, but I keep that to myself.

Everyone spins my way, including Wyatt.

"Ah," Mr. Archer says. "Interesting idea. What say you, Wyatt?"

His eyes don't leave me for a long second, and I ache for there to be something else behind his attention. His lips part, and this is it. Will he shoot me down? Has the door closed? Or is there still enough of an opening that we might yet breathe life back into us at least as friends? Not that that would be my first choice.

"Alaina is a solid choice," he says, finally. "I have complete faith in Danielle's judgment."

After that, I stop listening.

I catch up to him near the elevators once the meeting is over.

"Wyatt!"

He turns right away as if he expected me. "Hi."

"Um, thanks for backing me in there," I say, the words sticking on my tongue now that we're only feet apart. His hair is impeccably slicked back, and he's let that five-o'clock shadow grow into intentional scruff. Very hot.

"Sure." He watches me warily.

"I wanted to…" We both step to the side to let others pass. "Do you mind?" I tip my head to the dead-end extension of the hallway. "We're kind of in the way here."

He rolls forward on his feet. "Sure."

I follow him a few yards from the high-traffic lane.

"Thanks." A thousand critters mill about my chest, refusing to fall in line. "Where was I?"

"You wanted…something?" He props his shoulder against the wall.

"Yeah." I take a deep breath. "I wanted to say I'm sorry. Really sorry. For everything."

He doesn't blink. "Okay."

"I was a jerk." My fingers go to the cut on my forehead, stroking it absently.

His frown deepens. "Does it hurt?"

"Not bad." I drop my hand.

"Good." He drums the side of his leg. "I'm sorry, too. It is what it is."

No, that's not... "Have you talked to Loel?" I ask to keep him with me a little longer. "Has he heard anything?"

"About?"

"I don't know. The fire? I have no idea what to do until I have the report."

"I have no reason to doubt Loel's assessment. I think someone started it."

"Intentionally?"

He hesitates. "Look, Dani—I'm not going to tell you what to do here, but if I were you, I'd consider who has something to gain from all this." He glances at his watch. "Sorry, I've got a meeting in two." For a second, I think he might hug me, but he doesn't. It's like finding out that big present under the tree wasn't for you in the first place.

I smile to conceal my disappointment. "Gotcha. I guess I'll see you around."

What are you going to do now? Iris says in my head. *Give up?*

46

I GIVE WYATT and Mia space the rest of the week, escaping into work during the day and felting in the evenings. A figure has taken shape, and now I can't stop. I'm hoping the creative outlet will help inspire a plan for how to get back in their good favor, but when the fire report lands in my lap the following Monday, I'm still none the wiser.

"Will you sit with me when I read this?" I ask Iris that evening.

"Of course."

I slice open the envelope and withdraw a stack of paper, scanning the where-and-when summary until I get to the conclusion. *No indication of electrical involvement, traces of accelerant, multiple origin sites, possibly criminal...*

"They recommend a referral to the police for investigation," I say, dropping the document onto the table. Since no insurance company is involved, this decision is now up to me.

Iris bends forward to read it for herself. "Are you surprised?" she asks when she's done.

Am I? "I don't know. I still thought maybe it was my fault for flipping that switch." Truth is, I wanted that to be the case—an accident—because Wyatt's words have been percolating in my brain. *Who had something to gain from this?* There's only one answer and its implications are bigger than what I want to deal with right now.

"What are you thinking?" Iris asks.

"Nothing good."

That sharp smell at the house that night—at the time I wrote it off as stemming from a new phase in the construction process, but what if it wasn't? And the noise that drew me out onto the deck—it could have come from a gas tank. I picture the night, the moon shadows dancing, the flag, Sam showing up.

"He was still wearing his clothes," I say, more to myself than to Iris. Of all the things that night, this makes the least sense to me, because didn't he say I'd woken him up?

"Who?"

If Sam was that concerned about the other neighbors hearing me, would he have taken the time to get dressed? And why the urgent need to get me out of the house unless…

Unless.

"I think Sam started the fire," I say. "I don't want that to be true, but it's the only thing that fits. The lawyer couldn't help him, he had the most to gain, he was there…" I look up at Iris. "Does that sound completely out there?"

"No. He had both motive and opportunity, and there's an eyewitness placing him at the scene." She pushes the report back to me. "And of course, dogs don't lie. They always sniff out the bad eggs."

"But arson? I don't know."

"Sounds like he might have been pretty desperate. And I'm sure he didn't want to hurt anyone physically. You going there that night was probably a case of wrong place at the wrong time."

I nod. Still, the leap from Sam, my ex-fiancé, to Sam, arsonist, is awfully long. Is that what I drove him to? Because if he was that desperate, if the house was upsetting him that much, I'll have to take some of the blame.

"What are you going to do?" Iris asks.

I shrug. "I don't have any proof."

"If you tell the police, they'll find it." She brushes something invisible off her thumb. "If that's what you want."

There has to be another way. As much as what he did is a crime (if he did it), there's a part of me that understands why. If it wasn't for all the money lost, I honestly don't know that I would even miss the house. Now that it's gone, it's not much more than a dark vortex I've managed to escape.

"Does he know that you suspect him?" Iris asks.

"I doubt it."

"Then maybe you should talk to him? If he comes clean, you can go from there."

I shake my head. "As soon as he knows what I'm thinking, he'll go on the offensive and lawyer up. I couldn't afford a slander suit—especially right now. His family is loaded."

The moment the words are out of my mouth, it dawns on me. He's rich, and I need to get our money back. If I'm able to prove he did this, maybe that'll motivate him to set things right.

I share the thought with Iris, who is, if not convinced I have this in the bag, then at least on board with trying. She moves her chair to the open kitchen window, takes out her cigarette holder, and lights one up with an apologetic wave.

"Sorry, this makes me a bit too excitable." She blows out a blue puff of smoke. "Do you have a plan?"

"Not yet." This is Mia's strength—out-of-the-box thinking, persuasion. She should be here.

A flare goes up inside me. She should *be* here. She'll love this. This is how I fix things with her.

I get up and gather the papers. "I've got to go."

"Oh?"

I grin. "I'm going to talk to Mia. I think we'll be fine." No, I know it. From now on, no more running my own race. I'm going to do things differently. Together.

"I'll be back," I holler on my way out.

I *am* back.

47

MIA IS IN her pajamas with a plastic bag wrapped around her head when she opens her door. She takes one look at me, then pivots, but she leaves the door ajar, which I take as an invitation to enter.

"Roots?" I ask. It's a monthly ritual to preserve the golden-brown hue of her hair. As a kid, she was white-blonde.

"Always." She sits in front of the TV and tosses back a handful of peanuts. One goes down the front of her shirt, but she ignores it. "What's up?" she asks.

The way she fixates on the screen could make a person think she's thoroughly vested in which singer gets voted through by America, but not me. When she's really into something, she stops snacking, and right now the peanuts are disappearing hand over fist. All I need is to bait the hook.

"I know you're still mad at me, and you have every right to be," I start. "But hear me out, okay? Five minutes. I have an idea for getting the money back."

She pauses the show but keeps chewing.

Now extend the line... "It might involve a midnight heist."

Her head swings my way, and the sinker disappears beneath the surface. Time to reel her in.

I explain everything, the implications of the fire report, my suspicions regarding Sam. Her eyes widen when I point out that he was fully dressed the night in question.

"There's no way," she says, then continues with an uncanny imitation of him, "'Early bird catches the worm.'" She puts the bowl of nuts down. "I can't believe it. I don't know if I should be impressed at the cojones or want to strangle him."

"Well..."

"Don't answer that." She gets up and paces. "Okay. We find proof he did it, let him know he's toast, and then what? Turn him in?"

"Better." I smile. "Blackmail."

A diabolical grin blooms on Mia's sweet face. "I love it when you talk dirty. How?"

"We give him a choice," I say simply. "Turn himself in or buy back the property from us above cost to cover the investment."

"You're brilliant!" Mia jumps me on the couch and smothers me with kisses.

"Ouch, my leg."

"Sorry." She scoots over. "But if we turn him in, wouldn't he have to pay anyway?"

"Sure. But..." I dig my teeth into my lip. "I guess I..."

"You feel bad for him?"

Leave it to her to figure me out like that. I hold up my thumb and forefinger an inch apart to give her a measure of the affirmative.

"Say no more. I'm game. As long as we wear all black when we break in."

I smile. "Ah, your old ninja dream."

"Finally coming true!"

I hug one of the throw pillows to my chest. "But seriously—do you forgive me?"

Her face is neutral, head slanted, evaluating. "Hmm…"

I smack her with the pillow.

"What?" she laughs. "Maybe I want you to suffer some more."

"You're terrible." *Smack.*

"Okay fine." She raises her hands for protection. "I forgive you. Truce!"

"Thank you."

"When's the mission?"

"I'm not sure yet."

"Let's do it soon. *Under the cover of darkness,*" she says with the deep cadence of a movie voice-over. "Iris can be a lookout with the dogs."

"I don't know if we should involve her."

"Oh, come on. She'll enjoy it."

I did commit to be pro-teamwork going forward. "I'll ask."

"Cool. How do we get Sam out of the house?"

If what he said was true and he's ended things with Catrina, he's not likely to be out and about much. "We'll have to give that some thought."

"Thanks for saying *we*." Mia winks.

We. There's someone else I'd also like to use that word with. I haven't seen Wyatt since our last conversation, and I can't wait much longer. He's probably writing me off completely as we speak.

"Hello? Where did you go?" Mia waves a hand in front of me.

"Sorry. Spacing out."

"Wyatt?"

I gawk at her. "How do you do that?"

She bows with flair. "Raw talent. No, but seriously, you need to fix that. He's your guy."

Hearing her say it matter-of-factly like that increases the urgency. "I know."

"You do?" She squeals. "I knew it. Ha! Matt owes me ten bucks."

"You're betting on my love life?"

"Not on your love life—on you coming to your senses. There's a difference."

"Ah, thanks for the vote of confidence. I guess I'll have to have a word with your boyfriend."

She throws a peanut my way. "You should go see Wyatt now."

"It's nighttime."

"Okay, *Sam*."

"And he pulled out of our joint project at work. What if he doesn't want anything to do with me?"

"Assumptions, speculations, excuses." She counts them off on her fingers.

I put my hands up in surrender. "Fine."

When I don't move, she gives me a pointed glare.

"Now?" My pulse picks up. She's serious.

"Yes now. Dude, get out. Go get your man."

She ushers me out the door faster than I can say "grovel," and like that, I'm en route to Wyatt's place. Only problem is, I have no clue what I'm going to say when I get there.

48

IT'S PAST NINE when I pull into Wyatt's garage and find an empty guest spot. I turn off my engine, willing courage to form from nothing.

"I don't want to be with Sam," I say out loud, trying the words. *No.*

"I've been such a fool." *Ugh, too melodramatic. Come on, Porter. Think.*

I shake out my hair, stretch my neck. That's when the edge of my vision snags on the bundle underneath my purse in the passenger seat. The Husky flag. I grab it and wrap it around my hand, bring it to my face. Recoil at the smell. The pièce de résistance of The Spite House.

For when you rebuild, rebuild, rebuild…

As if it might bite me, I shove the purple-and-gold fabric aside. No, I want nothing to do with it. Not anymore. I'll get rid of it when I get home. Or…

I straighten with a jolt. That's it!

I jump out of the car, singed flag in hand, and set course for the elevators. This flag may not be white, but it will have to do. It's my best shot. The fresh hope propels me forward until I'm five steps away and a car comes zooming down the aisle, "Wicked Game" blaring. I stop, knowing right away it's him. No such thing as a Chris Isaak coincidence...

Wyatt parks in his spot near the elevator bank, looking at me through the window. He opens the door, and I love how he unfolds before me—long legs first, then a strong arm finding leverage on the door, his solid torso rising.

"What are you doing here?" he asks after shutting the door behind him.

I walk closer when he won't, trying not to let my weak knees get the better of me. "Can we talk?"

He squares his posture. "Sure. Is everything okay?"

This is it. For real this time. "I wasn't clear last week. I really am sorry for the way I've acted. It wasn't fair to you— lying about what I was doing to Sam, how defensive I got about it, assuming the worst about you. More than once. If I could take any of it back, I would."

He looks away, jaw working. "Dani..."

"No, let me finish." I breathe in. "I like you a lot." My eyes seek and find his. "Just as you are. But I totally understand that you might not feel the same way. Anyway—here." I reveal the flag behind my back and hand it to him.

He accepts it. "What's this?"

"I don't need it anymore. I'm not rebuilding. No more spite house. You were right—I was stuck in the past." On several levels. "Also, for complete honesty, I forgot to send in the insurance papers."

"What? How?"

"It slipped my mind. I'm not making excuses." I bring my hands together in front of me and squeeze one in the other.

He might regret expressing such confidence in me with Archer now. He wouldn't be wrong. "Oh, and obviously I'll still help your nan with her drapes. That was the deal—house or no house." I take a step back, then another. "That's all, so... thanks for listening."

I'm about to turn when he says my name.

"Yeah?"

He shakes out the flag, folds it. The muscles in his arm play in the overhead light. "My nan lives in a retirement home."

"Okay?"

"She only has one room, and the home supplies the drapes. I kind of made the other stuff up."

A small, confused laugh bubbles up my chest. "You what?"

"Yeah... I..." He squints. "When I ran into you that day after your paintball thing and you said there was no wedding, I kind of hoped it might be a sign. I'd noticed you before at work—not in a creepy way—and I wanted to get to know you better. This was my chance. I thought you'd say no if it was a no-strings offer to help."

He'd noticed me... My heart expands. "I might have," I concede. "But that's sneaky."

"Are you mad?"

I study him—this complex man. "No way. Maybe a bit impressed."

"Really?"

For a long moment neither of us speaks. The events of the past months swirl around us, but we're through the twister now, finally removed from the storm.

"I really want to kiss you right now," I say, then clap my hand to my mouth. I'm not sure I meant for that to come out.

His gaze flashes, but something is holding him back. "Then why did you end things?"

I stare at him blankly. "I didn't. You did."

"What? No."

"You said you were done," I remind him.

He gives a firm shake of the head. "Because you made it clear I was limiting you. I know what that means."

"No, that's not at all what I..." Oh fuck it. I go to him and wrap my arms around his waist. Drink in his scent. He, too, has been stuck in the past. "I'm sorry," I say into his shirt. "I'm sorry, I'm sorry, I'm sorry." I look up, still holding on to him. "But you left the Rose project. I assumed that was because you didn't want to work with me."

The flag flits to the ground and then his arms envelope my shoulders. "I decided to be straight with Archer. About us. To eliminate any conflict of interest if there was a chance we'd still...figure things out. He was understanding. I should have given him more credit."

"Oh." Hope grows ever stronger, sprouting fresh shoots in my chest.

"I was trying to be practical."

Of course.

"And optimistic." He kisses my forehead softly. "So, to clarify—the house is no more? Sam's in the past?"

"Almost completely." His silent question is instant, but he doesn't have to spell it out. "There is one more thing I need to do to set things right," I say. "Before I can...move forward."

I free myself from his embrace and tell him about our plan. He listens quietly, and when I'm done, he nods.

"As soon as you mentioned Sam was there that night, I had my suspicions. I'm sorry. That's got to be a hard pill to swallow."

"It's not great. Although if he did do it, I'm sure he's feeling all kinds of bad about it. He's a lot of things, but he'd never intentionally hurt me."

"So, you and Mia will hunt for proof. When?"

"Not sure. We need to get him out of the house. Haven't solved that part of the plan yet."

"But soon I hope."

The anticipation in his expression has me reaching for him again. "Yes. This week. And then we can…"

"Talk more?" He looks at me like *that*. Like I'm not real. If he had a mirror, he'd see he's the unbelievable one.

I place a kiss on his lips and linger there, and it's like finally having that ice-cold glass of water after a long hike in scorching sunlight. His hand caresses the side of my face until suddenly, he laughs against my skin.

"What is it?" I ask, smiling back.

"Here we are, in a fucking garage again."

I break away and grin at the sleeping cars surrounding us. "I'd suggest going upstairs, but I meant what I said—I need to settle this house stuff first. Otherwise, it won't be right."

"No, I get it." Wyatt takes a measured step back. "You are free to go, *Ms. Porter*. But rest assured, I'll be awaiting your call."

49

ON THE NIGHT in question, Mia, Iris, and I go over the plan at the kitchen table. Mia says she's made sure Sam will be out of the house for enough time, so at 9:45 p.m., we'll drive over to his neighborhood with forty-five minutes at our disposal. Iris will park in a church lot at the other end of the neighborhood and take Cairo and Cesar for a walk by the house to confirm the coast is clear. And then—enter the two ninjas.

Mia can't sit still. Her leg bounces up and down until I steady her knee.

"You're making me more nervous," I say. "Be cool."

She spreads out her fingers and moves her hands forward slowly as if pushing an invisible ball. "I am. Totally cool." It lasts about fifteen seconds, and then she gets up, announcing she needs to pee.

"What will you be looking for?" Iris asks while Mia is gone.

"I'm not sure. Anything out of the ordinary, I guess. Things someone would use for arson. I know it's a long shot."

"I don't know about that. He isn't exactly a career criminal."

"Eh, venture capitalist. Po-tay-to, po-tah-to."

"Fair point." Iris taps her forehead. "Just not the kind that gets his hands dirty."

Mia returns from the bathroom. "Is it time yet?"

"Almost. I suppose we could start rounding up the dogs." Doing something is better than doing nothing after all.

We leave at exactly 9:43.

Sam's neighborhood is dark and quiet when Iris drops me and Mia off near the back of The Spite House lot. We'll wait there under the cover of the elm until Sam leaves. The air is still tainted with the smell of burnt wood, but only the outline of the ruins is discernible in this light.

"How are you getting him out of the house again?" I ask Mia.

She's huddled next to me, her black hood pulled down over her forehead. "Need-to-know basis," she whispers. "Don't worry about it. Damn, I need to pee again."

"As long as it works… And you don't need to pee."

Finally, at 10:20 my screen lights up the night. The eagle has left the nest, Iris texts from up the block.

"We're a go," I whisper to Mia. "Ready?"

"Born ready."

We stay close to the fence as we creep onto Sam's property and around the back. If we're lucky, he's left the patio door unlocked. If not, the laundry room window has a wonky latch that I'm hoping we can jimmy open. I lead, and Mia follows. Forty-five minutes. We'd better hurry.

The door is a no-go. Very locked.

"Maybe he's turned paranoid living all alone in this big house," Mia says with a sneer. "Not so cocky now, *buster.*"

"You know this isn't a 1920s gangster movie, right?"

She rolls her eyes at me. "Where's your sense of fun? Jeez."

"Let's try the window."

"You're never going to get it open."

"Thanks for the confidence."

"We didn't even bring any tools. What are you going to open it with?"

Damn it. She's right. "We're terrible burglars."

Mia smiles. "I don't know if that's a bad thing, cuz."

True, but now what? I jiggle the window to no avail.

Mia backs away from the house and scans the second story. "Psst," she says. "There's an open window."

"Where?" I join her and she points. It's the main bathroom.

"Come on, I'll hoist you up." Mia drags me to the back of the garage. "Climb up here, jump up onto the overhang, crawl along the gutter, and you're in."

"Pretty sure you have me confused with an Olympic gymnast. I'm not doing that."

"Yeah, you are." Mia bends down and weaves her fingers together to create a step. "Stop whining and grow a pair. This is our only chance. I'd do it, but let's be real—you're not hoisting me anywhere. You've skipped out on way too many arm days lately. Now, come on."

What choice do I have?

My first attempt at finding purchase on the edge of the garage roof goes better for me than for Mia. I have to brush off a layer of slimy leaves and moss in order to get a good grip, and she's downstream, so to speak.

"Ugh! Gross!" She spits and squirms to rid herself of the debris, almost dropping me.

"Sorry," I call.

"I'm sure you are," she grumbles. "Hurry up and climb, will you?"

After that, I'm on top of the garage in no time, and now there's no backing out. The only way I'm getting down is through the house.

"Jump," Mia coaches. "You can do it. I believe in you."

Oh crap, here I go.

While likely not the most graceful parkour move ever seen, I do manage to get onto the main roof overhang after a fair bit of wiggling. My arms are jelly, both from adrenaline and muscle exertion, so I pause to collect myself before I start my crawl to the open window.

Mia follows on the ground—ready to catch me if I fall, I hope—whispering encouragement every step of the way.

"Only a few more feet now—come on."

"If I die, I'll come back to haunt you," I say between my teeth.

But then I'm there.

I don't waste any time climbing inside. Twenty-five minutes left, maybe thirty if we're lucky. As I'm checking the time, Sam calls, and I almost drop the phone. "Straight to voice mail," I mumble, tapping the screen, then run downstairs to let Mia in.

She flies into my arms. "Oh my God, that was badass. I never thought you'd actually do it."

"Oh, ye of little faith. Now, let's focus. If I was a piece of arson proof, where would I be? You go check the garage, I'll take the laundry."

"Aye, aye."

We split up, but she returns not two minutes later with a triumphant smile on her face. "I've got something." She's waving a pair of gardening gloves above her head—a pair I've never seen before. "They stink of gas, so I bet this is what he used."

"Get a bag from the kitchen and put them in there. Did you see any gas cans?"

"Everyone has gas cans in the garage."

"He drives a Tesla."

"Good point. What about for a lawn mower?"

Shoot. "Still. Doesn't hurt."

She nods. "I'll keep looking."

I rifle through the dirty laundry, but there's nothing unusual. The clothes he wore that night are nowhere to be seen. Maybe he's learned to do his own laundry. Not that it helps me now.

With no other bright idea, I open closets at random. Cleaning supplies, towels, batteries, winter coats. It's not until I get to the walk-in closet in the bedroom that I spot something of interest. In the back, behind all his shoes, is a plastic grocery bag with a small red cone sticking out. I rummage it open, and several pairs of painted black eyes stare back at me. It's four of Iris's garden gnomes. Poor mankini gnome's shiny behind hidden up here in the dark, and I had no idea. "You son of a…" I mutter. I bring the bag with me downstairs, where Mia is busy going through kitchen drawers.

"I don't think you'll find anything there. But look." I hold up the bag. "Did you find more stuff in the garage?"

"Two gas cans. I put them by the back door. But that's all." She grimaces in apology.

"I don't think it's enough," I say.

My phone buzzes in my pocket. It's Iris. How's it going? Fifteen minutes…

Gloves, gas cans, gnomes, I respond. Do you think the dogs could sniff something out?

Not how dog noses work.

"There's got to be something else," Mia laments. "He burned down our house for fuck's sake."

"Unless he didn't." I peer into the shadowy corners of the house. "What if we're wrong?"

"No. I feel it in my bones."

"Not exactly hard proof."

Thirteen minutes. My heart is racing.

The screen lights up again. "No, stop texting," I groan. "We don't have time."

"Here, give me." Mia reaches for the phone.

I need to think.

"Iris says she's outside," Mia tells me. "She asks if you've checked the cameras?" She frowns. "What does she mean?"

Cameras? I look out the window where I spot the dogs near the street. Then it clicks. "Oh. My. God—the cameras!" I set the gnome bag down and run into the office, Mia on my heels.

"What do you mean?"

"When we first moved in," I say, my fingers flying across the keyboard. "I thought the house was too big for comfort, so I had a security system installed. Sam thought it was total overkill—I mean you saw, he never even turns the alarm on— but I did it anyway. If I can remember the password… I'm sure he hasn't changed it. I doubt he even remembers they're there."

"But wouldn't those cameras only show this house? That's not helpful. We need to catch him in the act."

I tap the keys, waiting for muscle memory to set in. "Not necessarily." I try the first word that comes to mind. No luck.

"Hurry up. We don't have much time." Mia goes to the window.

"I know. Stop stressing me out." I type in a variation of the same word, replacing the *S* with a dollar sign. The screen changes, and I'm in the cloud. "Yes!" I shout. This must be how hackers feel. "It's all here." I scroll through the list of en-tries, thankful I programmed it to keep footage for two weeks before deleting. I locate the feed from the date in question. "There. Look at this."

The time stamp reads 11:03 p.m. and the greenish night-time vision shows Sam leaving the house dressed in the same clothes as when I met him not an hour later. In his hands are the two gas cans.

"Holy shit," Mia says right next to my ear.

I turn to her with a smile. "I think this is enough. I should be able to access it from home, but let's film it with the phone, too, in case." I rewind and she records it, and we're almost done when a notification pops up.

"Oh no, Iris says he's coming," Mia gasps.

I close the browser and shut everything off. "We have enough. Let's go."

50

WE'RE OUT THE back at the same time the garage door opens and take off along the fence at full speed.

Once beneath the tree, Mia rests her hands on her thighs and laughs. "I think I'm going to throw up, but that was totally worth it." She straightens and offers me a high five.

There's movement near the street, and Iris and the dogs emerge from the shadows. "Did you get anything?"

"Sure did." I show her the video footage. "I think we should confront him right now. I don't want him to discover someone was there and call the police or anything. Let's get it over with."

Sam opens the door, flinching at the sight of the three of us standing on his porch.

"You're here?" His expression changes from surprised to angry in a second flat. "What the hell? I was worried?"

"About?"

"Some bartender called to say they'd confiscated your keys,

and you gave them my number to call for a ride. I drove all the way downtown."

A bartender? Mia got Matt to help? I glance at her, but she gives nothing away. "Nope, I'm here. Stone sober." Sam must have tried my cell when he couldn't find me.

"Then what the hell was that about?"

"Maybe we thought you needed an...excursion."

"Why?" He steps forward but stops when Cesar emits a low growl. "Those damn things again." His nostrils flare.

"Be nice," Mia says sharply. "They wouldn't hurt a fly—which is more than we can say for you."

Sam cocks his head toward my cousin. "Always a pleasure, Mia. What are you talking about?"

I reveal the bag with the gloves and gnomes from behind my back, and Mia sets the gas cans down in front of her.

"Found some stuff," I say.

Sam's eyes widen.

"Your story about why you were over there—" I point "—never sat well with me. I wasn't that loud, you're never up late, and you were still dressed. And why the urgent need to get me out? You knew it was going to blow because you set the fire."

Sam stills, then crosses his arms. "That's absurd."

"Am I?"

"Everyone has gas tanks at home—that doesn't prove anything."

"You took my gnomes," Iris says.

"Fine, whatever. They're an eyesore, and now you have them back. Speaking of which—you broke into my house?"

"Don't change the subject. I know you did it and soon everyone else will, too."

"You have no proof."

"No?" I hold the phone up to him. "See the date?" I hit

Play and relish the color draining from his face. "I assume it's a coincidence you left your house carrying those gas cans that night, then? At a time when you told me you were sleeping?"

"Where did you get that?"

"Remember that security system you didn't think we needed?"

His head jerks as he scans the porch ceiling. One of the cameras is mounted in the far corner closest to the garage.

His chest rises and falls. "That still doesn't prove anything."

"Doesn't have to, because here's the thing—even an investigation would drag your name in the dirt."

His mouth opens but he doesn't speak.

"Fortunately for you, we're going to give you a choice."

"A choice?"

"Either we turn over this evidence to the police, or...you buy the lot from us. We pretend it was an accident and I don't press charges."

"What?" he sputters. "But I don't want it."

"Do you want your reputation?" Mia asks. "Your job?"

"And you don't know for sure that a court would acquit," Iris chimes in. "It would be a gamble."

Sam looks between the three of us, pink rushing back into his cheeks. "This is extortion."

I examine my nails. "I prefer to think of it as fair retribution. If you'd bought that lot, like I asked, none of this would have happened. We need our money back. It's not like it's going to hurt you financially."

"Plus some extra," Mia adds. "For pain and suffering. A blocked view versus arson..." She uses her hands to show the much heavier moral weight of the latter.

Sam glares at her.

"Oh, give it a rest," she says. "You almost killed Dani and you know it."

"We're prepared to give you until noon tomorrow to think it over," I say. "If we don't hear from you—this goes to the police. Come on, ladies."

We're down the steps when Sam calls my name.

I spin around. He's moved into the porch light, and maybe it's the shadows, maybe not, but he's suddenly younger. A scared little boy. He shoves his hands into his pockets, takes them out again.

"I don't need to think about it. I'll buy the lot. You name your price. But I need your word this will never go anywhere. We never talk about it again."

I straighten, my crew flanking me on either side. "I promise."

He nods once. "For what it's worth, I'm sorry. I messed up."

There are a lot of memories in the man before me—in his blue eyes, his dress shirt, his drive, this house. Before all this, three years of mostly good stuff. A pretty long chapter.

I nod back. "I'll be in touch."

We walk to Iris's car in silence until Mia jumps in front of me and grabs my shoulders. "I know that was emotional and all, but do you realize we did it? We'll get our money back. Woot woot!"

Her enthusiasm is contagious, and, finally, the muscles in my neck relax. "We did." I let an airy laugh free. "I can't believe I climbed a roof tonight!"

Iris balks. "You did what?"

"Long story."

"We need to celebrate! Do you have any champagne, Iris?"

"You know it. The real kind." Iris winks.

The car ride home is jubilant, with Cesar and Cairo adding happy barks when our laughter gets too boisterous. Before we go inside, I stop Mia.

"You'll have to thank Matt for me. That was a smart way of getting Sam out of the house."

Mia smirks. "Oh no, it wasn't Matt. He's working a bachelor party tonight at the rec center."

My mind churns. "But if it wasn't him..."

"You really haven't figured it out?" Mia grips both my shoulders as if she's about to shake me. "Who else could it be?"

The answer hits me like an anvil. "Wyatt? But..."

"He called me at work. Said he wanted to help."

That wonderfully sneaky man. For once, I'm speechless.

"It's okay, hon," Iris says ahead of us. "You can go. But I'm not promising to save you any champagne."

Mia hugs me. "I'll have a glass for you. Or two."

51

I CAN'T GET to him fast enough.

The car, the road, the garage, the elevator.

My heart.

"She told you," he says with a grin before I fly into his arms.

I cling to him, my legs locked around his waist. "She did. I can't believe you did that. Thank you."

"Really, it was the least I could do after making you doubt I was on your side." He finds a wayward strand of hair at my temple and tucks it behind my ear as he sets me down on the floor.

"I like the beardy look," I say.

"Yeah?" He rubs his chin like he's pondering a significant mystery.

"It's very 'dangerous suave.'"

He laughs. "I have no idea what that means. I just didn't feel like shaving for a few days. Come on." He takes my hand and leads me to the couch. The TV is on, but muted. Some travel and food show I don't have time to identify before he deploys his signature stealthy maneuver and hauls me into his lap.

"Smooth." I giggle as his scruff tickles me.

"I thought so. Now tell me about tonight—did everything go okay?"

I nod. "He's going to buy the lot."

"That's a relief. And no more unfinished business?"

"Not a bit."

At that, he gathers me in his arms and arranges us side-by-side, half reclined. "Then let me finally tell you this." He caresses my jaw with light fingers. "Dani, I'm sorry I told you I was done. More than you'll know. I'm not done. Not even close."

A burden I didn't know was still there rolls off my back, and I wiggle closer, into the warm nook of his neck. His freshly showered skin smells like minty evergreen. "And I'm sorry I suggested you were holding me back when you're obviously doing the opposite."

"Pushing you forward?"

I swat his arm. "Let's say *motivating* me to move on."

He settles me on top of him. "Just to have it said, though. If we were…together, there might be things you want to do that don't work for me. I never want to be an obstacle in your life, hindering you when you could soar."

It will be a while before I stop beating myself up over how little I paid attention to what he was telling me all along. This whole time, he was worried I'd be another Madeline, while I was making him out to be another Sam. "Your health stuff *never* bothered me," I say. "You know that. I just want to be with you."

He enfolds me into a bear hug and holds me there. "Mmm, I've missed you."

"I've missed you more."

"I'm sorry about the house."

"I'm not." I peer down at him. "Do you want to hear something sappy?"

"Always."

"At some point, the build stopped being about Sam and turned into being about you instead. Because I got to be with you. I think subconsciously that's why I ordered the Carrara—to delay things. When the house was gone, I was more upset that *you* were gone. Plus, without it, I would have never gotten to do this."

I lay siege to him, and, as always, his soft lips trigger that hunger low in my belly. Without breaking contact, I use my hands as leverage on either side of his chest and push myself up until I'm straddling him. I walk my fingers up his torso, across his taut abs and rigid pecs, and grind my hips down once, never releasing his gaze. His eyes close on a hissed inhale. Whoever invented sweatpants was a genius.

"Sappy is my new favorite," he says, voice thick.

When I move next, he meets me, a wicked smile unfurling. He runs his hands up my thighs to my hips, before trailing in beneath my shirt. I let him pull it off and help with his. His abs stand out in magnificent relief when he crunches up to sitting and wraps his arms around me. He palms my ass to get even closer and kisses me higher and higher until the room spins.

"I'm really sorry about the loft thing," he whispers against my neck while deftly undoing my bra. He slides the straps down my arms and takes one of my nipples in his mouth.

"I know," I say, gasping. It's not a lie.

"And for being a jerk about your mom mistaking me for Sam." He switches to my other breast.

I let out a low moan in place of an answer.

"I wasn't sure where your head was at…" He looks up at me, his tongue circling against my skin. "And I didn't like it."

His teeth tease me as his hands dive into the fabric covering my backside, pressing me to him. My pulse kicks up another notch.

"I'll forgive you, if you forgive me."

"Deal," he growls. "Damn, I missed you. Did I say that already?" He urges me to my knees, and in that brief parting, I read on his face what I'm sure is already being broadcast on mine. What's between us isn't merely a want, it's a need.

I *need* him to be mine.

The rest of our clothes come off in a flurry of stretched limbs and eager hands, and this time, he's prepared, reaching into the drawer of the side table and returning with a condom.

"Sit," I say, my voice husky as I take it from him, and then, finally, I'm on top of him again.

He groans when I sink onto him, his fingertips digging into my hips. "Fuck." A vein in his forehead swells.

I lift slightly. "Oh, I intend to." I give him a smug smile before lowering myself again.

He chuckles—a breathless sputter that comes to an abrupt stop when I pick up the pace.

As we move together, chest to chest, he grips my right hand in his and for a moment we're tangoing, the rhythm in our blood urging us faster and faster. I have spaghetti arms and will not respect his dance space.

He brings our linked hands to his lips and rests them there, and the tenderness makes my heart burst. In the midst of this onslaught of primal need, he's found a way to show me it's more. *We're* more.

I slow and he opens his eyes.

"Are you good?" he whispers. He releases my fingers and reaches for my cheek instead.

I lean into his palm and nod. "Better than good." I rise up all the way and come back down.

He shudders, then angles his mouth to mine and helps himself to an unhurried taste of me. Our tongues meet, and after a sultry stroke, he clutches my hips again, spurring me on. I don't take much persuasion.

"Don't close your eyes," I say. I want that unbroken connection. To navigate this tightening spiral together. It's like I'm being read. Like he wants to know how the different parts of me are linked. How they communicate. His touch explores my body, while his eyes do the same to my soul.

It doesn't take long before wave after wave of the most intense orgasm rocks me, my body clenching around him until he joins me with a groan. We steady each other as I collapse against his shoulder, our labored breathing one sound.

He trails gentle kisses against my slick skin, his heartbeat reverberating aftershocks deep within me.

I rest my hand at the nape of his neck.

"I think you've picked up some moves in your new career as a bartender," I say after a while, sitting back a little. "Consider me both shaken and stirred."

Mischief brightens his features. "Ah yes, my new alter ego."

"What I don't get is how you knew that was going to work? I'm not exactly known to be a boozehound. Recent wallow binges notwithstanding..."

He interlaces our fingers. "You really want to know?"

"I do."

His thumb rubs across the back of my hand. "If someone had called me to come get you from anywhere even when we weren't talking, I would still have rushed to your side." A bashful smile. "You've gotten under my skin, *Ms. Porter.* I figured after several years, you'd be firmly stuck under Sam's, as well."

"Is that so, *Mr. Montego?*"

"Uh-huh." He bites his lower lip. "I think that's what happens when you fall in love with someone."

Heat rushes to my face. "I see."

"Do you?"

I nod. "I'm falling for you, too."

"Oh thank God." He leans in for a kiss, and I can't seem to wipe the smile off my face as I meet him.

"I just remembered," I say as we separate. I free myself from his embrace and walk barefoot over to my purse, from which I extract a parcel wrapped in tissue paper. "For you." I hand it to him and curl up at his side.

He squeezes it. "It's soft. Did you get me socks?"

I laugh. "A little too soon for such a lack of imagination, don't you think? Open it."

He does, and when he sees the felted figure I've been work-ing on—an alpaca with a tiny garden gnome on its back—his expression goes from amusement to disbelief to tenderness in the span of three seconds flat. "It's Bud," he says. "You made this?"

I smile. "I didn't set out to, but it appears you've gotten under my skin, too. I even *craft* Wyatt things now."

He runs his fingertips over the shape of Bud's head and across the gnome's pointed hat before setting it down on the coffee table behind me and pulling me close. "I love that you do. And I love the little gnome, too. It pieces you and me to-gether in wool." He nuzzles close, his arms strong and sure around me. "Thank you."

"You're welcome." I touch my lips to his shoulder then say under my breath, "And since you've now demonstrated you're not at all put off by my nerdy pastime, I would also like to inform you that, while I do have a job that's a bit of a time-suck, and a cousin who'll kill me if I go underground completely, I'm free this weekend. And the weekends after that. Provided you're open to renegotiating the terms of our agreement, that is."

A wide grin blossoms on his face.

"I'm sure I can find a way to fit you into my schedule."

EPILOGUE

EIGHT MONTHS LATER...

THE LACED EDGE of the white satin skims the floor as the supposed bride-to-be does a practice lap around the room.

"You look gorgeous," I say.

"I know." Mia runs her hands over the bodice of the dress in front of the mirror.

I lower my voice to avoid the attendant hearing us. "Isn't this the dictionary definition of *jinxing it*, though? You haven't been together that long."

"Almost a year. And I'm not planning entrapment here, only trying on a dress."

"That happens to be white."

"Exactly." She lifts her hair off her shoulders and piles it on top of her head. "No, I liked the last one better. It made my boobs look incredible."

"When don't they?"

She turns to me, eyes dancing. "Aww. You should try some on, too."

"Ha! Nope. For me that would *definitely* be jinxing things. I'm perfectly fine with where we are right now."

"I hear ya. Cohabiting and everything."

"Not yet, we just started looking at places."

Mia starts humming "Here Comes the Bride," so I toss a garter at her.

The shop attendant frowns at us from behind her desk.

"Are you nervous about your mom meeting Wyatt?" Mia asks from the other side of the dressing room door as she's changing into the next dress.

My aunt is coming out to visit Mia for her birthday at the end of the month, and she's somehow pulled off the impressive feat of convincing my mother to join her. "A girls' trip," my mom called it when I was home for Christmas. Next, pigs will fly and hell will freeze over, but who knows? Maybe there's still hope for her after all. I'd like to think seeing me happy and hearing about how different my relationship is with Wyatt could have inspired this small step, but who's to say?

"As long as she manages not to call him the wrong name, I think we'll be fine," I say. Truth is, I'm looking forward to it. I think Wyatt's the one who's nervous.

When Mia's satisfied her longing for tulle, I drive her home and head back to Iris's. An epic bark fest is going on in the backyard, so I make my way around the house, ducking when an orange projectile flies past my head, followed by Cesar and Cairo. When they spot me, they decide the ball is old news.

"Hi, boys." I scratch their necks, trying my best to stay upright. Nothing like two excited Great Danes to test your balance.

Wyatt jumps up from the ground, brushing his jeans off. "Hi, babe. You done with Mia already?"

I push through the large canines. "So it would seem. What's going on here?"

"I thought I'd teach them fetch, but it's not going great."

"That's probably for the best. I doubt Iris will keep that up when she gets back."

Iris is currently exploring France, fulfilling a lifelong dream of hers and Ellen's. When the sale of the lot went through, she decided she was done putting it off and asked if I'd dog-sit Cairo and Cesar. It was the least I could do after everything.

It also turns out Wyatt loves dogs nearly as much as Iris; he's been over daily, helping out. Not that there's much to do— we walk them, feed them, love on them—but sharing this everyday routine has made Mia's new hobby of dress-browsing seem slightly less absurd. One I could even get into, at some point in the foreseeable future.

"Do you want to do takeout tonight?" he asks. "Or go out?"

"Takeout and a movie sound good." I reach up and pick a leaf from his hair. "Such roughhousing, *Mr. Montego*. Where has that urbane architect I once knew gone off to?"

A devilish smile forms as he hoists me up around his waist as if I weigh nothing. "That wasn't roughhousing," he says, nibbling along my neck. "But if you want, I'll show you how it's done."

The dogs trail us into the house, probably thinking this is some new fun game for them.

"Go lie down," Wyatt tells them. "The grown-ups are busy."

He brings me all the way to my room and closes the door with his hip. A moment later, I'm on my bed, draped in him.

"How does this go again?" he mutters against my cheek. "Oh, that's right. Like this." He rolls us so I'm on top, kisses me, then rolls another 180, settling on me again. "Pretty good, huh?"

"Meh." I try to stifle a smile.

He pulls away. "Meh?"

"I always thought it was better done naked." I flutter my eyelashes. "But what do I know?"

"Hmm." His hands roam up my body until they find the top button of my blouse. He undoes it. Nods. "You know, you might be right. Let's try it."

I sit up and take his face in my hands. Let my lips sweep across his.

"Yes, let's."

★ ★ ★ ★ ★

ACKNOWLEDGMENTS

AS MUCH AS writing can be a lonely calling, the process of taking a book from idea to publication is most definitely a group project, and I have many amazing people to thank for finally realizing this dream.

You would not be reading these words if not for the incomparable support of my stellar agent, Kimberley Cameron. Thank you for always believing in and supporting me and my writing! And to my editor, Melanie Fried—thank you for working tirelessly to make Dani and Wyatt's story the best it could be. I forever value your guidance.

To the whole team at Graydon House/HarperCollins: Leah Morse, Pamela Osti, Gigi Lau, Mary Luna, and Lucy Davey, thank you so much for all you have done and keep doing to make *Love at First Spite* jump off the shelf and into readers' hands! And thank you to Elsa Sjunneson Henry for providing a very valuable authenticity read of an early version of the manuscript.

Now, this book is a Rompire baby. It was conceived, incubated, and hatched in the warm, nurturing embrace of the best group of writerly friends any person can have. Alexandria Bellefleur, Amy Jones, Em Shotwell, Julia Miller, Lana Sloan, Lisa Leoni, and Megan McGee—without you, I would have long ago run out of words, not to mention perished during quarantine. My days are brighter because you are in them. Special thanks to Amy, Julia (a.k.a. playlist maven!), Lana, and Megan for reading early versions and offering invaluable feedback, and to Lisa for your always educational advice on hidden bias.

I would also not be at this point in my writing career if not for PitchWars, so shout-out to everyone involved in this awesome community, but especially the class of 2017 for still being the most supportive and enriching group of fellow creatives I could ever hope to be part of. You are populating my bookshelf quite nicely! A particular thanks to my PW mentor, Vanessa Carnevale, who held my hand through my first big revision experience and ensured it didn't put me off doing it again. And again. And again.

With writing, no words are wasted and there's always a trajectory of growth from one book to another. For that reason, I want to thank my other CPs, Jessica Holt and Melissa Wiesner (and everyone else who's ever read parts of my WIPs and shared their thoughts), who didn't necessarily beta read this book, but who nevertheless have been instrumental in my writing journey with always insightful notes, enthusiastic support, and writerly tips. You rock!

To Alexandria Bellefleur (again!), Kate Bromley, Brooke Burroughs, and Denise Williams, who provided early blurbs, everyone who reposted exciting book news, and those who answered random questions along the way—thank you so much! Shared joy is the best kind of joy and even brief connections in the writerly universe have boosted my spirits throughout this process.

There are obviously people outside the writing world without whom I couldn't have done this. Thank you to every English teacher I've ever had for nursing my love of the language. To friends and family members who've encouraged me since my first unwieldy endeavor into fiction years ago by asking to read my words and suggesting they weren't complete crap. And a special thanks to Tobi for always being there through ups and downs and round and rounds, for getting me, and for always cheering me on. "We'll be best friends until we're old and senile. Then we'll be new friends all over again!"

To my parents—turns out growing up in a home filled with books can lead places! Thank you for letting me spend all those hours in my room reading and for never objecting to yet another trip to the library.

To my kids who are not yet old enough to read this book, but who nevertheless offer hugs and high fives for every win and always encourage me to "go for the gold" even when that means they have to fix their own lunches because I now have deadlines. I love you times infinity!

And to my husband, Brian. (Yes, you get two mentions in this book—especially well-earned since it might otherwise be title-less!) Thank you for not marrying someone else before I could meet you. You're my soul mate, my best friend, and a wonderful man, and I'm a very lucky woman. Thank you for working your butt off so that I can play around with words on my computer all day. No but seriously—your support and belief in me means more than I can ever express. I love you and there's no one else I'd rather do this life thing with.

Last but not least, Dear Reader—thank you for choosing to read my book out of the millions available to you. It truly means so much. I hope you found it an enjoyable escape for a few hours and that it left you with a smile on your face.

You'd better believe that simply knowing *Love at First Spite* is out there in the world has left a smile on mine.

THE STORY BEHIND LOVE AT FIRST SPITE

I DON'T CONSIDER myself a vindictive person. Do I sometimes hold a grudge? Sure. Did I occasionally engage in sisterly tit for tat growing up? You betcha. But, generally speaking, I'm more inclined to let karma do her thing undisturbed.

This is why, when years ago I read an article about buildings constructed as a means of payback, the concept stuck with me. The Alameda Spite House, The Montlake Pie House, Boston's Skinny House, The Virginia City Spite House... The list goes on. All designed to wreck a view, one-up someone, or stake a claim on land rightly owned. All designed out of spite.

Looking at pictures of these houses, it's easy to feel both the desperation and the triumph of the feat, and I find that duality fascinating. To most of us, this is next level revenge—the love child of a carefully nursed grudge and a refusal of common societal norms. But, to a select few throughout history, nothing less would suffice. Who were these people? Why couldn't they move on without making these bold gestures?

Unsurprisingly, the answer was most often found in the remnants of a relationship gone bad, and so the idea for *Love at First Spite* was born—a romantic comedy about Dani Porter, an interior designer who simply refuses to turn the other cheek when her fiancé cheats on her.

Dani is like most of us—a novice to grand revenge schemes. But what she lacks in experience, she makes up for with a ride-or-die cousin and a landlady with money stowed away for a rainy day, neither of whom care much for unreliable men. Together with her wing-women, Dani dives headfirst into building a small (but tall) vacation rental on the vacant lot next to her ex's house to mess with his view and his peace of mind, and to prove to herself she's not one to be stepped on.

Now, a story about revenge can veer into many different genres, but with a romantic comedy in mind rather than a sinister thriller or introspective literary novel, as Dani sets out to get even, she falls for the stern architect helping her draw up the house. The question is, how do you open your heart to someone new while dwelling on the past? Answer: you don't. Consequently, the closer Dani gets to her goal of building The Spite House, the more she wonders if winning revenge could mean losing something infinitely sweeter with her new fling…

One piece of information I've always found missing from the articles about real-world spite houses is what happened after the build was complete. Did the vindictive person get satisfaction? Did the parties make up? Were they able to move on?

Writing this book was my chance to have some fun answering these questions, and in true rom-com fashion, Dani's revenge journey is a bit of a roller coaster. As for the aftermath of her spite house, I hope readers will find the resolution both entertaining and thought-provoking. A tongue-in-cheek cautionary tale for what might transpire if instead of love at first sight, you go for love at first spite.

THE SPITE HOUSE PLAYLIST

"White Wedding"—Billy Idol

"You Oughta Know"—Alanis Morissette

"My House"—Flo Rida

"Out of My Head"—Loote

"Shut Up"—Greyson Chance

"Messy"—Kiiara

"There Are No Gnomes in Sweden"—King Luan

"Just Friends"—Virginia To Vegas

"Hurricane Love"—LA WOMEN

"Gives You Hell"—The All-American Rejects

"Wicked Game"—Chris Isaak

"Dream House"—COIN

"L.O.V."—Fitz and The Tantrums

"Burning Down the House"—Talking Heads

"Hungry Eyes"—Eric Carmen

Find it on Spotify:
http://bit.ly/LoveAtFirstSpite

LOVE
AT
FIRST
SPITE

ANNA E. COLLINS

Reader's Guide

GRAYDON
HOUSE

1. Early in the book, Dani and Wyatt both claim not to be "the dating kind." What purpose does this self-belief serve in their respective lives? Would their relationship have been different without it? How so?

2. Themes of revenge and forgiveness feature prominently in the book. Is revenge always bad and forgiveness always good? Do you think Dani did the right thing in exacting revenge on her ex in this way? If not, how would you have liked to see her handle the breakup?

3. Wyatt tells Dani that he deliberately puts on an unapproachable persona in the office because it "makes things easier." What do you think he means by that?

4. Wyatt has Ménière's disease—a degenerative disorder of the inner ear that causes hearing loss, vertigo, and tinnitus. Why do you think he wants to hide it from his coworkers at the beginning of the book?

5. Initially, building The Spite House brings Dani and Wyatt together, but later it drives them apart. Do you think they would have ended up together without The Spite House? Why or why not?

6. Sometimes people come into your life when you most need them. Discuss the different ways Mia and Iris support Dani. Who in your life is your Mia or Iris?

7. In what way does Dani's relationship with her parents inform and influence her romantic life and choices?

8. By his own admission, Wyatt knew all along that The Spite House had something to do with Dani's ex, Sam. How do you think he justified keeping this knowledge to himself, especially as he and Dani got closer?

9. If you were to build a spite house, who would you spite and how would you do it?

10. Who would you cast in the movie version of *Love at First Spite*?